Ghastly Business

Ghastly Business

LOUISE LEVENE

BLOOMSBURY
LONDON · BERLIN · NEW YORK · SYDNEY

First published in Great Britain 2011

Copyright © 2011 by Louise Levene

The moral right of the author has been asserted

Bloomsbury Publishing, London, Berlin and New York

36 Soho Square, London W1D 3QY

A CIP catalogue record for this book is available from the British Library

ISBN 978 1 4088 1065 1
10 9 8 7 6 5 4 3 2 1

Typeset by Hewer Text UK Ltd, Edinburgh
Printed in **** by ****

www.bloomsbury.com/louiselevene

March 1929

Chapter *1*

A trio of pigeons had gathered on the pavement outside the public house on the corner and were breakfasting companionably on a pool of chilled vomit. The grey gathering fluttered clear as Dora dashed on past the deserted news-stand where the rain-stained placard for Saturday's evening paper was still promising 'Alley Murder: Girl Named'.

One of the other paying guests at Warwick Square, a Miss Digby, had been lodging with Mrs Frith for the best part of a year and seemed to have passed every spare moment memorising the routes of London trams and omnibuses. Miss Digby had had her doubts about the 24 but the bus came in seconds (rather than the twenty minutes Dora had been urged to allow). She'd be early if anything but the horrid, panicky first-day-of-term feeling in her stomach was getting steadily worse.

The bus was nearly empty – so much so that Dora began madly imagining that it was only Sunday after all. No. Heaps more people got on at the next stop by the station. A weasly little man in a rainy grey raincoat and a soft hat sat down on the seat in front and immediately started emptying his mind in the direction of another passenger.

'I *can* get the later London Bridge train and change at Clapham Junction but it's a bit of a sprint over the bridge even when it's on time and if I miss the connection then I'm relying on catching the jolly old 24 the instant I get in – not something on which any sane person would rely, I think you'll agree.'

It was obvious to anyone listening that the chap had deliberately left a chuckle-sized gap in this gripping narrative but his chum was in no mood to play nicely. Silence.

'Of course I could save the best part of forty minutes if I caught the 7.48. I once asked the old man if I could start and finish a quarter of an hour later and he told me I should move somewhere with a better service and did I value my position or did I *not* value my position with the department. And, of course, they fine you if you're late in his office.'

Crikey. *Fines* for lateness? Detention was bad enough. Dora wondered what other penalties lay in store in the world of work. Where did they stand on laddered stockings? Or boaters on backs of heads? Or hands in blazer pockets?

The other man, who had an angry-looking pustule on the side of his neck where his freshly starched Monday morning collar rubbed against it, had not been listening as closely as Dora but had nodded automatically – if gingerly – at decent intervals. A nod was safe enough. The chances of the chap-he-knew (but knew not at all) saying something to make him shake his head in violent disagreement were clearly very, very small. The boil didn't even have a mustard plaster on it. Dora hastily transferred to a seat by the platform.

A few stops later and both men toddled off to another day doing whatever-it-was. After the bus had made the turn by the black mass of the Abbey their places were taken by a trio of elderly charladies fresh from polishing the Foreign Office and the Admiralty, smelling strongly of soft soap and sweat. The three squeezed fatly on to the long seat. One of them had salvaged Saturday's *Evening Star* from a ministerial waste-paper basket and they fell ravenously upon the crumpled newsprint as if sharing a helping of fried fish. They tutted in delight over a girl who had been found strangled behind a parade of shops on Peckham High Street in the small hours of Thursday morning ('Alley Murder: Girl Named'). Girl named Mavis, apparently.

The *Star* had plumped for 'Blonde found dead in alley'.

Too old for 'schoolgirl', too young for 'mother of three', too well brought up to be 'hostess' or 'barmaid', she came within a whisker of being 'Peckham girl' (to *Star*, *News* and *Standard*) or 'London seamstress' (to the nationals) had she not spent that fortnight picking hops near Maidstone last September and turned her bingled hair from mouse to gold.

The bare headline had obviously shocked and saddened the charladies, but the details – nineteen, blonde hair, pink blouse, red jacket – seemed to be eating away at their sympathy, and the facts in the case became a hateful game of Lotto in which each vied with the others to find something in their own lives to match the story in the newspaper. All three spoke in loud aitchless voices, not seeming to mind that the whole omnibus could hear them. Dora opened her book and buried her eyes in Bertie Wooster but it was impossible not to listen. You couldn't really call it eavesdropping.

None of them thought too highly of Peckham although there *were* some quite nice parts where a sister (not the one who'd married the glazier, the other one) had had quite a cosy two pair front out Sydenham Hill way, but Peckham? There were streets down there where decent women wouldn't, didn't, daren't, even, and as for alleys . . . The dead girl, Mavis? – someone's brother's boy used to go with a Mavis – worked for a wholesale milliner's in the Commercial Road . . . This got one of them started on a hat she'd once bought, but they soon tired of that and were back up their Peckham alley reflecting that three in the morning was a Fine Time of Night to be out gallivanting in pink artificial silk blouses and red jackets. 'Nineteen,' sniffed one, accusingly, her bosom rolling beneath her old brown coat like puppies under an eiderdown.

The *Star*'s description of the victim as 'hatless' gave all three of them pause, and 'attractive-looking girl' did her reputation no good at all. Nor did the word 'blonde', which seemed to damn her utterly on the apparently unanswerable grounds that if it were her natural colour they'd have said 'fair-haired'. According to the one sitting in the middle, one of the Sunday papers had said that the police were questioning some young man she'd been stepping out with as well as the cinema's chief cashier. (Married man. Two children. They were the worst.) And there had been 'interference'. The word caused their mouths to fold inwards round their gums as if they'd just bitten into a pickle sandwich.

Injury had then apparently been added to insult when the victim's body was taken to Southwark mortuary and subjected to a 'post-morton' by Alfred Kemble. This got all three of them frightfully excited. The fattest of the three remarked that 'old Kemble' could tell you what you'd had for breakfast, at which point the one with the black curls (very much not her natural colour) who hadn't uttered so far piped up that she hadn't had no breakfast and all three of them fell about laughing, their uncorseted shapes squishing into one, the happy holes in their cheery red faces looking as though a bored child had blacked out half their teeth with a lead pencil.

Dora looked anxiously out of the window, afraid that the bus would decide to vary its advertised route and deliver her into some strange part of town. That she would miss her stop and be late on her very first day. *Fined*. Fined how much? She only had three shillings in her purse.

She squinted at the buildings visible between the charladies' bobbing heads just in time to see Landseer's lions whiz past, which was vaguely reassuring. Dora had lived in London all her life, but most of that life had been spent away at school and her mental map of the city was only very sketchily filled in. She knew the bookshops and school outfitters within walking distance of her father's house in Harley Street and the short taxi rides to museums and railway stations were familiar enough, but places like Pimlico and Goodge Street were *terra incognita*.

The bureau woman had given a string of instructions as long as a French dictation (most of it in the imperative). Dora had taken it all down as best she could but Mrs Frith disliked her PGs using the telephone and it had been a fearful rush. Something about 'four turnings past the Corner House', but they'd already passed at least two of those. She might just as well have said 'pillar box', 'telephone call box', 'tree'.

The conductor was whistling the one about the poor getting the blame. Every now and then he would take it into his head to call out the name of some landmark or other – more for his own amusement and glorification than to inform his passengers, who all knew perfectly well where they were and where they were going.

'Excuse me.'

He finished the verse before stopping to listen.

'Have we passed Goodge Street?'

'Chair-ing Crawss Road!' He almost sang the words then swung across the platform and up the stairs without answering. Jolly rude.

The charladies were still engrossed in Kemble and his post-mortem. The one sitting in the middle didn't mind so much when it was murder. Not like her poor old mum (God-rest-her-dear-soul): 'Lo-co-mo-tore-Ay-taxi'. She pronounced it like a Roman prayer, uncomprehending but somehow conscious of the power of the words. Old Dr Bennett had known that all along. No need to go chopping her about. The sniff came easily enough on a cold morning but it was harder to suggest tears with no handkerchief.

One of them remembered that it was old wossname who had done the post-morton on her uncle and that she didn't hold with all that cutting people about unnecessary. At which point the other two conceded that they had to have a bit of a look round when it was Sudden. Oh indeed, huffed the other, Sudden was the word all right: the poor old sod had been run over by a tram. No need to go cutting him open from ear to ear (a long soda-reddened forefinger drawn dramatically down her coat buttons) to find out what killed him. Sudden.

The inside pages of the charladies' newspaper had revealed that a motor car had taken a wrong turning over the Bristol harbour wall and sunk into twenty feet of water, plunging two men and an Airedale to their deaths, which reminded the one with the loudest voice (Winnie, her name was) that she used to live next door but one to an Airedale and that they barked a great deal. More exciting still was the news that a human leg found in a striped cotton bolster cover on the bandstand at Clapham Common was not, as the police had (not unnaturally) assumed, in any way connected to the dismembered body in the Portslade biscuit tin case.

'The limb was that of a well-nourished male' – well, that was Minnie's old man off the list. As they launched into another chorus of hysterics, Dora accidentally caught the eye of the one holding the newspaper.

'Goodge Street, dearie? Two more stops. Can't miss it – just by the Tube. Know where you've got to get to?'

It was doubtless more kindness than nosiness, Dora told herself, but when she muttered 'hospital' the woman had the infernal cheek to cock her head in sympathy, as if for two pins she'd have taken a nice medical history but settled for saying that it was straight down Goodge Street and you 'couldn't miss it'. People always said that, but you probably could.

She rode the last two stops on the platform, terrified that the char would start talking to her again. She spent her walk along Goodge Street rehearsing how best to introduce herself: Dora Strang from the agency? Or would Miss Strang be more the thing? The new filing clerk in Mr Hubbard's department? The new filing clerk in the Willcox Wing? Or just clerk? 'Filing' sounded a bit feeble. Or assistant? 'Assistant' was a bit swank; the bureau did say it was strictly Filing.

'Wing' turned out to be a bit swank, too. The building was a four-storey red-brick monstrosity, one of the many satellites of the main hospital. The latter was an unnaturally clean, newly built edifice which took up six whole blocks but still needed half the neighbourhood to house its various clinics and laboratories.

Racks of flasks and tubes and beakers could be dimly glimpsed through the wired and frosted glass of the ground-floor windows. The street door was pinned open with a rusty red fire bucket, its sand garnished with cigarette ends. Two men in holland overalls were shifting crate after crate from the back of a small green lorry, up the front steps and into the passenger lift. They were watched by a uniformed porter who lived inside a draught-proof sentry box thingy to the right of the main entrance hall. There was a second lift in the far corner behind him but it was elaborately padlocked, with a painted sign saying 'not in use' strung from the chain.

'Mr Ubbard's department?' The porter, who had reluctantly limped out from his hutch to keep an eye on the delivery men, looked strangely affronted at Dora's request. 'He'd like to have a department. "Mr Ubbard's department!" Third floor, second on the left, Room Eight. The key's on the ledge over the door.' She'd have to wait for the lift – he jerked his head in the direction of the delivery men – unless she fancied the goods lift? He winked as he said this and pronounced 'goods' in a rather rum sort of way.

The third-floor corridor smelled as if a lot of disinfectant had been used to hush up some indefinable unpleasantness, like chlorine poured into a drain: an uncompromisingly medical smell. Dora's father had always tried to mask the scent of his trade. Many of his contemporaries were perfectly satisfied with hunks of carbolic soap in their surgery washbasins. Leopold Strang's were supplied with virginal rose-scented tablets with 'Made by the Blind' embossed (surprisingly neatly) on each cake. Sachets of lavender and sandalwood lurked in the shelves of the beechwood cupboards that lined his consulting rooms, and great bowls of flowers – stocks, freesias, lilies – were renewed weekly. If anything, the overriding whiff was of the starch that the laundry used on the dainty linen runners freshly laid along the examining couch (Regency in style and made to his own specifications). Dr Strang could not abide 'aseptic' Wigmore Street fittings.

Room Eight was cold and peculiarly dark. Most of the half-hearted February daylight was blocked by the six-storey bulk of the hospital opposite, but there was a faint electric glow from the window above a door in the far corner marked 'Strictly No Admittance' that gave a ghostly shimmer to the room and its furnishings.

Nothing Regency about it – nothing aseptic either: just a lot of smoked oak desks and filing cabinets crowded together on the scratched green linoleum. Each of the four desks had its own telephone, but the instrument on the typewriting table next to the door was twice the size of the others, a bloated black machine whose elongated shape held room for a dozen extensions to which calls could be transferred. It began ringing the moment Dora looked at it. Jolly loudly. The actual sound came not from the 'phone itself but from a large bell on the wall behind her. She had hopes that someone in the adjoining room might answer but a noisy minute passed and the ringing continued. Dora looked around the empty office, shrugged and pulled a face in a silly, theatrical way like a housemaid in a play. She pulled off her hat and cautiously picked up the heavy black receiver but the beastly thing carried on regardless. She squinted helplessly at the various switches, as numbersome and baffling as the buttons on an accordion. Clerk? Hall? Port? Mort? Main? Hubb? Lab?

'Lab' looked fairly promising so she pressed it. The telephone bell didn't stop but she heard an answering whimper from the room next door. Blast. Dora jumped out of her skin when the receiver in her hand began barking at her.

'Can somebody not answer that infernal telephone?'

'There isn't anyone here. Apart from me, obviously.'

Dora felt the cold Bakelite of the mouthpiece mist up against her lips as she stammered apologetically into it. 'I only arrived this morning. From the agency. I don't know how to work your telephone, I'm afraid'.

The 'No Admittance' door sprang open. A tall, thin man burst through it and almost ran across the office to the desk where Dora was standing in the half-darkness. He wore a white canvas overall, a long white rubber apron and matching surgical gloves, like a mad scientist from a book jacket. Without a word, without even looking at Dora, he yanked the receiver out of her hand and jabbed one of the buttons (she didn't see which) with his rubber finger. The ringing finally ceased.

'Yes? Yes, this is Kemble.'

The man gave Dora half a smile and rolled his eyes impatiently. 'Yes. Yes. My clerk will collect the exhibits tomorrow morning and the photographer is sending over his enlargements. The coroner knows all about it. Yes. Most emphatically. The marks on both breasts and nipples were absolutely conclusive. My report from Southwark was quite clear: After, not Before.'

It was absolutely ghastly. Breasts. Nipples. Dora could actually feel the colour flooding across her face and neck and she was sure the man was looking at her as he said the words. And then, ghastlier still, she began to feel the tickle of tears somewhere in the back of her face. She couldn't blush *and* blub. The man was still jawing away into the telephone about haematomas and whatnot. She still had her coat on and her instinct was to grab her hat and run. At least get a breath of air before she made a complete fool of herself. The agency had said quarter to nine after all and it was still only five past eight . . . She retreated into the corridor, re-locking the door behind her.

Downstairs the men were still busy squeezing their crates through the open door. Dora didn't really need to look at the polish-encrusted brass plaque on the railings to know which department they would be going to.

The hospital, like a grand old playhouse, had a different entrance for every class of life. There were a couple of Royces parked in the forecourt and Dora saw a pair of morning-coated grandees doing a spot of charity work before their Harley Street appointments began. The sick themselves either went in horizontally via the ambulance bay round the back or limped through the apologetic side door into the outpatients department. Visitors, when their hour came, probably used the main entrance where they could gaze at a great wall of artless art – Charity and Compassion ministering to Chronic Dyspepsia, or some such – or play games of surname lotto with the list of the hospital's Glorious Dead while they waited to be told which ward to visit.

Nurses were relegated to a side entrance. Probably weren't allowed to use the front one without a patient in tow. Probably *fined* or given lines or made to sew their pockets up. A whole flock of them, wearing their capes, thick black belts, stiff white collars and starched caps like deranged damask dinner napkins, had arrived to start work in one of the clinics. A matron in dark blue sailed past them, borne along by the great white wigwam of linen pitched improbably on the top of her head. One of the nurses dashed in front of the group to open the door for her, like some fourth-form creep sucking up to a house mistress.

Dora's collywobbles had eased off somewhat and she suddenly found herself absolutely ravenous. She had only been in residence at Warwick Square since Friday and so far Mrs Frith's breakfasts had consisted of meat rissoles, atrocities devised with malice aforethought by the author of one of Mrs Frith's most trusted guides on catering matters: 'Cold Meat and How to Disguise It' (it was seldom a very convincing disguise). Rissoles were one of the pamphlet's cunning culinary dodges for using up the remains of a Sunday roast by eking out the scraps of lamb, beef or what-have-you with mashed potato, breadcrumbs and a suggestion of parsley (which remained a mere suggestion as Mrs Frith didn't grow it and wouldn't pay for it). Mrs Frith had clearly got the whole business down to a fine art. Indeed, the remains of the roast in question had already been eked within an inch of its life in the attempt to serve eight for Sunday luncheon so that the proportion of leftover meat to be found in each rissole was practically homoeopathic.

Mr Stone, who occupied the room below Dora's, had only moved in a fortnight earlier but was already growing mutinous and talked of looking for rooms elsewhere (so Miss Digby said, anyway). Dora had no such chance of escape. She seemed to have been under Mrs Frith's wing for most of her life since her father had first taken the wretched woman on as his secretary when his daughter was twelve years old. The whole job-in-London business ('Theodora's little experiment', as her father insisted on calling it) had been on the understanding that she was securely lodged *chez* Frith.

By the time Dora had done the full circuit of the hospital the hunger pangs were so acute that she decided to risk a cup of tea and some species of bun in an enterprising little tearoom that had recently opened opposite the main gate to lure anxious relations and malnourished medics. The café smelled pleasantly of toast and tobacco. Several doctors-in-waiting were nursing pots of tea and neat squares of implausibly yellow cake. The students were learning the wisdom of keeping one's profession a secret. All sorts of riff-raff – women especially – were forever trying to save shillings on the panel by cadging free advice, and so their white coats had been prudently left hanging on their common room hooks, but the wormy bulge of the stethoscopes in their pockets and their weakness for talking shop soon gave them away. The waitress certainly wasn't fooled. More hot water for the doctor, Hetty.

The teacup was made of a white china so thick that Dora could not get her forefinger comfortably through the handle, which had to be pinched between finger and thumb like a cup from a dollies' tea set. She cut her bun in half, then in half again but it remained wilfully adhesive when she tried to wipe her mouth with one of her old school pocket handkerchiefs (*three dozen, plain white, clearly monogrammed*). She had only managed to soldier through one segment before glancing at her wristwatch to find that it was nearly twenty to nine. This left her almost (but not quite) enough time to sprint the five hundred yards back round the corner to the Willcox Wing and waste the vital minutes between Punctual and Late explaining herself to the day porter. The new man had clocked on at half past eight and hadn't never been told nothing about no new clerk (did three negatives make a positive?) and his grasp of the telephone system (after four years on the job) was as shadowy as Dora's.

'Young lady here says she's the new filing clerk in "Mr Hubbard's Department" ' (he too seemed personally offended by the thought of this Hubbard person's elevation). 'I've heard nothing about this from the Bursar's office.'

By the time Dora had climbed the three flights and reached the now familiar green door it was nearly nine o'clock.

Chapter 2

'Not a very good start.' The voice came from the big desk under the window. The wall clock in the office read two minutes to nine. Beneath it sat a man with an undecided, ratty-looking moustache and what Dora feared was a celluloid collar, who looked up from a pile of newspapers and pointed at her with the surgical scalpel he held in his right hand. Behind the thick lenses of his spectacles his eyes looked like the last two pickles in the jar. Dora smiled ruefully and made her excuses.

'Strang. Dora. Dora Strang. I'm sorry I'm late. The porter downstairs wasn't expecting anyone. I showed him my letter from the bureau but it still took rather a long while to explain.' Hardly the breezy, confident introduction she had rehearsed.

'It might help if he could actually read,' chuckled a cheery disembodied voice. Behind the desk opposite the door a skinny tow-headed chap in flannel bags and scruffily scuffed Oxfords about half the age of the moustache character was sitting on the floor, muttering strange oaths and wrestling with the bottom drawer of one of the filing cabinets.

Old moustache-features had sunk the blade of his scalpel into a crack in his desk and was now buzzing the main switchboard.

'Porter's desk, Willcox Wing.'

Dora walked across to where the young man was sitting and frowned encouragingly at the drawer. His leg was stretched out across the floor in front of her and you could just see where he had inked the skin of his heel to mask the hole in his sock.

'Hello. You might try pulling the middle one right out. Then you'd see what was blocking it,' offered Dora.

'It's been tried. Everything's been tried, from French chalk to brute force. Hubbard here had good money on wax candle ends, didn't you, Hubbers? Brought them in specially in their own little tobacco tin.' He scrambled to his feet and dusted down his flannels. 'It's no good. This is a job for Maintenance: big men with very large tools and very small frontal lobes.'

He gave the cabinet a parting kick and the bottom drawer glided smoothly open, neatly catching his shin bone as it did so.

'Or not, obviously.' He folded himself in half to rub at the sore place. 'I swear this furniture's haunted – especially that desk,' he nodded towards the table with the big telephone, 'jinxed by the ghosts of the last four incumbents, all of whom left in mysterious circumstances without giving the usual notice . . .'

The other man had got through to the porter on the telephone.

'Mis-ter Hughes,' he managed to make the 'mister' sound like a rather snide private joke, 'Hubbard here. Are you detaining any other young persons seeking employment in this department? We seem to be minus one typewriter. You are quite sure?' His accent was almost-but-not-quaite, an affectation that was almost (but not quaite) endearing. He replaced the receiver and carried on fretting to no one in particular. 'I shall have to telephone those fools at the bureau. They advertise themselves as specialists. I distinctly requested a male clerk . . .'

'Aren't you the typewriter?' puzzled the friendly young man.

'No. Filing.'

'Vazard, sorry, Alec Vazard.' He wiped his dusty hand on his tweed jacket. 'Helping out in the department.' Dora shook hands carefully. Her headmistress had been a stickler about handshaking: too firm or too fishy and you'd be made to do it again. Mortifying.

'That's Hubbard over there, fount of all knowledge. Our lord and master is out at the moment but he lives through there in Room Nine.' He gestured towards the 'No Admittance' door. 'Filing clerk, eh? That'll be a novelty. Months since we had one of those – eh, Hubbard?' He winced in the direction of a low cupboard in the far corner bearing a stack of tin trays with letters japanned on to their ends: 'Path in, Path out, Kemble' and, most precariously of all on the open top deck, a huge slippery heap marked 'Filing', which had long ago reached its safe maximum and was surrounded by supplementary piles of pasteboard folders plus two shoebox-sized cartons containing hundreds of six-by-four index cards filled out in a fantastically neat yet resolutely illegible hand using green ink and the finest possible italic nib.

Vazard lowered his voice. 'You'll have to watch it with that filing system. Every one of the big man's cards to be cross-reffed in triplicate thereby forming the great departmental cross-index. Entirely of Mr Hubbard's own devising. It's supposed to mean that you can find any person, cause of death, date of death, district or collar size all at the flick of a fingertip. A beautiful thought, I'm sure you'll agree, and dashed useful should you wish to track down all the peritonitis in Poplar, but as you can see . . .' he cocked an eye at the stack of unfiled reports, 'the system's only as good as its slaves. I've even had the odd crack at it myself. We haven't had a bona fide filing clerk since the last poor soul – Harris, I think her name was – shook the dust from her feet back in August. Mrs Culvey did her best, I suppose . . .' He tailed off as if her best hadn't really been very good.

'So are you Dr Kemble's assistant?' asked Dora.

'In a way, but don't let Hubbard hear you say it. I don't even qualify till next year – if then. I'm still going to the regular lectures but I'm spending part of this term attached to the lab; after that

I'm down for a stretch of hard labour in obstetrics. I help out with the odd spot of morbid anatomy if they ask me nicely. Take samples, make slides, write up reports, that type of thing. We all muck in as required. In an ideal world we'd have someone who could do shorthand *and* typing but no sooner do we land one than they head screaming for the hills.'

'Will you go in for pathology, do you think?'

He paused as if about to answer at length but thought better of it, perhaps conscious that housemen had better things to do than make conversation with clerical pond life.

'Dunno. Ask me again at the end of term – if you're still here, of course ...'

Hubbard was now to be heard telephoning to Dora's agency from the large instrument on the typist's desk, whining that he had been assured that not one but two of their operatives would be available to commence employment first thing on Monday morning. His little soup-strainer was tickling the mouthpiece as he spoke.

'Nonsense, madam, no one in my department' ('*e'd like to 'ave a department*) 'could possibly have requested any such thing.' A well-bred voice could be heard squeaking in protest at the other end of the line, like an indignant swanee whistle. 'I don't care if she's the fifteenth. I don't care if she's the fifty-fifth. The fact that you are having difficulty supplying anyone truly suitable is your problem not mine and, if I may say so, says very little for the calibre of potential employees on your books.' The voice in his hand became more shrill at this. 'I don't doubt that she is, madam, but that does not alter the fact that you have sent this extremely busy department *one* female when *two* male operatives had expressly been requested.' He replaced the receiver.

He looked crossly up at Dora.

'Is your name strange?'

The main door behind her opened as he said this. It was the tall, angry breasts-and-nipples character. He hit the room like a stiff breeze and Hubbard and Vazard were suddenly at attention, like dogs in hopes of a walk.

He had swapped the white rubber apron for the full Harley Street fig: striped trousers, black morning coat, gold watch chain and dove-grey spats. The immaculate sartorial picture was spoiled by the fact that he carried a very large, well-polished Gladstone bag in his right hand. He was quite a bit older than Vazard, with a gaunt but rather distinguished face and dark hair combed straight back. His face was lined but only faintly, the wrinkles sketching his habitual expressions: a few lines above the quizzical left eyebrow, a little crescent to the right of his mouth made by that wry half-smile. Dora could never tell people's ages but he was definitely more young than old. Not fifty. Forty? She thought of her father's sixty-five-year-old forehead chequered with decades of surprise and vexation.

'Morning Hubbard, Vazard. This the new typewriter?'

Hubbard opened his mouth and closed it again, obviously reluctant to admit that no such article had been delivered. Vazard looked faintly discomfited that Dora should be spoken about in the third person but neither appeared ready to risk a proper introduction. The man struck a match and lit a gasper, somehow managing to frown and smile at the same time. 'Miss . . . Strange, I think you said? Welcome to Morbid Anatomy.'

On the whole his manner was businesslike but perfectly amiable. Not a peep about their earlier meeting but he'd obviously recognised her. 'I think this young person had better begin by learning to master the telephones, don't you, Hubbard?' Dora shrivelled with embarrassment but he made no further reference to their earlier meeting. 'Come along, Hubbard, lots to do. No calls please, Vazard.'

And with the big black bag leading the way he sailed through a door marked 'Supplies' with Hubbard clomping along behind.

Jolly peculiar-looking shoes. The soles were unusually thick and the uppers unnaturally deep, like the boots that cripples wore.

'You might as well sit over there for now.' Vazard pointed to the desk by the door. 'I don't expect the new typewriter will start until tomorrow – even supposing they find one at all, male or female. Hard to believe that the agency will be pulling out all the stops for poor old Hubbard somehow. This is far from being their first conversation.'

This temporary promotion earned Dora the smoked oak desk with the big telephone and the typewriting machine. It was ringed with yet more filing cabinets and card index boxes: A–Bot, Bou–Cho, Chr–Emb. There was also a blotter, an inkstand, a pencil-sharpening machine like the sort that form mistresses always had bolted to their desks and a miniature merry-go-round of rubber stamps: a date stamp, 'paid', 'pathology', 'urgent'.

' "Destroy yellow"?' wondered Dora.

'One of the great mysteries. Hubbard won't admit to it but it's believed to be a hangover from an earlier, Neanderthal stage in the evolution of the Great Filing System.'

There was no sign of life from the supplies cupboard.

'What goes on in there, exactly?'

'What?'

'Dr Kemble and Mr Hubbard. They've been in that cupboard for five minutes nearly.'

Vazard had rather a nice laugh.

'It connects to the lab from the other side. They'll have all sorts of specimens to prepare. The chief's working on this alley murder business.'

The two-week gap between secretaries had offered a window of criminal opportunity during which someone had pinched the typist's chair. Vazard was still lurking helpfully.

'On past form it will almost certainly have been one of those adjectival blighters in Dispatch. Same spot as this only in the basement below. The chair you're looking for had "Maintenance" scratched into the back with a dissecting knife, if I remember rightly.'

'Maintenance? Shouldn't it go back there?'

'Good Lord, no. Not unless you fancy trying to requisition a new one in triplicate from the jolly old general purposes committee. Possession is nine-tenths and all that. Besides, Maintenance never sit down: they *loaf*. Expert at it. I've studied their habits in the yard at the back: leaning against walls with mugs of hot tea like a minor industrial study by Ford Maddox Brown. When they're not doing that they're down holes or up ladders. Wouldn't know what to do with a chair if they had one – which they don't, of course – unless they've pinched it back from Dispatch. I'd offer to go myself but I suspect your, ahem, maiden charm will get better results. Make sure you get someone to carry it for you.'

Dispatch were all out dispatching at that time of day and the old man left in charge greeted Dora's request with the enthusiasm of a Jack Russell who has just been shown the worming powder. He was eventually persuaded to manhandle the missing chair in and out of the passenger lift but he did it with a very ill grace.

Dora sat down once back at her desk. Vazard had had to disappear to a lecture on The Splinting and Irrigation of Compound Fractures but had left a large pile of filing and half a box of virgin index cards on the desktop, together with a yellowing sheaf of paper detailing the proper use of Hubbard's famous filing system. She felt like the miller's daughter in 'Rumpelstiltskin'.

It seemed she was to mark up cause of death and victim's name in capital letters along the top of the first case card (the more juicy cases had as many of six or seven each) then make new cross-reference cards for victim, mortuary and date. The pathologist seemed already to have double underlined cause of death in the top right-hand corner of the first card so it was supposedly just a matter of copying it out (always assuming one could decipher his spidery green script), but any subsidiary causes or pre-existing conditions that he had also seen fit to underline would also require a separate card. And that was the easy part.

Hubbard had based his classifications on a system advocated by a large American hospital. There was a definite logic to it but fire seemed to dominate their thinking for some reason, taking precedence over all other causes of injury: 'If a patient is injured directly or indirectly on or about a conflagration, the number 166 must be assigned to the diagnosis, e.g. a fracture of the femur produced by the fall of a passenger elevator in a burning building must receive the number 166 and not 174B.' Your wife might induce a fatal heart attack as she beat you about the head with your favourite golf club but if the house happened to be in flames at the time fire would remain the primary terminal event.

Mrs Culvey had obviously made a vague stab at the cross-referencing and had left a dozen or so cards in the box ('cradiac' arrest: not a natural typist). Far quicker to do them by hand in any case – saved all that fiddle with the platen knob. The thoughtful Vazard had left a dipping pen on the blotter but the inkwell held nothing but black crumbs and Dora began to rummage through the desk in search of a fresh bottle. The topmost drawer contained the usual inky jetsam: chewed ends of pencils, a hairy blob of sealing wax, a dried-up stamping pad, a fountain pen with a ruptured bladder (84c), a pair of knitted blue gloves with no fingers and a grey ink eraser – the sort that was supposed to correct typing errors but which, Dora had long since discovered, merely gouged a hole in the paper where the mistake had been. A single cough lozenge had glued itself to the base of the drawer and was covered in petals of pencil shavings like a miniature dinosaur.

Dora began scanning a bundle of cards. 'Victim a well-nourished female, hair chemically lightened and bent by the action of heat, significant cervical scarring, no signs of any pregnancy carried to term, hands and feet were well kept and she had worn well-fitting shoes, both nipples missing, letters h-a-r-l-e-t scratched in dorsal skin with sharp, square-ended instrument. Punctures and lacerations to birth canal query instrument. Scar tissue. Evidence of previous lacerations to cervix and vaginal fornices.' Cross reference: St Pancras.

Dora's stomach curdled in panic the first time the telephone went. Vazard had shown her what to do but sticky memories of Kemble's gloved hand around the receiver (gloved against what?) prompted her to wipe it with her handkerchief before she pressed the correct button. She could barely make out the cockney whisper at the other end but she was to tell Hubbard that there was one lined up in Alexandra Ward and to look lively. The line went dead.

Hubbard had gone off to pick a fight with the bursar's office and, with no Vazard to ask, Dora was at rather a loss. The doctor had distinctly said no calls, but the Man of Mystery made whatever-it-was sound frightfully urgent. She decided to risk it and pressed *Lab*.

'Very sorry to disturb you, Dr Kemble, but a man called Whitfield has telephoned. I didn't quite understand the message but he says he's *found one* in Alexandra Ward.'

Had he, by Jove. Moments later the pathologist was in the office, peeling off his apron and wriggling into one of the white coats hanging on the hat stand.

'Get me Vazard's stethoscope off the rack there, would you? Might as well look the part.'

He slung the borrowed apparatus around his neck then opened Hubbard's top desk drawer and slipped what looked like a screwdriver into his right-hand pocket. Hubbard returned just as he reached the door.

'We finally have our guinea pig, Hubbard old man. I'll be back as soon as I can. See if you can't organise some sort of nuisance call to Alexandra. Give me a few minutes to get across.' Then he dashed from the room and thundered down the stairs.

Hubbard began watching the office clock obsessively the moment Kemble left the room. After five minutes had passed, he used Dora's telephone to buzz the main switchboard and ask for Alexandra Ward and then angrily demanded to know who was responsible for an abandoned trolley found in the basement subway between Willcox and the main building and could they kindly get a porter to remove it. He held the receiver in his right hand and was waving his left arm for emphasis, causing the front of his jacket to flap open. Dora turned her head and moved her chair a bit further away.

Vazard was back from his lecture and already hard at work copying something out of one of the files he had liberated. She coughed feebly.

'I'm sorry to be so useless but do you happen to know if there is any black ink anywhere?'

'Couldn't say exactly but you can generally find everything your little heart could desire in Supplies – provided that your heart's desire is in the filing paper and formaldehyde line. I'll have a look for you.' He paused. 'Is it really strange?'

'Is what really strange?'

'Your name. Is it in fact Strange?'

'No. No. It's Strang. It seemed churlish to fuss.'

'Oh dear. May already be too late. There was a similar blunder about three typewriters ago. Resulted in her being called Mrs Tempry for the two weeks she was here – may have been one of the reasons she left.'

He was interrupted by an unmistakable clattering sound just outside the door, where a Mrs Arnold was having her daily argument with the tea urn, the trolley and the passenger lift.

'Morning, Mrs A. This lady is replacing Mrs Culvey. Miss Strang: Mrs Arnold.'

Mrs A looked a slimmer first cousin to one of the old ghouls on the omnibus. What would Dora fancy? There was a big plate of iced buns and teacakes on the shelf below the cups and saucers. Dora was ravenous again but decided that sitting at her desk tackling a Chelsea bun the size of a bath sponge wouldn't be quite the thing, and settled for a cup of tea while Mrs A committed to memory the fact that Miss Strang liked strong, with, without.

Big Chief Kemble came back just in time for elevenses (without, two sugars, iced bun). Hubbard (without, without, bugger all) sensed his return somehow and emerged simultaneously from No Admittance.

'And how are you, Mrs A?' The pathologist placed his cup and saucer on Hubbard's desk and slipped the screwdriver thingy back into its drawer. It had a blond wood handle.

Mrs Arnold had bunions and corns and adenoids and haemorrhoids and fibroids and the beginnings of a peptic ulcer but she mustn't grumble (not to him, at least). Nice enough gent in his way but no sense queering your Christmas box over it. It wasn't like he was a *Doctor* doctor. She had once made the mistake of answering his automatic enquiry with the earth-shattering news that the pain was all down one side and much worse in cold weather. Dr Kemble had remarked that nothing would give him greater pleasure than to establish the exact cause of her complaint but that she would have to oblige him by dying first.

Even the fabled supplies cupboard had no stocks of ink so Dora resumed tidying the desk while the furious Hubbard went in search of some. The middle drawer was wedged shut by a batch of error-covered post-mortem forms. When she finally managed to jiggle it open it revealed a ream of lemon yellow typewriting paper and a tray of congealed and inky copying gelatin. A conscientious secretary was supposed, in theory, to melt the stuff down and use it again. Dora peeled the tissue free of the bakelite tray, rolled up the dried jelly and filed it neatly in the waste-paper basket. The only other thing in the drawer was the Hektograph copy that the jelly had made: a rather interesting-looking speech on 'Purifying the germ plasm' to be delivered to the Human Betterment Foundation. She placed the yellow sheets carefully to one side.

There were demerits for messy desks and cubby-holes at Dora's school, and while the typewriting academy didn't go as far as putting its young ladies in detention, the instructress was forever pointing out that A Tidy Desk meant A Tidy Mind (which it very probably did in her case). An efficient secretary kept her personal effects to the barest minimum – a box of aspirin and a comb covered most eventualities – anything more was Unprofessional. The late Mrs Culvey was of a very different opinion and appeared to have departed in the wake of a full-scale fire drill. She hadn't actually left her hat and coat on the rack but she had blithely relinquished a tin of fruit dragees, a paperbacked detective story, a box of face powder, a comb containing quite a number of chemically lightened hairs bent by the action of heat, a new pair of rather decent-looking silk stockings and a full bottle of Coty scent.

Dora laid a sheet of foolscap over the gelatinous mess in the bin and placed the powder and scent carefully on top in case the charlady might like to have them. She decided to keep the stockings (her size). Dora looked uncertainly down at her own lisle calves. She had imagined her predecessor rather in the mould of her old stinks mistress: mannish coats and skirts, heavy brogues, bobbed hair with an unshaved neck, and she frowned as she tried to picture the spendthrift Mrs Culvey, wearing scent and powder and silk stockings to come and (mis)type cards in a laboratory. Rather rum.

Hubbard had managed to wangle a bottle of ink from the hospital typing pool, whose manager had given him the number of yet another agency. He was soon regaling some unseen female with a long and very detailed list of all the unsatisfactory personnel supplied by the other agencies he had tried (probably not the best tone to have taken, in all honesty).

Nothing was said as to when or where Dora should lunch. Vazard had gone to watch an amputation over in the main building, leaving Dora alone with Hubbard. Hubbard consumed what he liked to call his 'dinner' at his desk at one o'clock sharp, and he arrived each morning with an old Oxo tin supplied by his mother, with whom he lived. Today's offering consisted of two sandwiches of butterless vita-bread filled with the remains of the previous day's boiled beef and cabbage greens, which gave the office an unpleasantly Frith-y whiff.

Mrs Hubbard maintained that cheese and ham and tongue and corned beef weren't a Proper Dinner and that you wouldn't catch her wasting tinned stuff when there were perfectly good leftovers going to waste. The three tins of sardines in Mrs Hubbard's cupboards had been earmarked for Emergencies but had survived the entire war – including a bizarrely persistent succession of Zeppelin raids on Leytonstone – entirely unscathed. How grave would the situation need to be, Hubbard wondered?

When Dora tentatively asked if the hospital possessed a canteen he chewed on with almost bovine concentration, a scissored sheet of the *Daily Sketch* placed across his desk to protect it from stray strands of cold cabbage. Did he never leave the office during the day for a breath of air? enquired Dora, politely. Couldn't he telephone to the main switchboard and simply explain that there would be no one in the department between one and two? Or just not answer the telephone at all at that time? How many times did it usually ring? Most people lunched at one, after all. He still didn't reply – perhaps he was merely deaf?

Dora wondered about heading off to the main building in quest of the refectory (there was sure to be one) but the thought of braving its mysteries was altogether too daunting. Who sat precisely where was certain to be a minefield for the uninitiated and there were probably unwritten rules about what one did with one's tray. Perhaps a picnic from the teashop was the answer? Had Mrs Culvey brought sandwiches? Unlikely. Dora fished the tin of boiled sweets from the waste basket and sucked on one as she printed 'Syphilis', 'Rectal carcinoma' and 'Golders Green' on three rectangles of buff pasteboard in her best copperplate capitals. Two down, six hundred to go.

The majority of the post-mortems were routine investigations after hospital deaths from pneumonia or nephritis, but there was no end to the ills that flesh was heir to: disseminated suppurative encephalitis, elephantiasis of the scrotum, ruptured bladders. Kemble's insistence on examining every nook and cranny meant that the cross-referencing soon piled up. A man in his mid thirties, thick-set and coarse-featured, with extensively decayed teeth, a recent appendix scar and a bluebird tattoo at the base of the left thumb, had been discovered in a partially skeletal condition under a haystack on the Sussex Downs. He was trussed like a chicken with drum cord, hands tightly lashed behind him by means of an ingenious array of self-tightening slipknots, knees roped to the chest, head enveloped in an army coat strapped over nostrils and mouth by a webbing belt. The cause of death was exposure (accidental) but the cross-references ran to six cards: cirrhosis, urnings, perineal papilloma and a rather fine strangulated ischiorectal hernia. His cards also chummed up rather neatly with a surprisingly large group of men found hanging naked from the backs of their bedroom doors.

Sometimes there was no definitive cause of death even after all the cutting about. 'Male. Had worn ill-fitting shoes. Tubercular lesions on both lungs. Haemorrhoids. Dismembered with some skill into eight pieces. Head, hands not found.' There was nearly half a drawerful of headless men. What became of all those heads and hands? Was there a stash of cabin trunks somewhere simply filled with leftovers?

And there was poor Mavis, right at the top of the second pile. 'Female. Hitherto virgo intacta. Tooth marks breasts. Vulval lesions.' And no, of course she hadn't been out gallivanting around back alleys inviting the murderous men of Peckham to come for her: 'extensive bruising wrists; lacerations knees query gravel. Fingernail scrapings show traces of mammalian blood'.

Hubbard had placed his greasy sheet of newspaper in the wastebasket when he had finally finished his 'dinner' and was in and out of the pathologist's inner sanctum for the rest of the afternoon, leaving Dora alone with the dead. It was slow work but by four o'clock she had used the last of the three dozen buff cards Vazard had left for her.

'Already?' Hubbard's eye flew to the waste-paper basket (as Dora jolly well knew it would) in hopes of finding it filled with mistakes. There had been quite a number, as it happened, but Dora had hidden those in her coat pocket.

'It wasn't a full packet.'

He jerked his head in the direction of the door marked 'Supplies', unwilling to waste more words than necessary, and dived back through 'No Admittance'.

'Supplies' turned out to be more of a room than a cupboard with its own radiator and a frosted window on to the building's central well. The moment she opened the door the warm room released a whole new world of smells. The nice, dry, gymslippery aroma of the main office was still in place but the notes of gum-arabic and freshly sharpened pencils were all intensified as if you were sniffing them straight from the bottle and the innocent schoolroom cocktail was spiked with a very different set of scents. Smells that would have triggered hideous pangs of anxiety in any other girl: Lysol and Dakin's fluid and boracic lint and iodine and formalin and medicated cotton wool wrapped in dark blue paper.

The smell of check-ups, injections, medicals, sterilised hands on virgin flesh, just-slip-your-blouse-off terrors and the icy tease of the stethoscope being dabbed unseen on entirely unpredictable areas of the back.

The cupboard walls were lined floor to ceiling with shelves of stationery and fat brown bottles of chemicals. In the far corner against the wall were great sacks of sawdust and bales of tow and straw. Screwed to one of the shelves was a long bolt of thick brown paper with a special toothy gadget for tearing off the required length. And gathered on the floor beneath, under the lowest of the shelves, was an assortment of stout cardboard boxes and a tray full of labels and long red sticks of sealing wax. Dora scanned the stationery section until she spied a fresh packet of index cards. They were way out of her reach but there was a folding ladder tucked behind the door.

She had just climbed on to the top step when she was startled by a cough at her elbow and nearly fell. The pathologist had tiptoed in unnoticed from the laboratory side. His ungloved hands reached out to steady her. His head was level with the middle button of her cardigan.

'Size?'

He was *looking* at her. Looking at her *shape*. Rather bad form.

'What size are you? I need you – that is,' like a little boy belatedly remembering his manners, 'if-you-wouldn't-*mind* – for an experiment we're planning to do tomorrow.' He spoke very, very quietly, as if unwilling to be overheard, for some reason.

Dora was still standing on the stepladder, and the upward tilt of his head gave him a curiously submissive appearance.

'Would you mind very much? I know you're very busy with all those infernal cards . . .'

She continued to hesitate, confused and annoyed by his standing so unnecessarily close.

'Hubbard will chaperone, of course.'

It sounded suspiciously like an afterthought. Would Hubbard have been left undisturbed if she had consented more quickly?

He followed her out of the cupboard and into the main office, where Hubbard was hard at work with the scissors once more.

'Your young clerical friend here has agreed to give us a hand tomorrow, Hubbard. She's just the right size.'

Chapter 3

There was a jam jar sitting on the stairs at Warwick Square when Dora returned. A tiny brown paper funnel had been placed in the top and a strip of the same paper, about an inch wide, led from the inside of the funnel to the triangle of floorboard where the carpet made the first turn in the stairs. There was something black and sticky in the bottom of the jar. When Dora got up to the second floor she found that the legs of her brass bed were standing in four (matching) tins marked 'Portuguese Sardines'. The whole room – the whole house – smelled alarmingly of paraffin. Mrs Frith was on the warpath.

The widow Frith had been obliged to seek paid employment after the war. She had invested her husband's minuscule legacy in a tedious but eminently practical course of study which had made her mistress of Pitman shorthand, typewriting, the care and feeding of the out-letters book and other bureaucratic mysteries. She had then presented herself at an employment agency in the Strand where a Miss Winchett had put her in touch with various parties seeking experienced but inexpensive secretarial help. After a few false starts she had found an employer who met her requirements: a tight-lipped, stony-faced Harley Street widower looking for a firm-minded, no-nonsense lady to organise his appointments diary, deal with his correspondence and screen him from the whines and woes of his patients.

Dr Strang had been willing to overlook Mrs Frith's lack of experience and her unaccountable refusal to work on Wednesday afternoons and, overall, the appointment was a success. True, his new employee was possessed of an unmistakably hostile manner but that was always something of an asset in a medical secretary and the woman appeared perfectly efficient and biddable.

It was only three weeks after her installation that the doctor received his first glimpse of the Inner Frith when he had casually mentioned that his ten-year-old daughter would be coming home from school the following Thursday, or was it Friday? ... and that Mrs Gregory (Mrs Frith's predecessor) had always been quite willing to collect Theodora from the railway station and parcel her off to various relations of her late mother's where she spent the bulk of her vacations – 'vacs', he believed they were now called. Harley Street, he continued, was hardly the place for a schoolgirl (an assertion immediately contradicted by a crocodile of young ladies from Queen's College which had just that instant materialised beneath his consulting-room window and was, as he spoke, sensible-shoeing its way to a matinée at the Wigmore Hall).

During Dora's earlier childhood Dr Strang had hired a starched succession of nannies to bridge any gaps in her care, but he was unwilling to put himself to the unnecessary expense of an agency nursemaid for a great girl of ten. Mrs Gregory had also been happy, *more than* happy, to take charge of kitting Theodora out with frocks and hats and, er, hockey racquets and so forth – just an occasional visit to Whiteley's or Liberty's or the Neale people to purchase whatever it was that girls of her age required. More than happy.

Was she indeed. Mrs Frith had already grown decidedly weary of Dr Strang's constant invocation of this Gregory female. She had stared frostily back at her employer from behind her Morocco-topped desk and taken a deep, fortifying breath, conscious that their working relationship would be defined by the outcome of this exchange.

'You will forgive me, Dr Strang, but surely some female relation would be more suitable? Surely', she pretended to forget the stupid name, 'Pandora? would prefer to undertake such an outing with an aunt? Or a cousin?'

Dr Strang blocked that move at once. The nearest available aunt lived on the Sussex coast and never came to town. Never. She was an Invalid (Dr Strang had pronounced the diagnosis in a tone of habitual scepticism). Theodora perfectly understood that her papa could hardly be expected to spare time away from his patients to go shopping for Liberty bodices and what-have-you and she had grown quite used to Mrs Gregory taking her about. Dr Strang risked one of his rare smiles (a toothless stretching of closed lips) but it was utterly wasted on Mrs Frith, who pounced on the sainted Gregory and volleyed her straight back at him.

Could not this obviously excellent female be persuaded to carry on that aspect of her former duties? She and Miss Strang must surely be firm friends by now? The idea of anyone becoming friends, firm or otherwise, with Mrs Gregory, whose humourless *froideur* had always bordered on outright hostility, nearly cost Dr Strang a second smile but he aborted it in time. Mrs Gregory had retired to the far North of England and Mrs Frith must forgive him but he was afraid that there would inevitably be times when her duties would mean undertaking tasks that ensured the smooth running of the practice. Of course, if Mrs Frith's objections were *insurmountable* then he feared they must both return to the agency from whence she came – the line that usually followed hung in the air between them – although, he had continued pitilessly, her Wednesday absences might make it difficult to find another suitable position. *Particularly*, Dr Strang smiled the cruel but satisfied smile of a player about to croquet an opponent deep into the herbaceous borders, *without* the necessary references.

The following Thursday, Mrs Frith, mindful of the depressing number of excellent typists to be found in the box of cards on Miss Winchett's desk, was at Paddington Station to meet Dora. Dr Strang's telegram to his daughter had been a thrifty burst of literary modernism which warned her to expect 'unsmilingwidow, yellowhair, wheyface, repellent aspect' (the allusion was sure to be lost on Theodora but it amused him as he pencilled it on to the form). Mrs Frith in her turn had been told that Theodora had brown hair and that her uniform was green. Her employer (who had never personally met the school train) evidently imagined that this would suffice to distinguish his daughter from the 150 or so of her fellow students on the school special from Cirencester (the 'Sisters', as they liked to call themselves).

The fact that the child should have made so very little impression on her own father had led Mrs Frith to anticipate a mousy, submissive little body and she was altogether unprepared for Theodora as she trotted along the platform the following Thursday lunchtime. Hello, she must be Mrs Frith, she must call her Dora. Everybody did – everybody except Papa (wouldn't you know it?). *Theo-dora* – such a bore-a. Pity he hadn't had a dog first and got the dratted name out of his system. How did she do? Was she on nursemaid duty? What an absolute bore for her.

Once inside the taxi it became clear that the child was not remotely interested in the proposed shopping excursion (as any normal girl her age would have been). Instead Mrs Frith was given a sheet of foolscap with Dora's measurements neatly written in roundhand. Would she mind too dreadfully going on her own? Shopping was *such* a bore. 'Nice *plain* things. Papa will know straightaway I wasn't with you if you try any prettifying. I'm just Not That Sort.'

Mrs Frith hadn't been a bit surprised when the storm blew up over the girl wanting to go off to university. It was old Strang's fault for letting her stay on at school for so long. Higher Certificate, all that nonsense. It was exactly the same with convents, Mrs Frith had observed: leave them a moment too long and they were sure to go native. In the event, the university business had come to nothing – just as well. Failure had knocked a bit of the stuffing out of her.

The two of them had acted out the same Paddington farce six times a year until Dora's final term at school, when Dr Strang's retirement had chimed so conveniently with the death of Mrs Frith's mother-in-law, who had finally crossed the divide after a long and extremely unpleasant illness. This had allowed her to move from her small, dingy Marylebone flat to a large, dingy house on the wrong side of Warwick Square. Too large for her own needs, obviously, but ripe for uglification into a genteel boarding house.

Dora had spent a month sulking in her bedroom after the Somerville rejection letter came, until one morning her eye was caught by an advertisement in the *Morning Post* for a residential typewriting establishment. She eventually succeeded in persuading her father to finance the nine months' study which would enable her to earn her living in London, but he drove a hard bargain: should she ever actually find employment in town she was to lodge with the dreaded Frith.

Dr Strang had perhaps imagined that his old secretary's habits of economy and efficiency would stand her in good stead in the domestic sphere. A vain hope. Mrs Frith had trained for twelve months to become a shorthand typewriter; she had never been trained to keep house for ten. Her married life had commenced just as her husband left for the front and the short, frantic honeymoon had been spent in his bachelor rooms in Marylebone. They had dined out when he was on leave but the soldier's bride had sat out the rest of the war on toast (cheese or sardine or potted meat supplies permitting) and her widow's diet was a similar series of savoury snacks, which were the limit of her culinary repertoire.

Mrs Frith's mama had kept a cook, two maids and a jobbing gardener, but her daughter had enormous difficulty keeping servants of any description when she took over the house in Warwick Square. The string of cooks-general who condescended to inhabit Mrs Frith's lower ground floor were not impressed by the pathologically parsimonious cookbooks that Mrs Frith had found on the penny shelf of a bookshop on Victoria Street. They were accustomed to far more generous fare, or so they always insisted. The one before last was forever referring to a (doubtless imaginary) Mrs Crisp, whose culinary largesse was positively Lucullan: lobsters, capons, hothouse fruits.

Their landlady's relentless economies meant that the Warwick Square PGs were seldom in any particular hurry to heed the nightly gong. Their daily dinners were advertised in advance on a scrap of paper pinned up in the hall. Sunday evening's supper had been 'consommé' (a lukewarm puddle of watery Bovril) and 'curried liver', one of the more sick-making suggestions to be found in 'Dainty Dishes for Slender Incomes' (the companion volume to 'Cold Meat and How to Disguise It'). Dora had spent most of the meal carving the liver into thin strips that could be concealed under her knife and fork (a trick perfected in the Lower Third). Not so Mr Haddon, who had evidently been banged up in a maximum security preparatory school at an unnaturally early age. Warwick Square's dainty dishes must have compared favourably with the food to be found in whatever outer circle of scholastic hell Haddon minor had adorned because, so far, he had consumed Mrs Frith's burnt offerings with the ravenous enthusiasm of an Alsatian at a kitten-eating contest. Hoping to ingratiate himself with his hostess, he had complimented her on Sunday's liver.

'Delicious.'

There was a wince from the other PGs, who had already learned to steer clear of their landlady's conversational *bêtes noires*. Mrs Frith had read somewhere that the excellence of the food on one's plate was a matter of course, not comment, in a well-regulated household. Health, as Miss Digby had discovered to her cost when she once complained of a slight headache, was another taboo, but even the most anodyne topics did not guarantee Mrs Frith's good opinion. Mention the possibility of rain and a cold front would drift inexorably across the dining table, followed by a hard Frithy frost of contempt.

Mr Stone, whose late mother had kept an excellent cook, had been far less forgiving than Mr Haddon, and simply pushed the offending offal to the side of his plate and made an elaborate pretence of studying the EPNS mark on the blade of his knife.

'Where is Sheffield, exactly? North of here, I imagine.'

Mr Stone had a job of sorts with an art dealer in South Audley Street and seemed decidedly out of his element in Warwick Square. What he saved in rent appeared to be spent on ties and Turkish tobacco.

Monday's menu promised 'Hasty pie' and 'shape'. The pie (which was nothing of the kind) was served with Cabbage Mould, a Frith speciality consisting of the previous day's leftover greens packed into a pudding basin with a pea-sized quantity of kitchen butter and a great deal of white pepper and baked without mercy until it had taken the shape of the bowl. Mr Stone jabbed at it uncertainly with the tines of his fork but decided against eating it.

Dora's arrival the previous Friday had served up fresh conversational meat, and the table's interest still continued polite but steadfast four days later. Had she known an Angela De Vere during her time at school? wondered Miss Andrews, another hopeless spinster who was frightfully keen to maintain her credentials as someone with younger 'chums'. Mrs Frith did her best to ignore Miss Andrews altogether. Miss Digby had often speculated on the cause of this extra two degrees of chill but failed to register that Miss Andrews, for all her carefully laid trail of gentility (papa, shrubberies, Saturday-to-Mondays), cut up her meat with her forefinger on the blade of her knife.

How was Miss Strang finding her new position? This from Mr Nilsen, an American gent who had taken lodgings with Mrs Frith on the erroneous understanding that Warwick Square was only a stone's throw from the British Museum. Mrs Frith kept up the pretence, resolutely referring to Mr Nilsen's daily walk to Great Russell Street and routinely expressing surprise that he did not avail himself of a light luncheon back at Warwick Square – the very words conjured images of raised pies and baked ham and hard-boiled eggs. Only three shillings a week extra.

Chapter 4

There had been nothing about vulvas or *nipples* in the Monday evening paper, just 'police pursuing their investigation'. Dora had seen the report over someone's shoulder on the bus on her way back to Pimlico, but the man had pulled his newspaper closer to his chest when he caught her reading it, as if she were pinching his penny, so she bought her own the following morning. The human weasel in the grey raincoat was on the lower deck again and she heard him boring on about the lateness of his train and the alley murder developments. 'Nice-looking girl like that,' he tutted.

'Probably her husband what done it.' A fat woman taking up half of the broad seat by the door nodded knowingly at Dora's *Daily Mirror*.

'She wasn't married.' The whole omnibus clearly had the case at its fingertips.

'Fancy-man, then. Bound to be someone. Good-looking girl like that.'

They all seemed struck by the victim's appearance. Dora wondered what they meant by it. Did her good looks compound the crime? Or did beauty make violent assault somehow inevitable?

Like the *Evening News*, the *Daily Mirror* seemed unaware of bite marks or vulval lesions or *virgo intacta*. Even if the reporters did know what Dora knew they probably wouldn't be allowed to print it, but there were big gaps between the lines that jaundiced eyes would have known how to read. 'Marks on the body' was bound to mean marks somewhere unsavoury or they'd have said where.

The whole two-column report had been written in a kind of code: the victim's employer describing her as 'steady' and 'punctual'; the fact that she lived at home; that she had attended the cinema not with her 'fancy-man' but with her aunt and uncle and that her father had lost a leg (the left one) – didn't say where: Inkerman? Ypres? Wimbledon Common? Somewhere where legs were lost, anyway – all of which somehow testified to her virginity. A new photograph showed her in school uniform: felt hat, blazer, the same shy, sun-blinded flinch of a smile. She wasn't blonde any more. Not even 'fair-haired'. A keen girl guide.

Dora arrived at the office to find Hubbard already at work double-checking all the filing she had done the previous afternoon. Had he had any luck with the agency? Silly question.

'I know how to use a typewriter . . .'

Did she indeed. Given the state in which her predecessor had left the apparatus, Hubbard would be most surprised if anyone were able to make use of it. The cover had been lost and dust had clotted the workings. He had spoken to Maintenance but one might as well address one's complaints to the machine itself for all the difference *that* made.

The typewriter was an old sit-up-and-beg model even more antiquated and unwieldy than the contraption Dora had learned on at the secretarial place and a great deal dirtier. The tailored burlap cover was found wedged into the back of the bottom drawer of her desk together with a square of oily rag and a bent hairpin. Dora managed to winkle most of the caked ink and skin flakes out of the types but the keys still got hopelessly stuck together whenever she tried working up any kind of speed.

'Is there any oil?'

'Oil?'

'For the machine.'

Hubbard returned to his pile of envelopes as if she hadn't spoken, keeping his eyes glued to his desk until the pathologist arrived back twenty minutes later, full of the joys of spring.

'Morning all. Glorious morning. Everything satisfactory? Hubbard?'

'The typewriter wants oiling, apparently.'

'Does she indeed?'

Heroines in school stories always blushed to the roots of their hair – hard to know without a glass. Dora stammered an explanation.

'This machine. It needs oil. All the types are completely jammed together.'

'I think I can safely say that that is not my department, Miss Strange. Hubbard's your man, I imagine. However, does this mean that you can in fact type?' Dora nodded. 'And spell?'

Kemble at once began firing real teasers at her: diphtheria, inoculation, leucorrhoea – all the really beastly ones. Suddenly the whole room was buzzing with words in an impromptu physiological spelling bee. Vazard suggested ipacecuanha. Hubbard (predictably) had psoriasis and diarrhoea. Kemble was pleasantly surprised.

'How very, very gratifying. Mrs Harris had trouble with "sincerely" let alone "syncope", didn't she, Hubbard?' It had taken him three months to train Mrs Culvey's predecessor, he explained, and even then she was forever telephoning through to the laboratory wanting to know how he was spelling 'eczema' or 'ectopic' or 'Edgware', which would have been quite bad enough without a telephone voice trained by South Kensington's finest – 'Hair lair? Air hair lair Dr Kemble' – he was a very good mimic. Even Hubbard laughed.

'Anyhow, it was a relief when she left, all in all. So tell me, Miss Strange, why the extensive medical vocabulary?'

'My father. He er . . . Harley Street.'

Hubbard snorted and the pathologist pulled a face at the very mention of the address.

'Aha. The valley of the shadow of death. I'm well aware that the jury is still out on these matters but I doubt if even the most ardent Lamarckian would argue that the ability to spell "ipacecuanha" was hereditary.'

'I once thought of reading medicine . . .'

'But thought better of it? How very wise. Well, you're well off out of medicine, anyway. Ghastly business.' He nodded cheerily in Vazard's direction as if reinforcing a point already made. 'Halt and the lame knocking on your door day and night. That's the marvellous thing about pathology: your patients never die on you and you always get your money – such as it is. Well, if Miss Strange's typing is as handy as her spelling we can definitely find a use for her. Hubbard, furnish your colleague with whatever lubricant she requires. I'll have another try with that cylinder apparatus the bursar so kindly bought us and we'll see how she gets on with a bit of dictation.'

The whispery voice Dr Kemble used for the cylinder was quite different from the bluff, bossy tones he used in the office and completely at odds with the words. It was like a police log being read as a bedtime story: once upon a time there was a girl called Mavis . . . Dora swallowed hard, clicked off the apparatus and threaded a sheet of paper into her machine to make sure it was running smoothly. 'The quack had crazy qualms but made no reply; a queer Quaker has a quaint packet of purple paper; I sat by a pool as I read my verses in secret; I dreamed I saw you at my feast in a pink dress.'

A pink blouse and a red jacket . . . The crazy qualm passed and Dora ripped the scrap of paper from the typewriter and restarted the dictaphone. The pathologist had made the recording in an unnaturally slow whisper – barely forty words per minute – to be helpful? Or merely discreet? She was still typing the report when Vazard returned from his lecture. Dora's practice sheet caught his eye.

'I say, Miss Strang, poetry during office hours?'

'They use all the letters, or use the fingers alternately. Or something. Lazy brown foxes coming to the aid of the party, that type of thing.'

' "I dreamed I saw you at my feast in a pink dress". Sounds jolly. And what's this?' The smile contracted to a pout as he held up the Hektographed pages on the Purification of the Germ Plasm.

'I thought I might read it later. It looked interesting.'

'Know your enemy, eh? That's the ticket.'

She combed the earpiece back across her head and she was alone once more with the voice of Alfred Kemble and the girl in the Peckham alley.

'Lacerations to knees and palms of hands consistent with crawling or being dragged across rough, gravel-like surface. Stop. Haematomas on both wrists consistent with victim's having been seized and dragged some distance. Friction burns to right side of neck consistent with victim's apparel having been pulled or ripped sharply downwards. Stop. Worst bruising right-hand side of neck suggesting sharp pull at clothing from right-handed assailant, query. Internal organs normal with no signs of injury or disease.' (*Cutting her about unnecessary.*) 'Hair fair in colour although dark at roots but pending microscopic and chemical analysis bleaching does not appear to be chemical in nature. Stop. Bruises to throat, all of recent origin, consistent with strangulation. Primary cause of death query asphyxiation. Lesser marks to left-hand side of neck most probably friction burns. Vulval lesions and bite marks on breasts unquestionably inflicted *post mortem*. Stop. Seminal fluid found in birth canal. Stop. Traces of mammalian blood found under fingernails of right hand. Stop.'

She stopped. *Marks found on the body indicated that the victim, a keen girl guide, had suffered interference.*

After, not before.

The new agency had promised Hubbard a choice selection of highly skilled male clerical staff – accomplished stenographers, fluent in eight European languages, expert unicyclists, in evening dress – anything, *anything* to get the horrid man off the telephone. He was now hard at work, shears in hand, stripping the daily newspapers of all references to death in general and the department in particular and sticking them into a scrapbook with a pot of glue and a brush.

Dora crossed the room and handed him the typed report. He actually straightened his tie before ferrying the sheets next door: worm. Moments later her telephone buzzed.

'Step through, can you, Miss Strange?'

The 'No Admittance' door led into a room slightly larger than the office. A lab bench with two sinks was set up under the long, high window. There was a bare, enamel-topped table against the far wall with a cork noticeboard above it. This too was bare and the waiting drawing pins had been arranged to form the letters AK – another one of Hubbard's important little jobs, presumably. Dr Kemble's desk was in the corner opposite the goods lift (whose gate bore no padlock) and next to it were two sealed wooden crates.

'This will do very well.' He was obviously pleased, although the note of surprise was pretty insulting. 'And not a bad speed.' Could she type as fast as he spoke? Dora expected so (if he spoke at the speed he used on the cylinder).

'In which case we might consider taking you along to the PMs with the portable machine – if Hubbard can remember where he hid it. Might save a bit of time. You'd better come along to one of my demonstrations here first, make sure you don't have a fit of the vapours. That all right with you, Miss Strange?'

'It isn't strange.'

'What isn't?'

'My name. It's Strang, not Strange.'

'Strang?' He hesitated. 'As in Leopold Strang?' She nodded eagerly but the way his lower lip stretched back for the 'leer' of Leopold told her that this was somehow not the right answer. Some unpleasantness over a death certificate perhaps? Or was it just Harley Street he minded? He tapped the sheets of typing into shape against his blotter.

'I think I'd rather stick with "Strange" if you don't mind, but we shall need to find you an accommodating late husband. Influenza, perhaps. Coroners can get a bit windy about unmarried females running around the mortuaries, taking down their grisly particulars. Especially Ealing, for some reason. Silly old fool. Lot of nonsense, I know, but it upsets the staff – and the police come to that. Do you possess a ring of any sort?'

She held out her hands dumbly, showing a small knot of gold. Her mother's other rings had all been far too Christmassy for Dora's taste.

'Yes. That'll do.' He took her right hand in his left. His was very dry and warm and ringless with a pleasant whiff of sandalwood – no hunks of carbolic for him at least. He slipped the ring from her finger and replaced it on the opposite side. He kept momentary hold of her newly wedded hand. She looked away but when she looked back he was still watching her, a dissecting glance that took in the white blouse, the formless tweed skirt, the guileless twist of light brown hair.

'Mrs Culvey found the work extremely satisfying.'

Dora tried again to picture the fragrant, untidy-minded Mrs Culvey with her powdered face and dirty typewriter.

'Think of yourself as a bride of science, Mrs Strange, *child bride* of science. Now if you'll excuse me, I am already late for my luncheon with the Betterment boys.' He enveloped himself in his large overcoat and swept from the room.

Hubbard's Tuesday 'dinner' seemed to be cabbage-free but that was the most that could be said for it. Dora snacked glumly on a bun she had bought from Mrs Arnold's trolley before filing a peritonitis, a post-partum haemorrhage and two suicides. Dr Kemble's lunch was evidently more expansive and it was nearly dark outside when he once more summoned them into the laboratory. Hubbard had unpacked the mysterious wooden crates and the table against the wall was now completely covered in white metal trays. The first two held the contents of the girl's jacket pockets: a cheap embroidered handkerchief with a faint, sour scent of stale orange peel, a small box with a cracked cake of pinkish face powder inside, a grubby comb, a purse containing three shillings, a sixpence and three farthings, a purple cinema ticket, a single mint humbug. No lipstick. No scent. No latchkey (but if she lived at home she probably wouldn't have had one, not at nineteen). A smaller tray alongside held nothing but a long, white front tooth, knocked from the girl's mouth by the same blow that had broken her jaw.

The wall was now densely feathered with photographs that Dora found unreadable until she realised that they were close-up images of the marks found on the body: the monstrous bruise on the chin, the long, dark burn on the side of the neck, the teeth marks on the breasts. There was only one picture of the whole person, lying as she was found, blouse ripped open, one arm up across the face, shielding the sightless eyes.

At the left-hand end of the table lay a blue skirt, a red jacket, a muddy shredded stocking (just one) and the torn, bloodstained remnants of a pink artificial silk blouse folded to fit into an enamel laboratory dish. On the other side of the room in the in-tray on Kemble's desk sat a pile of six identical blouses, untorn and fresh in crisp little bags made half of cellophane, half of tissue paper, neatly piled up like the stock in a draper's drawers. Dr Kemble was wrestling with one of them.

'Now then, perhaps Mrs Strange will be kind enough to put this on for us?'

Dora was afraid for one ghastly moment that he expected her to undress first, but he was holding the blouse out by the edges for her to slip on over her clothes. She quickly unbuttoned her cardigan, immediately wishing she'd taken it off in the other room. Hubbard was lurking over by the lab bench, playing glumly with the taps, but Kemble was watching her as she squirmed free of the knitted sleeves.

'Yes. About the same size I should say. Possibly a touch small.'

She pushed her hands through the sleeves and fumbled the tiny covered buttons into their holes then stood opposite him rather crossly, awaiting instructions. Why the blazes couldn't Hubbard wear the blasted blouses? He was skinny enough and hardly any taller than Dora. Shorter, probably, without those ridiculous shoes.

'Now. If Mrs Strange could stand *just* here. Excellent. Now let us imagine the scene. It is dark. Mavis Shirley is making her way home from the cinema after bidding farewell to her aunt and uncle when a man – a man she arranged to meet outside? A man who accosted her in the street? – seizes her wrists and drags her into an alley behind a row of shops. We know from the deep scratches on the victim's knees that she was dragged part of the way, that a punch – most probably a right-handed punch – to the jaw broke the mandible, simultaneously dislodging the second upper-right incisor tooth.' As he spoke, his fingertips touched Dora's face to indicate the location of the blow. 'These injuries were inflicted before death. The abrasions on the neck, the bite marks and the, er, assault ...' He seemed irked by the need for euphemism. Why so coy all of a sudden? She glanced across at Hubbard, who was straining to catch the words. 'These things all occurred post mortem. The angle of the jaw fracture is consistent with a heavy blow from a left-handed assailant but only if the victim were standing directly in front of him at the time. Now, if our volunteer will just stand *here*.' He placed his fingertips on her shoulders and guided her into position.

'We need to establish whether the assailant was left- or right-handed. Luckily the victim's clothes were quite new and purchased locally so the police were able to acquire some more of the same sort. We're fairly sure that the murderer was a right-handed man, which would mean that his left hand would have been restraining the victim like so.' He grabbed both of Dora's wrists, as if expecting her to run away.

'Ow.'

The fingers loosened their hold and the thumb absently stroked the skin they had pinched. He then raised his right hand and slipped the fingers into the neck of her blouse. She felt her pearls pulling against the back of her neck.

'I think you have your fingers caught in my beads.' 'Pearls' would just sound swank.

He adjusted his grip and then, without warning, pulled his hand sharply downwards and outwards. The front tore easily enough but the collar, with all its stitching and interfacing, was fairly hard to pull apart. There was a loud ripping sound and Dora felt a burning pain on the side of her neck. The right side. She bit her lip and the pathologist immediately angled the beam of the desk lamp in her direction, reached for the magnifying glass on his desk and examined the shreds of fabric.

'We will need the microscope, Hubbard, but I should say the fibres have been pulled in the same direction. Better try the other hand to be sure. If our subject could just keep quite still ... I'm going to cut the shirt off so that we can preserve the tear intact.'

49

She could feel the chill of the blades through her clothes as he sliced up the back and down the sleeves with some peculiar-looking shears. He handed the remains to Hubbard, who tenderly laid the dissected garment on a fresh enamel tray and tied a label to it while the pathologist unbuttoned a second blouse. Dora put it on and stood opposite him.

He placed his hand (left hand this time) carefully inside the collar. He seemed to be standing slightly closer. Another hard yank at the neck. Another wrenching noise. This time the whole side of the blouse (the side with the buttonholes on it) tore away. Dora raised her chin clear like a wary swimmer keeping her face out of the water. As she did so she caught sight of the police photograph of the girl's body lying on the muddy cobbles of the alley. Dora imagined unseen hands pulling her from the pavement, grabbing the cloth, ripping away blouse and brassiere. Imagined the pain of teeth sinking into breasts. But no. Mavis Shirley had not been conscious when the man tore her clothes or bit her flesh. The marks on the breasts had been quite conclusive: after, not before.

'And the marks on the skin' – the pathologist's glass hovered over Dora's neck and throat. His warm breath gave off a clubbable smell of lunchtime tobacco and beer – 'will probably match those on the neck of the victim once bruising is complete.'

Bruising? No one had said anything about bruising. Only they had, of course. In spidery green ink and in the whispers trapped inside the dictaphone cylinder. 'Friction burns to right side of neck consistent with victim's apparel having been pulled or ripped sharply downward. Worst bruising right-hand side of neck.' Mavis's neck. And now Dora's neck.

'Mrs Strange is being a Jolly Good Sport, isn't she, Hubbard?' The words were handled unwillingly, with tweezers.

'Mrs Culvey was always a good sport, sir.'

Mrs Culvey. Her again. Would that have been Miss Mrs or Mrs Mrs? And what games had been played with the memorably sporting Mrs Culvey? No wonder she kept a spare pair of stockings handy.

Kemble was still tracking his lens across Dora's neck.

'The extent of the ripping is consistent with the blouse found on the victim.' Again the scissors snipped the fabric from her back. 'The fibres definitely face the other way, wouldn't you say, Hubbard?'

Hubbard's turn to take a peek. Hubbard did not smell of sandalwood. Hubbard smelled of old clothes, old cabbage and hair oil. Old hair oil.

'Couldn't it have been . . .' Dora's voice sounded wrong. Hoarse and peculiar. She cleared her throat but the 'Ahem', too, was stagy and strange. 'Couldn't it have been a left-handed man attacking from behind?'

And so yet another blouse was unwrapped and he stood behind her – very close indeed this time, very warm against her back. His left arm appeared in front of her and the hand moved uncertainly towards her throat, fumbling for the top button.

'Not a natural angle but he would have the advantage of surprise when he stepped up behind his victim.'

She could hear him breathe in – as if smelling her hair. Once again he gripped and ripped but in his haste his grasp included the collar of Dora's own blouse. It was her old school church parade Sunday best and it had been weakened by nine terms of merciless boiling and starching at the school laundry (*every fourth Monday unless hopelessly soiled*). The fine lawn ripped more easily than the artificial silk. The long lines of drawn thread-work tore right down the front like the perforations on a sheet of postage stamps. The tiny buttons pattered against the tiled floor of the laboratory like pearl hailstones.

The pathologist seemed scarcely to notice. He was at it again with the magnifying glass. 'I think we can safely assert that an attack from the rear causes fibres to shear very differently.'

The lens played over the embroidered forget-me-nots on her underthings and over the rosy skin above. She could feel the heat of the lamp on her skin.

'Unusually fine pores.' Yet again his voice was barely a whisper.

Dora struggled to breathe normally, to breathe from her diaphragm and keep her chest still. She swallowed hard, afraid she might burst into tears or scream or scratch traces of mammalian blood from the pathologist's impassive face.

'Unusually fine hole in my blouse.'

'Oh. So there is.' Normal volume had resumed. 'Sorry about that. Hubbard and I can get a little carried away.' Hubbard was pinning torn pink fabric to a large sheet of brown paper. If he had been carried away it hadn't been very far. 'Our guinea pig can help herself to one of the spares, can't she, Hubbard?' Another guinea pig. What happened to the first? Why had he needed the screwdriver?

Dora hastily pulled the torn scraps of her blouse together, grabbed at the cellophane packet he held out to her and stumbled through the door to the supplies cupboard.

She leaned her forehead against the frosted glass of the window as she slid the blouse out of its bag and began mechanically locating its pins in the dark: one at each corner behind the yoke; one on the front to hold the fancy cuff on display; another pinning the shoulder seams together. Like new school uniform. There was a rolled fire blanket wedged inside a red metal tube attached to the wall and Dora jabbed the pins into the dusty bit of asbestos sticking out at the top. She was just undoing the buttons when she heard the lab door click open. It was Hubbard, who at once turned on the light and began decanting a demijohn of Lysol into a large brown glass bottle, filling the room with vapour. He hadn't even glanced at her but she could hardly take her clothes off with him there. She retrieved a few of the pins to tack her own torn blouse back into place and cautiously turned the handle to the office door and peeped out. The coast was clear. She quickly stuffed the garment into a large manila envelope addressed to Kemble from the National Vigilance Association, clasped the package to her chest and ventured out into the corridor, where she bumped into a mousy middle-aged woman in a brown coat and hat emerging from a door marked 'Pathological Chemistry'.

'Excuse me, I wonder if you could tell me where the . . .' The brown female didn't even break stride. 'Down one more flight, second on the right.'

The Ladies' WC was a grudging afterthought carved out of the larger one marked 'Gentlemen'. It had evidently been added quite recently and the door to it was different from the others in the building. It had only one lavatory cubicle and one handbasin. The Pathological Chemistry people (who appeared to have less difficulty finding and keeping female clerical staff) had two typewriters in addition to a sort of glorified bottle-washer. There was also the lady who answered the telephones and did the books in Dispatch. Every one of them left their desks at the stroke of five, so the room was extremely squashed with all four excusing each other like mad in the tiny space round a mottled glass the size of a pocket handkerchief and dabbing at their faces with scraps of chamois leather. A couple glanced in Dora's direction and one of them giggled something about 'Kemble's latest' but no one introduced themselves. Hardly team spirit.

Dora had to wait quite a while before she could sidle into the cubicle and get her blouses off and on. Hard to know how best to dispose of the bundle of torn lawn. She could hardly leave it for the charlady to find and Lord knows what Mrs Frith would make of such a thing. She rolled it up tightly and stuffed it into the envelope.

She got back up the stairs to find that Hubbard had switched off all the lights and locked the door even though Dora's coat and hat were still on the stand. Absurd little man. Like a dog in a house with a new baby pretending that the newcomer didn't really exist. She found the spare key, put the cover on her typewriting machine and gathered her things together in the darkness. She glanced up, half-expectantly, at the window over the laboratory door but the light was already out.

Chapter 5

Mrs Frith had not been at her usual station by the open door of the drawing room when Dora returned and she had been able to sneak up the stairs unobserved. She shrugged off her cardigan and took a proper look at herself in the dead woman's blouse. The material was a bit shoddy but it seemed to fit all right – too well if anything, emphasising her shape in a rather vulgar way. Ugly red marks were forming on either side of her neck. An exact match of the bruise in the photograph. Arnica was the thing. Mrs Frith was certain to have some. Mrs Frith had *everything*. There had been some kind of plumbing emergency on Friday evening just after Dora arrived and the female PGs had been obliged to perform their ablutions in their landlady's bathroom, which smelled explosively of chlorine and whose capacious cupboards had been extraordinarily well stocked with medicines and various peculiar pieces of rubbery gubbins that even a doctor's daughter was hard put to identify.

She rubbed optimistically at the blossoming bruise. Mrs Frith would be bound to have arnica and asafoetida and *arsenic* like as not, but she'd also be bound to ask what it was wanted for, so Dora settled for tying a silk handkerchief around her neck, blushing afresh as she remembered the lens tracking across her skin. She had shoved the envelope containing her old blouse through the railings of a derelict house in the Belgrave Road, like someone disposing of the evidence of a nameless crime.

Dora had hardly finished knotting the square of silk when The Frith herself nosed into the tiny bedroom, opening the door the instant she knocked on it, in that infuriating way of hers. The landlady wore a large holland apron and a worried expression. Had Theodora seen the new maid's box? The question was posed completely out of the blue, like a random sentence of French prose or a typing exercise.

The new maid – Ivy? – had arrived on Saturday afternoon from her previous post with a Dulwich veterinarian and her box and her bundle had been the cause of some considerable alarm. The obvious course, explained Mrs Frith, was a small tin bath, two house bricks, some sticky brown tape and three pounds of sulphur. These eminently sensible precautions had presented no problem when the Austrian gentleman with the beard had taken the third floor back, last summer, but domestic staff were hard to find and it was so easy to get off on the wrong foot . . . She bared her teeth mid-flow in a grey-green approximation of a smile.

Which was all absolute rot, of course. The smile gave it away. This charade wasn't about the maid at all. The new girl's box would have come down the area steps, invisible to the PGs. Dora could not possibly have seen it and however heavily infested it may have been, the vermin would hardly have had time to travel to the third floor. It was *Dora's* luggage the landlady was really worried about. Weeks on end locked away in a college attic, cheek by jowl with all those other trunks. Probably *alive* with Little Visitors.

The landlady had left the door ajar. 'I thought we'd have boiled cod this evening,' she confided (quite unnecessarily) as she made her nosy circuit of the room. She was quick to notice some underthings drying on the back of a chair. Dora's linen went with the rest of the household laundry but she washed the smalls herself.

'These are a little fast, surely? Not at all the sort of thing we used to get for you.' She eyed the silky scraps with covetous distaste. 'More fitting for a *trousseau*, I would have thought.'

Mrs Frith talked about *trousseaux* with depressing frequency and would often discuss Miss Digby's marriage prospects – or lack of them. Usually in a regretful but very decided imperfect subjunctive (if she had ever married she would have been worn out with childbearing by now, that sort of thing). As it was, Miss Digby remained one of the nation's 360,000 surplus females of marriageable age. Mrs Frith herself was thirty-nine – and had been for some considerable time (or so the waspish Mr Stone maintained).

The landlady was holding a cracked willow pattern cup and she jabbed distractedly at its contents with a tarnished kitchen teaspoon as she spoke, her gaze fixed uneasily on the large trunk in the corner of the room which Dora had not yet unpacked.

Was there not sufficient space in the wardrobe? Her 'man' only worked Wednesdays and Fridays and Mrs Frith had hoped to get any boxes stowed away the following morning but Dora didn't appear to have emptied hers.

'I would have been more than willing to unpack for you, my dear, but the trunk seemed to be *locked*.' Part reproach, part accusation.

She continued her progress around the room, occasionally crouching down to tap spoonfuls of snowy powder into likely-looking cracks beneath the skirting board. The action was automatic and the cup almost empty (Dora's room was not the first to be treated). Why was it, wondered Mrs Frith to herself, that the common cockroach couldn't be lured to its death with potato peelings or eggshells or some other household waste instead of black treacle and icing sugar? The peculiar smell of burning potato peelings was supposed to be very noxious to beetles. Sadly, it was also fairly noxious to house guests ... And yet, despite the expense, Mrs Frith was secretly rather pleased with the icing sugar and plaster of Paris method. Occasionally the plaster immobilised the obnoxious little beasts before they got back to their lair and you would find them, stiff as a collector's item, on the scullery linoleum, overtaken by their last, unexpectedly heavy meal.

'I unpacked my clothes the day I arrived but there doesn't appear to be anywhere to put books, Mrs Frith.'

This was interpreted as a complaint.

'Mr Bartholomew had only the Bible and Bradshaw,' as if that should really be enough for anyone, 'but I think you'll find a shelf or two in the bookcase on the landing.'

'I'll empty the trunk this evening and leave it outside,' promised Dora, holding the door open as she waited for Mrs Frith to pass through it. Not exactly party manners but how else was one to get rid of her?

Dora had absolutely no intention of storing her precious books on the landing. The wardrobe drawer would do very well. It had a strongish lock and the key could be tucked out of sight above the fretwork cornice. Not a safe hiding place in any well-run house but Mrs Frith's unwilling chain of Daisies and Ivies and Violets had neither the time nor the inclination to dust the tops of wardrobes. Daisy (it wasn't Ivy at all; no wonder they didn't stay) was the current maid-of-all-work. Daisy only really liked doing for gentlemen, who would routinely have their rooms dusted to a standstill while the three spinsters in the cheaper rooms were lucky to get their washbasins emptied and one clean sheet per week. Miss Digby was very resentful and suffragettish about it but what Miss Digby didn't know was that gentlemen left tips on an altogether more lavish scale (five shillings at Christmas and Easter). Whereas frugal lady boarders like Miss Digby expected you to be grateful for a cast-off hat or a well-thumbed copy of *The Lady*.

The books stacked quite cosily into the big bottom drawer, each one tidily covered in brown paper with its title gummed to the spine on a white label. Dora had named her library with care. Nothing too earnest (Matron would have smelled a rat) but *Sir Charles Grandison* Volume III was a safe bet as were *The Tenant of Wildfell Hall* and *Cranford* and the works of William Cowper (not even swots read Cowper). It was a few minutes till the gong sounded at half past seven. Dora selected a book (*Adam Bede* Volume II according to the spine) tucked it under her pillow for bedtime and carefully re-locked the wardrobe drawer.

Dinner was soon over but the spectre of postprandial bridge hovered hideously in the air. Did Dora play? Miss Digby had asked when Dora moved in on Friday. People always said that, not would Dora *like* to play bridge, just *did* she play, as if every bridge player were some sort of reservist ever liable for the call-up. The Digby female, having press-ganged two of the gentlemen into service, showed no mercy and they had played for two fractious hours after that first frightful dinner. Dora had seen the Bridge Fiend twittering excitably in hopes of more cards as the coffee things were cleared away but she was determined to retire to her room and her book. Not a headache (one needed to ration headaches or they'd know one was shamming). Letters to write (not unreasonable after one's first two days at work).

The dark bedroom still smelled horribly of paraffin and boiled cod but when Dora switched on the light and tried to open the window she found brown paper sticky tape pasted all around the edge (a souvenir from the room's last fumigation). A grey worm of sash cord dangled uselessly from the frame.

She took off her blouse and skirt, put them on a hanger and brushed them vigorously to beat out the stink of the omnibus. Walking to work would be less smelly. Perhaps if she travelled a little earlier and a little later she might be spared the press of strange overcoats. It wasn't always accidental. Men were like that.

Once, when Dora was about sixteen, Mrs Frith had forgotten to arrange a taxi to take them both to Paddington and she had missed the school train. After a frantic exchange of trunk calls, it was decided that, as a responsible member of the Upper Fifth, she could travel unaccompanied just this once and that the under-matron would meet her in the village taxi at the halt nearest the school. One could hear the blush in the bursar's voice as she hissed a reminder about 'spending a penny beforehand' (girls were not permitted to use railway lavatories under any circumstances).

Dora and Mrs Frith reached Paddington to learn that her intended train had been cancelled and that the next, a slow one, was almost completely full. The porter managed to find her a space in a second-class smoker. A man, a slim, light-haired man with hollow sunburned cheeks and itchy, Pied-Piperish lips, had put his folded raincoat on the seat next to him and he moved it on to his lap so that Dora could sit down. There was something a bit rum about his jacket: too many buttons, pockets in the wrong place. Something foreign-looking about his young, bony, rather handsome face.

As they passed Didcot, the murky yellow light in the carriage flickered and all but died but the heating was still on full blast and suggestions that a window might be opened were shouted down by an elderly fossil in the corner seat with a tartan rug folded about his knees. Dora had felt herself starting to sweat. Her gabardine school mac was already bundled into the rack and as there was still more than an hour and a half to go she decided to wriggle free of her blazer. Mrs Frith, mean even with Dr Strang's money, had felt it would last the year but it was jolly tight across the back.

The heat had been fractionally more bearable in her gymslip and short-sleeved blouse. The man's arms were folded beneath his rolled-up coat and he seemed to be sleeping. Her forearm had brushed against his fingers as she settled into her seat. Even in that dim light she could see the downy golden hairs on the back of his hand, feel them tickle her skin – rather thrilling. The second touch was no accident. He had turned towards her, still pretending to sleep, and the fingertips of his loosely cupped right hand could stroke her arm undetected. As Dora turned her arm so that his fingers could play on the skin of her wrist she had seen his half-closed eyes watching the rise and fall of her chest under the tight pleated serge. He had shifted uneasily in his seat, leaning back a little.

When they arrived at her halt, the man (who was very tall) had stood up to help her with her portmanteau and as she got her coat from the rack he had allowed the lurch of the slowing train to swing his body against hers. He had reached past her, grabbing the luggage rack and his lips had brushed her hair. The whispered apology (definitely not an English voice) was like an endearment – or an invitation. She had squirmed back into her blazer and another man got up and busied himself helping her on with her coat as if wanting to come between them, as if he had seen – only he couldn't have seen – those caressing fingertips. She often thought of it.

Dora shivered into her nightgown and climbed into the cold and creaky bed, taking care not to step on the sardine tins. She retrieved her book from beneath the pillow and smoothed her ring back to the left hand, where sandalwood-scented fingers had placed it. She turned to a familiar page and sniffed the comfortable chemical whiff of the bedstead and imagined herself back in the laboratory, recalling the hand at her throat, the warm breath across her skin.

Chapter 6

It was only half past eight but everyone was already hard at work in Willcox Wing when Dora arrived next day. Vazard could be glimpsed through the open door of the supplies cupboard mixing various fluids and pouring them into specimen jars – the whole floor reeked of formalin. The chief had already dashed off a post-mortem that morning (septicaemia, Southwark) and Hubbard, who had accompanied him to the mortuary, was copying his garbled Pitman notes into illegible longhand so that Dora could type them on to the form. Quite a process. The chief himself was standing by Dora's desk speaking into the main telephone.

'I still have some tests to make. Well, yes, you could call it poisoning but unless I am very much mistaken I think we shall find that the poisoning was done by his own teeth.' There was a pause. 'Oh yes. Most certainly. A badly abscessed incisor tooth was forced deep into the gum as he fell. Highly toxic matter released directly into the bloodstream.' Another pause. 'Perfectly possible, I'm afraid. Haig died in exactly the same way, funnily enough: fall from a horse. *Why* this gentleman fell in the first place is another matter – hence the additional tests. I have taken slides of some lesions in the brain for microscopical analysis together with some other tissue samples but the underlying disease may not be significant. He may simply have been giddy with toothache – or whatever specific he was taking for it. He hadn't a sound tooth in his head and the pain would have been considerable.'

The pathologist began taking off his black morning coat as he spoke. He then undid his cufflinks, tucked the telephone receiver into his neck and, with a practised twiddle of his fingers, detached the whole of his left shirt sleeve.

The arm was that of a well-nourished male, almost hairless, and the skin smooth and unmarked except for a few little blossoms of vaccination scars on the biceps. Its sudden nakedness looked very much out of place alongside the starched collar, the flawless silk tie and the natty waistcoat and watch chain. Dora saw the muscles flex slightly as he transferred the instrument to the left ear. Hubbard stopped scribbling and bustled across the room to fuss with the other sleeve.

'I shall telephone tomorrow with any additional findings and you will have my full report as soon as my microscopic investigations are complete. You must forgive me but I have another ... patient waiting.' He nodded a swift greeting at Dora and swerved past her from behind the desk.

'Hubbard's new bureau have yet to find a suitable operative so I thought we might see how Mrs Strange gets on at this morning's morbid anatomy demonstration,' he boomed encouragingly at no one in particular. 'If all goes smoothly she can have a go with some live dictation.'

Hubbard retrieved the sleeves, carefully snapping them back into their laundry creases and the pair scuttled into the laboratory and closed the door.

Vazard had finished lining up the specimen jars on a little steel trolley and was wheeling it through to the laboratory when he caught sight of Dora.

'Septic theatre nine sharp. Sure you can face it? Don't feel you have to. It takes a very strong stomach. A lot of the chaps take a while to get used to it.' It was as if he wanted her to back out.

'Not for ladies' eyes, do you mean?'

No-no-no-not-what-he-meant-at-all (but it probably was).

Dozens of students could be heard trudging up the stairs from the basement. It was raining hard outside so they had all come in via the subterranean passage that linked Willcox Wing to the main building, one of a warren of steam-heated, grey-green corridors that joined the hospital to its various satellites. The tunnels enabled patients to be transferred invisibly between departments or to make that last ungentle journey when the rubber-wheeled trolley would be rattled at speed across the skid-marked linoleum, banged heedlessly through the great lift gates in the sub-basement and up to the third floor of Willcox Wing, where Dr Kemble's dissecting table lay waiting for them, white and cold and hard as a freshly starched hospital bed sheet.

The septic theatre took up the back half of the third floor of the building. A door to it led directly from the pathologist's laboratory but the students entered from the next storey, where a viewing gallery ran around the room beneath the vast rainy skylight above. The galleries were full by the time Dora reached the fourth floor and the students, most wearing gloves and scarves against the room's tiled chill, were jostling for a good view of the proceedings below. There were only two other women in the room, who stood together next to the exit, pencils already poised.

The space was dominated by an eight-foot ironstone slab, its supporting central pillar linked to a special drain that removed the waste to a disinfecting cistern somewhere in the building's large intestine. The floor was covered in grey linoleum that lapped against the bottoms of the walls like pie pastry. Vazard was fussing around next to a pair of porcelain-topped side tables: one arrayed with the jars and slides he'd been preparing, the other parked up against a shallow stone sink at one end of the slab. A larger trolley against the wall was laden with small sacks of sawdust, a bale of fluffy material and a quantity of sacking. Hubbard, clutching notebook and pencil and looking all wrong in a white laboratory overall, was sitting on a stool in the corner with his knees tucked under a little folding table as if he had picked that precise spot for a solitary picnic.

Sound travelled strangely in the hard, bare room, every whisper reverberating unnaturally against porcelain and linoleum. A few wags on the far side of the gallery struck up a hum of A in imitation of an orchestra tuning up but the laughter stopped dead as the great white chief emerged through his laboratory door, resplendent in his gleaming rubber suit. In his left hand he carried his leather bag, from which he produced a roll of instruments that he laid out in order on the table nearest the slab, like the place-setting for an elaborate (if chewy) banquet. Then and only then did he look up and address his waiting congregation. The white of his overall and the gleaming tiles on the walls cast a strange, snowy light on his face, throwing the massive brow and beaky nose into thrilling relief.

'Good morning gentlemen,' a semibreve of silence, 'and *ladies*. Now then, some of you probably possess a post-mortem textbook by an otherwise exemplary morbid anatomist who makes a case for conducting examinations with one's bare hands. Some of you are going to suffer some highly unpleasant and hazardous infections if you follow this advice. Not – and I speak from personal experience – a mistake one makes twice. However, even the most foolish and over-confident pathologist would hesitate to work bare-handed with the case we have before us this morning.'

He spoke rapidly and his voice was low but every word was perfectly audible in that peculiar acoustic.

'Spectacles are also an extremely wise precaution. A plain glass pair can be had very cheaply. I have known two men blinded by infected material being splashed about.'

Still the sheet stayed in place while he smeared his hands with carbolic oil and eased on the white rubber gloves that Vazard had tweezed from the cardboard box in which they were kept. Taking a scalpel in his right hand the pathologist held it poised above the shrouded shape in front of him.

'Now then,' yet another pause for effect, 'Ven-er-e-al Dis-ease' (a generalised squirm from the student body). 'There was a Royal Commission on venereal disease back in '13 which estimated that 10 per cent of the population of London was infected with syphilis. The report concluded from the notoriously unreliable evidence available that as many as five or six times as many suffered (whether they knew it or not) from gonorrhoea, which was responsible for 50 per cent of female sterility and four-fifths of all gynaecological disorders. The two venereal diseases between them accounted for 30,000 still births annually and half of all congenital or neonatal blindness.' His voice was accompanied by a soft scratching of pencils.

'If the number of soldiers infected with venereal disease in 1917 alone had been sent out on parade they would have stretched from London to Birmingham. 400,000 military cases were treated – *treated*, mark you – during the course of the war, men from all parts of the kingdom, men with sweethearts and wives all primed to undertake the further syphilisation of the race.

'The original Commission's findings gave rise, as I am sure you are all aware, to two very different bodies hell-bent on remedying the situation. The Society for the *Prevention* of Venereal Disease took a purely pragmatic approach. Having reluctantly concluded that nothing was likely to keep the average soldier away from his weekly ration of shall we say *recreation*, the Prevention society advocated prompt inspection and treatment of likely sufferers and the immediate swabbing (*sir-wobbing*),' he dabbed the air playfully with his scalpel, 'of the appropriate parts with permanganate of potash in ablution centres set up for the purpose. This certainly saw off most of the germs, and my sources in the Army Medical Corps told me at the time that the infection rate was thereby reduced to 2 per cent – even among the Other Ranks (who have only a nodding acquaintance with soap at the best of times). However, if any of you gentlemen – or *ladies'* (muffled sniggers) 'is jotting this handy specific on your cuffs,' he broke off to look accusingly at the gallery, 'I should tell you that the sale by chemists' shops of this patent purple purifier and all similar prophylactics was outlawed by those tomfools in Westminster over a decade ago. Anyone so doing liable for a £100 fine or six months' hard labour.

'There are currently estimated to be something in the order of 450,000 syphilitic persons in England and Wales and the figures for gonorrhoea could be as high as 3 million – although to judge from what I see on my slabs, a fair number succumb to both diseases.'

He glanced almost fondly at the rubber-sheeted shape – obviously itching to get started – but he soldiered on with his lecture.

'The second body busied into being by the parlous' – *parlous*, he used the word as if he disliked it, as if he disliked those who used it – 'by the *parlous* state of the health of the nation in general and the military in particular was the National Council for *Combating* Venereal Disease, now operating more primly as the Social Hygiene Council, whose literature doubtless fills your waste-paper baskets. These good people felt that education served only to arouse prurient curiosity in hitherto innocent young men and their answer to a problem as old as time was clean thoughts and manly sports.' The rhyme alone earned a laugh from his embarrassed audience. 'In fact, as you will soon appreciate, by far the best means of keeping the male population out of the lock hospitals would be a parti-coloured picture postcard of this.'

It wasn't called theatre for nothing. With a flourish, he finally whipped back the yellow rubber like a music hall magician. The gallery gave a great gasp and the doors on both sides clicked shut behind several first-years whose breakfast was no match for what lay beneath the sheet. The rest – especially the old hands in the front row – leaned forward for a better look with the horror-struck relish of schoolboys savouring a maggoty blackbird. Kemble registered the departures but continued his lecture.

It was the most revolting thing Dora had ever seen. Not just the monstrous mess between the man's legs (although it was almost certainly that which had caused half a dozen of the students to stumble toward the exits) but everything about the body on the slab. Not a single part looked as it should. Every inch of skin was covered in hideous copper-coloured rashes and warty lumps. Part of her father's medical library was kept in the cupboard beneath one of his bookcases but he hadn't troubled to lock the doors and the young Dora had spent many a morning scanning the colour plates while Dr Strang was out paying house calls. The most disgusting was a large-format volume that came with a special set of stereoscopic spectacles that caused all the ulcerations to leap out in relief. But the body on the slab was worse – and that was just the outside.

'The most cursory external examination invites a diagnosis of tertiary syphilis: the limpet-like rupiae on the torso, the obvious distortion and collapse of the facial bones, the necrosis of the tarsals brought about by the ulceration of the feet, not, er, to mention the bifurcation of the urinary meatus by an infiltrating guma.' The tips of his gloved fingers moved the thing experimentally from side to side as if deciding where it looked best.

'Now were this *gentleman*,' he used the word the way Hubbard 'mistered' the hall porter and a laugh ran snobbishly round the gallery, 'possessed of any known relations – friends, even – (we can, I think, assume that he must at one time have had a great many *acquaintances*),' more dirty, nervous laughter, 'his physician might have been tempted, in that muddled way they have, to classify the cause of death in a manner that would spare the family the shame. One seldom sees "tertiary syphilis" on a death certificate and the euphemisms are legion – aortic aneurysm, pneumonia, pyaemia, chronic meningitis, softening of the brain, mouth cancer, general paralysis of the insane, locomotor ataxia' (*God-rest-her-dear-soul*) 'and (my personal favourite) "general debility" – one can take one's pick. Gonorrhoea is passed off as "pelvic abscess" or "peritonitis" '. Faces are thus saved and official statistics rendered entirely meaningless.

'In the majority of instances the terminal event in a case this advanced would probably be pneumonia or, if hospitalised, infected bedsores might easily give rise to terminal septic absorption or (again very common) catheterisation might lead to an ascending infection terminating in septic pyelonephritis, uraemia and death – one is spoiled for choice, quite frankly.' ('Py-e-lo-neph-ri-tis, ur-aem-i-a and death' muttered the student to Dora's left, hastily scribbling it all down.) 'All perfectly possible. We shall see, shan't we? I am aware that you have a lecture with Professor Bewdlay at noon. I shall endeavour to be swift.'

There was a communal fidget as the students made sure of their sightlines and the pathologist got down to business.

'As you will doubtless remember from last week's demonstration, the pathologist should stand to the right of the subject, hold the knife in his (or *her*) right hand ...' He affected to peer into the gallery to see whether his two female students had stayed the course '... and prepare for the primary incision. Unless, of course, the pathologist should happen to be left-handed in which case' – he took a long step back and batted the slab through 180 degrees on its supporting pillar while simultaneously tossing his knife ambidextrously from hand to hand – 'he should stand to the subject's left.' A red-headed student standing in front of Dora stifled a bravo.

'As we saw last week, the skin of the neck is placed on the stretch between thumb and forefinger and a median incision made from just above the thyroid cartilage,' his hand and arm glided across the flesh, 'as far as the pubic bone.'

The two-foot incision was made with astonishing speed, the tissue parting under the blade as smoothly and inevitably as the flesh on a Dover sole beneath the practised stroke of a fork. The watching housemen gave a unison purr of appreciation, as if Nijinsky had just leaped in through the theatre window. The ginger chap actually clapped his hands together but (luckily for him) his woollen mittens deadened the sound.

The pathologist worked fast, opening up thorax and abdomen with a flick of the knife, a few strokes of the saw. The ribs were snipped free with a large pair of peculiar-looking scissors (the same scissors that had snaked across Dora's back in order to cut away the dead girl's blouse). The whole mass was lifted out then one organ after another was palpated, weighed and placed on Vazard's little china table and the longest, largest of the knives sliced along its length. 'Avoid using a strong stream of water when washing the intestines.'

'Sound advice in any sphere,' whispered Dora's neighbour.

'If any of you opts for a career in pathology, the instrument makers will try to sell you so-called "specialist" blades but you should always remember that a butcher is also a specialist and that his tools can be had for a fifth of the cost.'

Pausing to admire the fibrous banding of the subject's typically hobnailed liver, he carved himself a thin slice.

'Always cut with one sweep of the belly of the knife. Draw, don't press the blade.' He detached his sliver of liver and dropped it into the glass jar that Vazard held in readiness.

He spoke as rapidly as he worked, so fast that there was little chance that his students would gain a great deal from the demonstration. All but Hubbard had abandoned any attempt at note-taking but they stayed to watch just the same, blowing on their hands to warm them, transfixed by his deft demolition of the body before him.

'We should also note that our subject today is a textbook case not only of his primary disease but several other conditions. Syphilis aside, he was not what we would call a picture of health: pigeon-chested, knock-kneed, round-shouldered, flat-footed, sabre-shinned, hammer-toed, cauliflower-eared – pretty much everything but tennis elbows. He also sports boils, bunions, chronic dermatitis, a duodenal ulcer and what may once have been haemorrhoids (although with an anal fissure of this magnitude that would have been the very least of his worries) plus countless traces of what would appear to be more than one species of biting insect. Do not allow yourself to become too excited by the discovery of small tubercular lesions on the lungs, by the way. The pathologist should always bear in mind that these will be found in 90 per cent of town dwellers even when they have died of something else entirely – unsurprising given that the bacilli are found in nearly a quarter of milk samples. The same goes for syphilis itself. Many a subject dying from another cause will show signs of the disease.

'When drawing the testes upwards into the abdomen care must be taken not to buttonhole the scrotum' (much wincing in the balcony stalls). 'Dear old Dr Box in his 1910 manual advises us that if, as in this case, the testicles are to be removed and retained by the pathologist, they should be replaced with dummies. He doesn't say what one should use for the purpose or why on earth this should be necessary and, as one of his students, I'm afraid I never quite had the nerve to ask him. One understands the family's need to view the body but I think a line should perhaps be drawn . . .'

The extent of the man's vile disease meant that more than two hours had passed before the head was reached.

'Watch him open the skull,' whispered the student on Dora's left, 'no coronets, no chisels even: just a knife and a hacksaw. Like he was peeling his breakfast egg.'

As the freckled skin of the forehead was rolled down to keep it clear of the pathologist's saw, the face on the slab took on a pained, puzzled expression.

'As one would expect in a case this advanced, the brain is sadly diminished in size and the texture quite unlike the healthy specimen we observed last week. The convolutions are shrunken and the entire mass collapses when placed on the table like a blancmange on a warm afternoon' (he placed it on the table as he said this and the entire mass duly collapsed as advertised). He continued speaking as he took yet another sample.

'I have known pathologists who strove to replace the brain in the skull but most prefer simply to tuck it into the abdominal cavity and to substitute a small sandbag approximating the organ's weight – roughly fifty ounces in the healthy male. Unfortunately this will entail carrying three pounds of sand about the place, a particular nuisance when called away to a case. I suggest that you improvise.'

There was an unpleasant silence while the doctors-to-be in the gallery wondered exactly what was meant by this. Wondered what they might have to hand when, as general practitioners, they persuaded unwilling families to let them establish the cause of death on the cook's kitchen table. *Improvise?* Coal? Tapioca? Golf balls? Conkers?

Kemble seemed almost to sense the mood: 'I should warn any humorists among you that exhumations, although extremely rare, are not entirely unknown. I myself was once called upon to perform a second autopsy on a body whose brain cavity contained two large jars of thick-cut Oxford marmalade and I confess it was hard to take the physician's findings seriously after that.

'Incidentally, I need hardly remind regular patrons of this theatre that relations and any other concerned parties should always be urged to consent to the fullest possible investigation' (*from 'ere to 'ere*). 'Country dwellers are particularly resistant to post-mortem investigations with the result that in life, as well as in penny-dreadful murder mysteries, the rural poisoner will be on his (or her) third or fourth victim before the local sawbones thinks to ask for a post-mortem.

'Now then. You will all have observed the collapse and distortion of the facial bones during your preliminary inspection of the body. Dissection of the bones of the skull . . .' the sudden practised twist of the wrist as he prised away some bone from the base of the brain reminded Dora of her father's cook dressing a crab '. . . reveals severe ulceration of bone and cartilage. This has affected fauces, hard palate and nasal septum so that the nose, mouth and pharynx form a common cavity.'

Dora held her handkerchief to her mouth, inhaling deeply as if the lavender water were ether.

'The rather fine gold molar is hard to square with the evident poverty of the subject. It is customary in these cases to donate any such teeth to the hospital benevolent fund. The extraordinary thing,' mused Kemble as his gloved fingers continued to probe what remained of the man's head, 'is that modern medicine would appear to have passed our subject by. Nigh on thirty special hospitals in London alone and yet syphilis has manifestly run its course unchecked. I doubt that even Salvarsan – our magic bullet – could maintain any realistic valency in a case this advanced. One shudders to think how many others he may have infected before matters reached this stage.'

He looked up at the clock on the theatre wall. 'Your lecture awaits, gentlemen, and I have more samples to prepare. Quite a few museum pieces today, eh, Dr Vazard?' Vazard was inserting yet another pencilled scrap of paper into a specimen jar before corking and sealing it.

'In the normal course of events I or my assistant would attempt to leave everything as we would wish to find it, restoring the body to some semblance of normality. The cavity should, as Box adjures us, be packed with tow or newspaper. The incision should be discreetly stitched with twine, orifices plugged and all traces of other matter swabbed away. "It must be as if you and your instruments had never been" says Box ... This is undoubtedly best practice particularly if the bereaved have plans to view the body but as there are no relations in this case and as one of the specimens being retained for study is the subject's skull, I see little point in observing such niceties. Good day, gentlemen.'

The students filed off, growing chattier and more ribald as they left the dissecting room behind. Dora's knees were stiff with cold and she had to hold the banister as she walked woodenly down the stairs to the third floor. Every time she closed her eyes she saw the same full-colour stereoscopic image, that unrecognisable thing split almost in two. He hadn't died particularly young. He would have had years of apparent health. Years of unsuspected disease ... The vomit had reached the back of her throat before a powerful gulp, deep breath, count to ten, got matters back under control.

'I say, Miss Strang. Are you all right?' Vazard had finished labelling jars and was on his way to the lecture with the others. 'You've gone the colour of that paint.'

'I didn't ... It's just that I hadn't.'

'Of course not. Although I did warn you. "A nasty but necessary business" as the other professor always puts it. All part of the training. You'd hardly want anyone probing your insides if they didn't know what they were looking for, would you?'

'It isn't that. I know all that. It wasn't that,' her voice had sunk to a teary hiss, 'it's the thought of him. All those years without anyone knowing.' She could feel the angry tears brimming over the edges of her eyes.

The tide of departing students had drained away down staircases and into cloakrooms and Vazard took the clean handkerchief from his breast pocket and swiftly swabbed her eyes. The gesture was medical, not personal. He didn't look at her as he did it. He patted her arm almost approvingly and his voice lost its starchy edge.

'I think some species of restorative might be in order. I'll see you back at the office once this dratted lecture's over: chronic diseases of the lung – practically light relief.'

Chapter 7

'I shall be lucky to last the week. I only got three of those blessed cases fully cross-reffed yesterday and that took most of the afternoon.'

Alec Vazard and a fellow named Curtis were sitting in a public house along the street from Willcox Wing and, much to her own surprise, Dora was sitting between them. Her final year at school had been stiff with supplementary subjects intended to prepare her for the life beyond: the correct use of the telephone, household accounts; the servant problem (hiring, firing, keeping), plus an intensive course in how a lady conducted herself in a range of social situations: how to extinguish conversation in railway carriages, who sat where in a theatre box, the proper pecking order at funerals. Sitting in public houses with relatively strange unmarried gentlemen had not been on Miss Parker's syllabus.

Dora's first instinct had been a polite refusal but Curtis was a chaperon of sorts and she had been rather dreading another lunch hour. She spent most of the short walk to the pub trying to decide what to ask for while Vazard and Curtis discussed the finer points of the morning's lecture. The only alcoholic drink Dora had ever tried was her aunt's sweet sherry, which had tasted exactly like candied envelope gum. She decided that she'd far rather just have a glass of lemonade but did public houses even sell such a thing?

They had sat down by the etched glass window of the Saloon bar and a man in a green apron immediately trotted across to their table. His wet black hair was striped with great oily furrows where the comb had passed through it. Vazard stammered out an order for two pints of something called 'half and half' and then the man asked him what Madam would like. 'Madam' not 'Miss'. With the beastly quick eye of his trade he had automatically registered Dora's wedding ring.

If Dora's father had had his way, his daughter would have been a real Mrs something-or-other by now.

Leopold Strang had had little contact with his only child. Dora had never taken up his time professionally and she vividly remembered being left to scratch and sniff her way through what papa had dismissed as 'the usual catalogue of childhood ailments': whooping cough, measles, mumps, chicken pox, scarlet fever, diphtheria. Even her father had to admit that she had an excellent constitution; unfortunately her mama did not. Dr Strang had been advised that boarding school was the best place for a motherless child of six and Dora's holidays (quite absurdly frequent and prolonged – or so papa maintained) were spent in the guest bedrooms of school friends or with her Aunt Jacaranda, mama's older sister.

This arrangement meant that Dr Strang had only to endure the occasional lunch or dinner as Dora passed between one posting and the next, but her father hadn't exactly made the most of their meetings. There would be an exchange of armed civilities over the soup but the meal was invariably interrupted by telephone calls or by Cole bringing in the post. Papa would then dice his food into forkfuls, slice and gut the envelopes and arrange them in a neat pile on his left, continuing to eat with his right hand as he read. The bad habit had been formed when Dora was (in his opinion at least) far below the age of reason but he saw no occasion to break it when she reached the fifth and sixth forms. He had little time for chit-chat (as he called it). Such inane *politesse* was bad enough with his patients but at least they yielded two guineas a visit.

Papa had cut up very rough indeed when he first learned of Dora's university plans, but it was his own silly fault in a way. He had always kept his medical library in his private study together with all the other books in the house (many of them, like the syphilitic atlas, thrillingly unsuitable). Poor papa assumed that Theodora's constant search for holiday reading matter was being satisfied by the calf-bound yards of Scott and Thackeray and Dickens, until the day he found her curled up in his favourite armchair reading bound back numbers of *The Lancet* with a medical dictionary at her elbow.

He took to locking the study door but the damage had been done and Dora began cramming in earnest for a medical career. Dr Strang realised that he had picked entirely the wrong school for her. Other men's daughters managed to survive their teenage years intellectually unscathed – Westonbirt was the place, apparently – but Theodora's mistresses seemed to regard every *subgraduata* on the scholarship board as a great big enamelled merit badge. The first he had heard of the whole degree nonsense was when the principal of some women's college had written what she clearly imagined to be an emollient and persuasive letter. In it she had admitted that, as Theodora had yet to reach her majority, she would not ordinarily be accepted as an undergraduate without parental consent but urged him to give it.

The woman made great play of the girl's 'intellectual promise,' but her father saw no sign of it. She retained information easily and parroted it with confidence, but he was reminded of his late wife's apparent 'cleverness', how she had used her smiles and small talk to conceal a mind like a patent mousetrap: quick, retentive, but essentially limited in scope.

Dr Strang had written back to the college to say that, in his view, Theodora was not mentally equipped for a degree of any kind and that he remained to be convinced that medicine was a suitable field of study, let alone a career, for females. The principal had been so incensed by his second point that she failed to address his first and her reply urged him to reconsider. She did not, however, make a firm offer of a place, just some flummery about Dora being likely to 'flower' if allowed to stay on at school for the entrance examination and the fact that her headmistress had written in glowing terms, quite confident that Dora would reach the required standard if she applied herself.

As if that brainless bag of tweed would have had any idea what the study of medicine required. Dr Strang's only previous exchange with the headmistress had been a rather distressing correspondence which he had initiated on Dora's first arrival at the school – distressing on her side at least; he had rather enjoyed it.

Ugly memories of his own miserable, malnourished schooldays had prompted Dr Strang to insist that Dora supply him with full details of the domestic regime. The laundry policy left a great deal to be desired. He had written to point out (in quite unnecessarily sick-making detail, in Matron's opinion) that the school's policy of allowing only one pair of white under-knickers per week was not acceptable and could a daily change please be made? Matron had written back blandly to insist that constant changes of under-linen were entirely unnecessary and that Theodora would be issued with clean things every Sunday like the other girls. Her father's reply, penned and posted so swiftly that it arrived that same afternoon, pointed out that, while money-saving, this unsanitary policy was a recipe for a lifetime of candida, leucorrhoea and chronic urethritis. The correspondence had ceased forthwith but a punitive supplement had thereafter been added to Theodora's termly laundry bill.

Dr Strang's retirement from practice coincided with Dora's final term at school. He had moved from Harley Street to a large and comfortable house on the outskirts of a market town in Sussex. In previous years it had always been his habit to spend three or four weeks of the early summer on the French Atlantic coast, but his daughter was hardly Biarritz material and he decided to forgo his usual holiday in hopes that a summer spent in Sussex might woo the child away from those foolish thoughts of university.

Dr Strang's new neighbours were both sociable and inquisitive and June, July and August saw a flood of invitations to tennis parties, strawberry teas and dances for the distinguished-looking widower and his unmarried daughter. Their first few sorties were not a success, with Theodora doing her best to spend the entire time sitting around in an ill-fitting brown frock answering in monosyllables while affecting to read back numbers of *Country Life*. It transpired that she had only two dresses (neither of them remotely becoming) and Mrs Frith, by then mistress of her Pimlico establishment, had been recruited one last time and dispatched to Whiteleys for a mixed box of frocks and hats (her reward being a hat of her choice, which the thrifty Frith found irresistible). Theodora had worn the clothes without a glance but no amount of pin-tucked lawn (the closest she ever strayed to demi-toilette) could render her sulky little face one whit more appealing in her father's eyes.

Once, in a rare attempt at fatherly banter, he had warned that without smiles and wiles the young men would look elsewhere, but the child, now a prig as well as a bore after all those hours of swotting, was undismayed.

'I hope they do, father. I hope they do. I don't want young men to talk to me. I don't want to dance foxtrots and prattle about motor cars. I want to sit for a degree.'

He couldn't very well *beat* sense into her. He would very, very much like to have done but it was 1927 and the moment for heavy-handed fatherhood had passed, along with carriages and between-maids and all the thousand and one other things that made the past so miserably alluring. And besides, the very prospect of packing her off to university was itself becoming more attractive as he found that he disliked having her about the house. Very, very much. He had always found her presence irksome; now that he was obliged to endure many more hours in her company he discovered her to be neither use nor ornament.

She had been known to make other people laugh with what were said to be quite witty remarks but when these were repeated to him in a more audible tone he was unable to see any humour in them. She was pointlessly skilled at indoor games of various kinds and could beat him hands down at cribbage, bezique and piquet. She had even learned contact bridge, or whatever they called it, from a little book she'd bought from the stationer's in the high street, and when she had made up a 'four' at a dinner he'd bullied her into attending Major Kerr-Stanley had damned her with the highest praise: 'Excellent card brain, that girl of yours: thinks just like a man.' She didn't *look* like a man. Which ought, in an odd sort of way, to have been some comfort, but Dr Strang really mightn't have minded so much if she had: spectacles, an incipient moustache, thick ankles for those blue stockings. That at least would have held some sort of professional interest; that at least he could have understood.

In fact she looked very much like her late mother, but with women it was never just a matter of bones and skin and hair and teeth but of furs and frocks and lace collars and ear-bobs and shy smiles and light laughs and the angle at which the blessed chin was worn: the whole trinket box of late Victorian charm. The fact that Theodora should possess the raw materials yet make so little attempt to advertise or improve upon them made her somehow immeasurably more unattractive than a sallow, squinting little chit in lip rouge would have been. At least they would have been making an effort to appeal, to join the dance.

The final straw had come at a dinner that Dr Strang had been obliged to give for his relentlessly hospitable neighbours. He had invited three local fossils and their wives together with any young, unattached offspring they might have cluttering up the house. The girls looked as though their idea of heaven would have been an afternoon trying on hats and frocks in Whiteleys. Theodora Strang was immediately marked down as an alien species and after a brief, simpered greeting, they ignored her totally. The young men were initially nonplussed by her failure to fuss or fascinate, but she seemed a good enough sport and they began practising conversational gambits to use elsewhere on easier prey: shows they'd been to, a motor they'd once driven. Then one of them boasted of going up to the 'varsity next year, which was when Theodora announced that she too would be going to Oxford as soon as Papa could be persuaded to give his formal consent.

Leopold Strang's face had ticked from Changeable to Stormy on receiving this sharp blow to his *amour-propre*, while the flustered ladies wittered unhelpfully about so many gels going off to be educated these days – *not* that one actually knew any but one *heard* about such things and how in their day it had simply been a governess and a little light *plume de ma tante*. They had looked pityingly at poor Dr Strang and the unfortunate Theodora, and stole smug, sidelong glances at their own daughters.

To the exasperation of all those involved, both of these had been christened Elsie. The girls' middle names being Wilhelmina and Chastity (for inescapable, aunt-related reasons), there was little chance of either family giving ground in that direction, and so their friends called them Ellie and Ella to their faces (which they didn't mind too much) and Something Else and Precious

Little Else behind their backs (which they would not have liked one bit).

Something Else was an overgrown, decidedly plain brunette rendered almost presentable by a half-decent dressmaker and an expensively maintained head of Marcel waves. All that now remained was to find an eligible young bachelor in the Hastings area over five feet ten inches in height – 'a tall order' as one local wag never tired of putting it. These were in alarmingly short supply and the larger Else spent most of her time at dances, a delphinium among the wallflowers, hoping that someone would have a tall friend staying Saturday to Monday. There was also talk of wintering in London with a distant cousin in the hope of widening the field.

Precious Little Else was generally considered a safer bet in the matrimonial stakes: small, slightly plump and enjoying the brief, sunny spell of prettiness one so often observed in short, fat girls of eighteen. By twenty-five she would be an overblown mother of three or four, still bravely wriggling into girlish frocks and by thirty she'd be jowly and stout and buttressed with whalebone and patent elastic. It was her physical destiny. Endomorphs. Dr Strang had read half an article in *The Lancet* about them. The big bony plain one would wear a great deal better but young men didn't look at these things scientifically and so Little Else was already six proposals up on her tall friend since they both came out (if you could call a subscription dance at Tunbridge Wells 'coming out').

Dr Strang, in a fit of insane optimism, had once made enquiries about the possibility of some kind of season for Theodora. Mrs Frith knew an honourable Mrs something or other widowed at Passchendaele who would, for a consideration (an outrageously large consideration in Dr Strang's view), shepherd motherless girls through presentation at court and the various compulsory figures of the London season. He had got as far as paying a call on the woman, who lived in a state of suspended grandeur in Rutland Gate. He found her obnoxiously mercenary and risibly convinced of her own importance in the world (whatever he was, Leopold Strang was not a snob). He'd rather settle for a dance at Tunbridge Wells – not that the process had given much air or polish to Little Else, he noted. The girl, who wore both powder and rouge, had looked as smug as her mama when the conversation had somehow turned to blue stockings, actually glancing down at her legs and back up at Rick or Dick or Nick or whatever the Markham boy called himself. Was blue her colour? Deliberately drawing the young man's attention to those fat, silky, pattable little calves. Something Else's mother had sniffed disapprovingly and Dr Strang had drained his glass in disgust. The sooner Augusta Bampton got the girl off her hands the better. Bold. Flighty. And to think it would now have the vote.

Theodora's surprise announcement about her university plans had the whole table in uproar. The other men all sided with papa and were united in their disapproval of women's education, but her father didn't seem to find their support very comforting and was clearly appalled that an entire tablesworth of virtual strangers should be discussing his personal affairs. She'd never seen papa so cross. He had all but exhausted his usual range of wordless signals to indicate that the general drift of the conversation was unacceptable to him. Nostrils had been dilated, eyebrows raised, lips pursed, knuckles whitened. Short of going cross-eyed and waggling his ears there was little more he could do to let them know that money and family business were simply Not Discussed. He was clearly determined to deal a death blow to Dora's scholarly schemes. Theodora, he announced pompously, did not have the mental capacity required for the study of medicine, and the effort to prove that she did would ruin her eyes, her looks, her reproductive health and any prospect of a settled future. She hadn't known whether to laugh or cry.

The Elses and their mamas dined out on this unseemly outburst for weeks. Months. Especially relishing Dora's furious reply that she would be going on hunger strike from breakfast next day and he could jolly well feed her through a tube. It had been as good as a play.

To Dora's everlasting amazement her father said nothing at all when she failed the entrance examination. She had not, of course, been party to the principal's regretful, almost apologetic letter, acknowledging that although Theodora had been a conscientious candidate who had obviously worked steadfastly etc. etc., her father's original assessment of her abilities had proved correct and that re-sitting the examination was not advised. The headmistress had said nothing at all. Most satisfying. Dr Strang merely enquired what Dora proposed to do next. Having by then privately concluded that marriage was unlikely be the automatic next step he had once so fondly imagined, he raised no objection when his daughter proposed a short course in typewriting at a residential college nearby. It was only when she had completed the programme that he showed any renewed signs of irritation.

Her search for paid employment and London lodgings would inevitably cast doubt on his paternal affections or, worse still, on his personal solvency. Another dinner was arranged at which both were painstakingly established. Theodora would be under the wing of Madeline Frith while staying in London. Mrs Frith (whom none of the Sussex people had met) was depicted in the light of his faithful retainer and Theodora's childhood friend. Dora's allowance would naturally continue in addition to the pin money earned at whatever little job she chose to amuse herself with.

There had been a slim volume in Dora's school library listing possible career opportunities for young women. It hadn't aimed high. Lady's paid companion and bath house attendant were among the suggestions, together with feather curler, an occupation that conjured a muffed and bustled age when picture hats were worn.

Dr Strang had no fixed idea of the genteel field in which unmarried daughters might respectably find employment. A publishing house, perhaps? Private secretary in a university department? Or a museum? It was a vague enough list but 'Jobbing filing clerk in a public hospital' was definitely not on it, and so when the post was found by the employment bureau the Sussex gang learned only that Theodora would be working 'at the University'.

Dora wondered whether her elevation to secretary would prove more presentable. Even the Bamptons would have heard of Kemble. Always supposing Mrs Strange could stay the course.

'A gin and French for Mrs Strange, please, Harry.' So much for the lemonade. Vazard was very tickled with Dora's new name (as was Curtis) and both of them had been using it repeatedly. It sounded very fast, spoken aloud in the saloon bar – as if she were some shameless and fascinating *divorcée*. The waiter brought the three glasses and two rounds of cheese sandwiches and replaced their dirty full ashtray with a dirty empty one. Curtis lit each gasper from the glowing end of the last, smoking three to Vazard's one and never offering to anyone else.

Curtis had come complete with Christian name when they were first introduced but Dora had already mislaid it. Harold? Curtis was a houseman like Vazard but Vazard, although technically still a student, was also an assistant demonstrator for the Pathology department.

'Young Vazard here has always been a demon with the old brain knife. Like a duck to water. The chief couldn't believe his luck. Got his hooks in at once.'

'I wasn't exactly beating rival candidates off with the proverbial stick, Curtis old darling. Morbid anatomy has never really been a popular field,' explained Vazard modestly, 'but the cash comes in jolly useful. Old mother Hubbard tried to argue that I was merely departmental assistant, knowing full well that the proper title's worth five bob a week more. Anyone would think it was his own money. Which reminds me,' he turned to Dora, lowering his voice, 'frightfully vulgar to mention it, I know, but you ought to make sure the bursar's office have you pegged as typewriter rather than filing flunky. You can bet Hubbard won't have uttered. As for not lasting the week? They all manage a week, don't they, Curtis? Remember the one who kept losing her breakfast? Mrs Strange here is probably made of sterner stuff and besides, our Great White Chief will keep very tight hold of anyone who can spell gonococcal gonorrhoea.'

While Dora was making an educated guess at the spelling she saw that Curtis had gone very red and that a man at the bar had turned to stare at them. Dora thought at first it was because she was the only woman in the room until she detected two female medics sitting with some chaps – the same pair she had seen at the autopsy (thick ankles, incipient moustaches). From this distance all four appeared to be wearing the same tweed, as though they had been grown on the seats from a culture. Unchaperoned public drinking did not seem to bother them unduly.

As Dora gazed enviously across at their corner table, Alec Vazard noticed the milky lustre of the double string of pearls peeping out from under the natty little scarf at her neck and the soft mess of brown hair at the back of her head catching the watery, bottle-bottom light of the pub window. How pretty she was.

'You could well have found yourself a job for life, Mrs Strange.'

'Perish the thought,' shuddered Curtis, taking comfort in his beer glass. 'I don't know how either of you can stand it.'

'You could say the same about surgery' (Curtis's aim in life).

No you jolly well couldn't, Curtis had puffed. Surgery was a Healing Art. Pathology was a Painful Necessity but people – people like Kemble anyway – went in for it because the patients never answered back and you could go on and on taking out bits and running them through the microscope until you eventually reached the right diagnosis. The detective work was all very well in its way but nobody ever got better. Wasn't that why one became a doctor? Vazard?

Vazard was staring somewhat crossly into space. He nodded but didn't reply.

'Does he really do a full post-mortem on every single case?' wondered Dora.

'Pretty much. Unless the family or the coroner tie his hands – say he can only have the stomach, something like that. We did just over a thousand last year. Every single one from soup to nuts.'

'But surely the cause of death must be perfectly obvious most of the time. I mean, if someone is hit by a tram or something.' (*Poor old sod*)

'Ah yes, Mrs Strange, but *why* was he hit by a tram? A seizure? Distracting agonies? An incurable condition that might tempt him to end it all? Tunnel vision caused by a brain tumour? Or would the size of his cranial cavity reveal that he was simply too stupid to negotiate his way from one side of the road to the other? You never know until you look.'

Dora took an uncertain sip from her glass of gin and tried not to pull a face. Vazard smiled encouragement.

'Do you good after this morning's horrors. Poor Mrs Strange had her first necropsy this morning, Curtis: tertiary syphilis with all the trimmings.'

Curtis chipped in to remark that the first time he saw The Great White Chief set to work with a brain knife one chap had fainted and another poor blighter had had an epileptic fit. Most encouraging.

Dora wasn't altogether sure about Curtis. He had made a trip to the bar to buy a second drink for himself (an unpronounceable half of half-and-half) and although he had *said* he wasn't hungry he had helped himself to most of Dora's cheese sandwich. He was constantly trying to needle his friend about his interest in pathology.

'You pathology coves make out it's all about science whereas what you really crave is the glamour of the courtroom. "Tell me, Sir Alec, in your twenty years as a pathologist for the Home Office, have you etc." '

'Nothing the tiniest bit glamorous about courtrooms, I can assure you – as Mrs Strange may soon see for herself. The old man 's giving evidence in the charm bracelet murder tomorrow and the biscuit tin business comes up any minute. He'll probably want you to ankle along and take notes.'

'Talking of ankles, I see the leg on the Wimbledon bandstand wasn't yours after all.'

'Far from it – unless the poor biscuit tin female had one leg six inches longer than the other and a rather fine tattoo of a Spanish galleon on her hairy right thigh. No, the evidence remains incomplete, although the Wimbledon police think they may have traced the sock – hand-knitted with rare skill, apparently – to a seamen's mission in Rotherhithe.'

The biscuit tin was not, as Dora had at first assumed, the murder weapon, but it made a more attention-grabbing headline than 'Portslade killing' (unless you happened to live in the Brighton area). Between mouthfuls of bread and cheese Vazard explained that the body of a blonde spinster (heavy, build, mid-thirties) had been dissected (without skill) into conveniently-sized portions, and a few of the smaller fragments had been distributed around the home of an elderly couple who lived in blameless domesticity in a small bungalow on the cliff road. The first batch was discovered in the biscuit barrel that gave the case its name, and when the old gentleman had opened the first-aid tin in search of some sal volatile to revive his wife, the box was found to contain one of the corpse's ears complete with a turquoise and coral earring. The other ear had yet to materialise. The rest of the body (give or take a leg) was eventually found in a rented holiday cottage nearby.

Vazard had accompanied Kemble down to Sussex and helped with the grisly jigsaw puzzle.

'Something about that stretch of coast seems to bring out the worst in the British male. I mean to say, you never hear of any Welsh trunk murders, do you?' To which Curtis replied that just because we didn't hear about them didn't mean they didn't happen and that the left luggage offices of Welsh railway stations were probably stiff with the dismembered corpses of well-nourished Welsh blondes of previous good character that no one could be bothered to claim.

The great man had carefully sifted all the Portslade evidence before establishing that various other highly significant parts of the corpse were not to be found. ('Steady on, Vazard. Mrs S still has half her sandwich to eat.') Much police time had been wasted trying to connect the poor old Darby and Joan with the victim but the link lay with the murderer ('Alleged murderer, old man, the trial isn't for a fortnight') who had lodged briefly with the couple a year or so earlier. He hadn't stayed long but it was long enough to learn their habits – church and a long walk along the esplanade at Hove every Sunday morning followed by lunch at the Sackville Hotel and a weakness for sal volatile in times of crisis – and long enough to develop an almighty grudge of some kind, but he could hardly have killed the woman as a practical joke. Certainly a lot of trouble to go to . . .

Perhaps one of Mrs Frith's PGs was nursing a similar grudge, mused Dora. Perhaps one day she too would find a nasty surprise in the biscuit tin and the famous Dr Kemble would call at Warwick Square with his famous black bag – 'eighteen former paying guests at the Warwick Square house are believed to be helping police with their enquiries'.

'What did he need the screwdriver for?' wondered Dora out loud.

Vazard appeared nonplussed.

'A strange-sounding man telephoned on Monday afternoon,' explained Dora. 'He said that he'd *got one* in Alexandra Ward and Dr Kemble dashed away with your stethoscope round his neck and a screwdriver in his pocket.'

Vazard looked slightly uncomfortable. 'Ah. Yes. Oh dear. Sounds like one of our little experiments in the charm bracelet case. He's keen to test his theory on post-mortem abrasions. I suspect the voice on the phone was one of his pet porters. First-rate science, of course, but matrons take a rather dim view of people gouging the alphabet all over their patients – even *ex*-patients. The chief isn't especially welcome on the wards. The patients even recognise him sometimes – and dear old Hubbard – hardly the cheeriest of sights if you're coming round from an operation.'

'What does Hubbard actually do?'

'Exactly as he's told, pretty much.'

'I mean, is he medically qualified?'

'Not so as you'd notice. He was assigned to a regimental aid post during the war and he was with Kemble when it came under heavy bombardment and the chief got badly hit in the leg. Hubbard carried him all the way back to the nearest clearing station. Saved his leg, probably saved his life, which is generally thought to explain his infestation of the department. He washes up in the lab, prepares the agar plates, sharpens the knives, puts

French chalk in the gloves, boxes up the specimens, polishes the knocker, that type of thing. And he sometimes takes the post-mortem notes. Taught himself shorthand from a library book – anything to be of use. The only problem being that both his shorthand and longhand are all but impenetrable – even to medics – so the whole writing-up business takes four times as long. The chief does his own half the time.'

'Mr Hubbard doesn't seem awfully keen on me. I expect I'm treading on his toes rather.'

'Jolly rum toes they are too. He once confided that he gets those funny-looking shoes from a special orthopaedic man: reasonable terms, discretion assured, guaranteed to add stature. Wore them the day he enlisted, apparently. By the time they discovered the missing inch and a half it was too late. As for not being keen on you, for heaven's sake don't take it personally: Hubbard is something of a misanthrope and a major cause of proctalgia.' Curtis chortled obligingly at this medicated quip. 'To the best of my knowledge he never addressed a single word to the late but unlamented Mrs Culvey. Used to leave her little messages in angry capital letters – like ransom notes. Best plan is a campaign of unquestioning efficiency and pathological politeness. It hasn't actually been *tried* – not by the clerical staff at any rate – but I suspect it might infuriate him into submission.'

'I once won the school cup for "Good Manners Under Difficult Circumstances".'

'Really? We never had one of those. Should stand you in good stead with Hubbard.'

As they headed back to the department she noticed Vazard glance at his wristwatch and quicken his pace.

'The chief can get a tiny bit snappy after lunch.'

He held the street door open as they trooped up the front steps of the Willcox Wing.

'And what were the circumstances exactly?'

'What circumstances?'

'Your cup for good manners. Did they engrave them on the side?'

The telephone was ringing as they entered the office and Dora edged behind her desk without having to answer Vazard's question.

Chapter 8

Thursday's breakfast consisted of herrings in oatmeal, a dish so utterly devoid of appeal that Mr Stone once again pushed his plate away untouched. Even the omnivorous Haddon seemed to draw the line at oily fish. Dora made a half-hearted attempt at a post-mortem (why would such a small creature need so many bones?) as she mentally pieced together the details of her dream.

She had been lying half-naked under the rubber sheet on the porcelain slab and she could hear Alfred Kemble's whisper echoing round the white-tiled theatre: *unusually fine pores; hitherto virgo intacta.* She could still see the white-robed, rubber-gloved figure of the pathologist looming above her, preparing to slice open the flowered silk of her underthings with one clean sweep of the knife and the distant faces of the housemen peering down from the gallery, eager to watch the great man perform.

Mrs Frith placed a herring-free triangle of toast and jam on one of her personal porcelain plates. The boarders ate their meals from a nondescript service with a scratched and faded pattern of flowers and pagodas while their landlady dined off an entirely separate set of Crown Derby bought at Liberty's January sale the year after the war. Her water glass was also from a quite different set. Nonsensical woman. She polished the rim with her napkin before filling it.

'I *said* did you sleep well?' demanded Mrs Frith, breaking through Dora's daydream. Dora couldn't speak for blushing.

'The Panamanian pygmy sloth spends twenty-three hours of any given day asleep,' observed Mr Stone, who had taken to introducing random snippets of resolutely useless information in hopes – so far thoroughly fulfilled hopes – of annoying their landlady. 'Well-known fact. And the average mouse,' he paused to make sure he had Mrs Frith's full attention, 'produces a hundred mouselets per year. White ones even more, apparently. Makes you think.' His glance strayed casually to the wainscoting.

Mr Stone was proving to be a major thorn in his landlady's side. During her first year at Warwick Square Mrs Frith had insisted on taking only female lodgers. There had been no shortage of mildly distressed – sometimes extremely distressed – gentlewomen, cheated of fathers and sweethearts by the Hun menace and eager for a refined but frugal roof over their heads. Unfortunately she was far from being London's only amateur landlady and the competition – much of it less wedded to cabbage mould, more generous with coals and hot water – was surprisingly fierce. She had taken her first gentleman entirely by mistake (what sort of person named their son Evelyn?). The paper and handwriting had given no inkling and by the time the man had arrived with his trunks (and a month's rent in advance) it was too late to do anything about it.

Dora resumed her struggles with the warty, oat-encrusted fish on her plate. Whenever she closed her eyes she found herself back inside her nightmare or reliving a moment from the previous day's post-mortem. Kemble's pigeon-chested, knock-kneed, syphilitic 'gentleman' was the first naked man she had ever seen – apart from the ones in the well-thumbed colour plates in her father's anatomy books. They too were flayed and diseased. *Think beautiful thoughts* (as Miss Parker was so fond of saying): Greek gods, cockney prize-fighters – but it had never worked: the sores and deformities always managed to leach back into her mind's eye and make an unholy mess of her bedtime reading.

Dora's daydreams caused her to overshoot her stop and by the time she reached the third floor, Vazard was sitting at her desk, cheerfully eviscerating the first post with a tongue depressor. Kemble and Hubbard were expected back from a post-mortem at St Pancras at any moment, he explained, and a driver was being sent to ferry the pathologist to the Old Bailey at nine sharp to give evidence in the charm bracelet murder.

Kemble breezed in moments later and nodded brightly to Vazard as he dashed through to deposit the precious bag in the laboratory.

'Septic abortion: not without interest. Is the motor downstairs? Splendid. I think Mrs Strange should attend. Hubbard can see to the telephones. Ought to be quite a good show if I say it myself.'

It was rather thrilling to be riding alone in a motor car with him. Dora waited for him to mention the torn blouse, to slide a mite closer along the seat (like the drug-crazed Arabian sheikh in *Cranford*) but he barely spoke as they sped across town and spent the unforgiving minutes consulting a small sheaf of index cards.

As they laboured up Ludgate Hill, he slotted the pasteboard bundle into his breast pocket, felt for the knot of his necktie and carefully shot his cuffs, ready to leap from the car and dart up the steps where a gaggle of trilbied press photographers was lying in wait to catch yet another 'Famous pathologist seen arriving' snap while the reporters fluttered around him with their notebooks: deferential, excited, *thirsty.*

Other people's photographic archives might suggest lifetimes spent lying naked on hearthrugs with a small stuffed bear or simpering behind ugly brides in unbecoming hats, but the pathologist's life would consist almost exclusively of skipping up or down courtroom steps. Every paper already had a file fat with almost identical pictures but they sent a man along just the same – they could hardly use an old one: it wouldn't be news.

By the time Dora caught up with him in the lobby, he had been engulfed by a tide of black barathea and was being chummily Kembled by lawyers from both sides of the case. He murmured a few words to a clerky-looking creature who ushered Dora up to the public gallery. The bona fide public had been queuing since seven o'clock and the seats were densely packed with sightseers. Only four of these were male: flat-footed, winter-vested, Hubbardy little men living on fixed incomes and smelling of mothballs and of the Hovis sandwiches gently ripening in their pockets.

A space was reluctantly made for Dora on the end of the front row by an old baggage clutching a quarter of mint imperials in a white paper bag. Dora was by far the youngest there and a woman across the aisle gave her a disgusted look, her lips narrowing like a librarian about to date-stamp a book she considered unsuitable. Dora took off her gloves and folded her hands (ring finger uppermost) but she didn't really pass muster as a matron. Perhaps if her hair were in coils rather than folded plaits . . . A short style would look less schoolgirlish but her father abominated shingling – the only time she had ever spoken of it he had insisted she take her meals in her room for the remainder of her stay.

The courtroom had the same sense of theatre that had made the post-mortem so unsettling, the same comfy hum of anticipation as men in wigs began filling up the spaces below. The closest Dora had ever come to a criminal court was a lower school production of *Alice in Wonderland* ('suppress that Dormouse!') and the fancy dress was rather exciting, although the old hand to her right was taking the opportunity for forty winks before the real fun started and one of the raincoaty chaps was doing the crossword puzzle in his *Daily Express*.

Regular witnesses in the case were made to line up on the long mahogany benches in the downstairs corridor, like slackers awaiting a wigging from the headmistress, but by the time Dora sat down the pathologist was already ensconced on a seat in the court below. He liked to hear all the evidence. The prosecution certainly didn't mind and the defence didn't dare complain.

There was a certain amount of Gilbert and Sullivanning about with trumpets and gavels and foolscap while the various officials were installed. Necks goosed even further forward as the prisoner was led into the rosewood cage of the dock – an undersized specimen with a yellow complexion and a shocking squint. He had been dressed for the occasion in a borrowed suit and cardboard collar but probably looked much better in his janitor's overalls. He wore very old, very highly polished Oxfords which he gazed at throughout the trial, wonderstruck by their shiny, shiny finish.

Everyone stood up and sat down again when the judge arrived. After a spot more oyez-ing, one of the lawyers got up on his hind legs and began braying in a peculiarly musical, toastmastery voice. He would, he sang, seek to prove that the prisoner in the dock, Oswald Albert Jelly, had opportunity, motive and means to commit a crime evil to a degree beyond all adjectives. The facts in the case were not in dispute, he said airily, then amused himself by telling them anyway.

The body of Violette Delgado had been found trussed up in a bamboo-banded trunk in the basement of a block of service flats near Regents Park. The woman had been sexually assaulted and stabbed (not necessarily in that order) on or about the evening of the tenth of January. The victim's injuries (injuries that had covered eight of the index cards now nestling in Dr Kemble's breast pocket) were of a particularly revolting kind and the word 'harlet' had been scratched deep into the skin of her back with a sharp instrument. An instrument of a similar description had also been used to inflict injuries on the victim's birth canal and it was these puncture wounds which had eventually caused the loss of blood that led to her death.

'Have a mint, dear. It'll settle your stomach.'

The first witness was an officer from the local police station who recited from his notebook with the halting, toneless delivery of a backward child learning to read. He had, had he not, been the first to open the trunk found in the basement of Hanover House? And was that body subsequently identified as Mrs Violette Delgado? It was. He had also (had he not) made a search of the basement quarters of the accused at Hanover House? Would he kindly tell the court what he found there?

'A wood chisel.'

'What else was found?'

'A large box formerly containing cigars.'

'And what, precisely, was this box found to contain?'

'Items.'

'Items?'

'*Items.*' A cough. 'Items of an intimate female nature.'

The policeman obviously reckoned that this would suffice but the prosecuting counsel wasn't letting him off that easily and, after a feeble squeak of protest from the defence, the sergeant was asked if he couldn't be a shade more specific? The old lady with the sweets fidgeted excitedly.

The policeman cleared his throat and reeled off the list like someone playing a parlour memory game: a broken comb, a collection of hairpins and a clump of yellow hair, a cotton pad of the type worn under the arms of a lady's dress or suit, a laddered silk stocking of the same manufacture as those found among the deceased's effects.

There were, were there not, several *other* items of a particularly intimate female nature? There were. Were these items clean and unused? They were not. Could he describe the condition of the items? Soiled. The court would apparently be hearing more about these items but as a result of these findings did the sergeant arrest and subsequently charge the accused? He did. When charged, did the accused make any statement? Oh yes. He said 'did murder Mrs Violette Delgado on the tenth of January last'. Those were his exact words? They were. 'Sensation in court,' scribbled the reporters, but it proved to be a fairly short-lived sensation because the defence then chipped in with a request for Sergeant er er to clarify his exact words to the accused together with the exact response given, at which it became clear that Oswald Albert Jelly was one of those infuriating people who habitually repeat the last half of any sentence addressed to them (sentence addressed to them). The defence then made as if to sit down and then affected to change his mind. Oh yes, and could the sergeant also confirm the full name of the deceased. Was it in fact Violette Delgado? Apparently not. Was it in fact Mary Margaret O'Rourke? It was. Was it indeed? The fat old lady's chins receded an inch or so on learning this highly significant fact, as if a change of name, like a pink blouse or a red jacket, somehow altered the crime.

Next to the stand was the head porter, a Sergeant Cooper, who described his discovery of the trunk in an unused basement storeroom. Had he opened this trunk? No he had not. And why was that? He had noticed a Smell. Sergeant Cooper wore medals, medals that almost certainly qualified him to identify the kind of smell that might emanate from a week-old corpse, and the prosecution let the subject rest. When taken to St Pancras mortuary he had, had he not, identified the deceased as a Mrs Violette Delgado (her name lived in inverted commas now). Dora saw the man's medals catch the light as he straightened his parade-ground shoulders another two degrees and gave a nod like an amen at the memory of what Kemble's ink described with such elegant economy. The face was not recognisable (*cold meat and how to disguise it*) but he had identified Mrs Delgado's charm bracelet and gold wristwatch.

How long had Sergeant Cooper known the accused? And was he satisfied with the defendant's work during those two years?

The sergeant seemed to take against the prosecution counsel at this point, clearly affronted at the implication that he would have tolerated anything less than satisfactory. The defendant, he admitted, was not the full shilling but was right as ninepence in other ways. A good worker, wouldn't harm a fly, kept himself to himself, good as gold and very clean in his habits. Tapioca for brains, he wouldn't deny it, but never any trouble. His quarters in the janitor's basement were kept neat as a new pin, clean as a whistle, right as a trivet. And of what did his employment consist? Hedges, lawns, brass, glass and, of course, the polishing.

Jelly was particularly sound on polishing, which seemed to take the lion's share of man-hours in the running of a modern block of flats: acres of entrance hall, miles of corridors. Jelly's special province had been the linoleum in the lobbies and landings and he would mow back and forth with his patent buffing machine, burnishing the fake marble till it gleamed like barley sugar.

The defence sensed an opportunity. How long had Mrs er-Delgado been resident in Hanover House? Aha. And during those eighteen months had she been in the habit of receiving many visitors? 'In the habit', as if having guests were a regrettable addiction like tobacco or cocaine or nail-biting. And was Sergeant Cooper able to recollect any regular visitors to the flat of Mrs er-Delgado? Not that he remembered. But a succession of different visitors? Objection. Was this relevant? He withdrew the question milord and the withdrawn question hung unanswered in the courtroom air like so much dirty linen.

A friend was found who had once worked with the pseudonymous Mrs Delgado in a West London *palais de danse*, who testified that (like the vast majority of dead people) she was the soul of charm.

The defence counsel then popped up with an ugly thought. 'Was Mrs Delgado ...' and he paused. Paused only for a millisecond but it was the pause used before pronouncing a code word of some kind and the whole courtroom was instantly on the alert for what came next, '*fond of society?*'

Apparently so. The fat lady had another mint imperial.

Mrs Delgado's face and hands had been mutilated in a crude attempt to conceal her identity but dental records from a very smart Wimpole Street man who had stopped or crowned practically every tooth in her head ten years earlier, confirmed that the body was that of Mary Margaret O'Rourke (he'd know that bridgework anywhere). Dora saw her neighbour's mouth plump out peculiarly as she ran her tongue guiltily across her own front teeth.

Next came a flying visit from an Oxford Street jeweller whose firm had supplied the latest trinket on the heavy gold charm bracelet she wore: a little wishing well with moving parts; new to the market, very popular. The man – an undersized specimen with brilliantined hair – clearly recalled selling exactly such a charm to a woman fitting Mrs Delgado's description. The defence wanted to know the price of this particular novelty (seven shillings) then went on to point out that there was a grand total of thirty-five charms on the bracelet that had given this unfortunate case its name. The minty female was actually counting on her fingers.

The next witness was the pathologist, and the public gallery gave a massed wriggle in order to sit a bit taller in the saddle while the great man gave his evidence. He made an impressive figure with his long, handsome head and his natty red carnation. There was a crisp swish as the press gallery collectively turned its notebook to a fresh page and the reporters' pallid faces troped irresistibly towards the witness stand, the evening men checking their watches in an effort to gauge which edition they could make.

Was he Alfred George Kemble? He was. Bachelor of Medicine and Surgery of the University of Oxford, a member of the Royal College of Physicians in London, lecturer on morbid anatomy, lecturer in forensic medicine and toxicology and medical jurisprudence, examiner in pathology and darling of prosecution lawyers? He was.

The prosecuting chap kept his questions very brief, lobbing them gently towards his star witness and then standing back while he unburdened himself of his observations and discoveries in clear, confident tones.

Could Dr Kemble please describe for them the condition of the body he had been asked to examine in the basement of Hanover House and thereafter at St Pancras Mortuary on the morning of the twentieth of January last? He most certainly could.

He had opted to address most of his testimony in the general direction of a pretty, fair-haired woman in the second row of the jury. Dora could see her shifting her seat uncomfortably – or perhaps comfortably? One couldn't be sure.

The body found in the trunk had been that of a well-nourished, well-preserved woman in her mid to late thirties. It was unclothed. The hair had had a permanent wave, the hands and nails were well kept, the body had worn well-fitting shoes, the toenails were painted and the armpits had been shaved – the punctilious use of the passive implied that the accused himself had removed the hair during some perverted homicidal ritual.

Had Dr Kemble been able to establish precisely when and how the accused had met her death? It was always difficult to be precise but, in his opinion, death could not have occurred more than two weeks previously. The rate of decomposition had been accelerated due to the very warm conditions of the basement room in which the trunk had been placed. He had nonetheless examined every organ and found no evidence of pre-existing disease, although there were signs of lesions which indicated a recent episode of pharyngeal gonorrhoea. The prosecution was hoping to carry smoothly on but the judge, who obviously had a healthy loathing of mystifying medical terms, intervened. Could

Dr Kemble kindly tell the court in ordinary language exactly what that entailed?

'Gonorrhoea, m'lord, a venereal disease.'

'Affecting what part of the body?'

'The pharynx, m'lord. The back of the throat.'

There was a silence you could have cut with rib scissors. Dora squeezed her eyes shut, trying to block out the picture of that dyed blonde head busying itself in a man's lap, the charm braceleted hand guiding its work. Like a scene from *Adam Bede*. One of the press men blew his nose rather abruptly but the prosecution chappie pressed on as though nothing untoward had occurred, anxious to shift the burden of guilt back to the accused. And what had, in Dr Kemble's opinion, been the cause of death? Well, in his opinion, death was due to a loss of blood following a series of penetrating wounds to the genital passage.

Brows furrowed in the press gallery. Their editors would never let them use any of this. Pencils hovered motionless above notepads as each reporter struggled to find some deceptively dry, euphemistic form of words that would plump back up into juicy fat life once the public's interest had drooled over them.

Was there anything inside the trunk which could have been used to inflict these injuries? No. What kind of weapon, in his opinion, would have given rise to injuries of this type? A square-ended sharp instrument of some sort. In his considered opinion could the instrument in question have been a wood chisel such as Exhibit One? A tray was passed round. Exhibit One had a blond wood handle, noted Dora. Could it, in his opinion, have caused injuries of this type? It was possible.

Could he describe the victim's other injuries? There was evidence of a violent sexual assault moments before or immediately after death. Had Dr Kemble observed any other marks upon the body? Rather. He began to catalogue the stab wounds, cuts and bruises, tracing each scratch, each gouge, each abrasion to its source with the skill derived from a lifetime spent assessing the damage done by hard surfaces in contact with soft. Dora pictured him in his overalls at the St Pancras post-mortem, cutting into the already half-dissected corpse, his thrifty butcher's knife slicing neatly through kidney and brain. *Cutting people about unnecessary.* What did Mrs Delgado have for brains now?

The marks observed on the wrists, elbows, ankles and knees were consistent with the body having been tied up and placed in the trunk in which it had been found. These marks had been made after death. Could Dr Kemble tell the jury about the marks he observed on the victim's back? He could indeed. The word 'harlet' had been scratched deep into her skin. The jury was at this point shown a photograph (black and white) while the gallery made do with its mind's eye (full colour). And how (in Dr Kemble's opinion) had these marks been made? They had been made with a square-ended metal tool one quarter of an inch wide. To judge from the limited extent of the bleeding, these marks had been made after death. Would he please look again at Exhibit One. The blade of the chisel was the same width as the marks made on the skin. Could the same chisel have made the marks on the back? It was possible. Was it likely? It was possible.

Having examined the many terrible injuries inflicted on the victim, had Dr Kemble formed a picture of the size and strength of her assailant? He had. The weapon was very small and very sharp. Only a few puncture wounds would have been needed for death to result and no unusual strength would be required. The nature of the fractures to the cheekbones, jaw and ribs and the angle of the puncture wounds had led him to conclude that these injuries had been inflicted at close quarters by a left-handed man of lower than average height. The jury's glance ticked inexorably from the pathologist to the runty, besuited figure of the accused.

The defence counsel popped up to point out that the unfortunate woman's injuries were, as his learned friend had so rightly said at the outset, not in dispute, and was it necessary to distress the jury with the details? No one doubted that an appalling crime had been committed, the question was whether his client could be proved to be guilty of it.

His Lordship then made a curious mooing sound like a dyspeptic Guernsey with wind in all four stomachs, and the other lawyer stroked at his gown in a rather sniffy way but held his ground before launching into the next phase of his questioning.

It was true, was it not, that as lecturer in morbid anatomy at a major London hospital Dr Kemble had a newly equipped scientific laboratory at his disposal? It was. And had he been able to offer his services to the police in the analysis of the material discovered in the cigar box found in the defendant's quarters? He had. Could Dr Kemble describe his findings to the jury? Again Dora noticed that when Kemble replied he addressed himself to the second row jurywoman, telling her all about the little dusty ball of combings found in the box. How microscopic analysis had revealed hair which exactly matched that of the deceased: dark brown hair chemically lightened with hydrogen peroxide, the individual hairs bent and twisted by the action of heat (this news was met by a contented told-you-so sniff from the mint lady).

'There was a brownish stain on the handkerchief which a specialist had revealed to be . . .' Dr Kemble coughed awkwardly and referred to his little card while the court held its breath in hopes of fresh horrors . . . 'Ceylon or possibly Indian tea, matching the type found adhering to the sides of the rubbish chute leading from Mrs Delgado's kitchen to the basement.' The sense of disappointment sighed into the courtroom like a gas.

Was there any other scientific evidence to link the contents of the box with the deceased? Oh gosh yes. The lipstick print on the scrap of paper undoubtedly belonged to the body in the trunk. The sanitary napkins – the scribbling ceased again at this point and a prim, is-this-really-necessary shudder rippled through the rest of the court – bore stains later identified by the Lattes process as blood type B, the same blood type as the body in the trunk.

Had the pathologist formed any opinion as to how the various items in the cigar box had been obtained? The pathologist looked positively pained and the prosecution hastily rephrased his question: was the appearance of the items in the cigar box consistent with having been retrieved from a domestic waste chute? It was.

The cross-examination was short. Had he taken the chisel found in the defendant's tool kit for analysis in his laboratory? Why ask if he hadn't? And in his microscopical examination of the wood chisel and of the other tools found in the room of the accused (who was an accomplished wood-carver) did Dr Kemble discover *any trace* of blood or tissue whatsoever? No. And was it his evidence that these marks could *only* have been made by a wood chisel? No. Could the marks on the victim's body have in fact been made by some other tool, a common screwdriver, for instance? It was possible. Defence seemed to feel he had scored a point but the listeners were not listening because the multiple mental image of the stunted little polishing freak in the second-hand suit and shiny, shiny shoes scrubbing his tools clean was so vile, so vivid you could almost have projected it on to the whitewashed wall of the court.

The prosecuting counsel had a little card index box back at his chambers containing the names and addresses of experts who could be relied upon to behave themselves. His next witness was one of these: a little Austrian alienist – almost a cartoon of a nerve specialist – who was invited to make sense of the possible connection between the contents of the cigar box and the contents of the trunk. He was a red-faced man with a clipped black beard through which his lips swelled fat and moist like the angry edges of an infected cut. He was called Green but he didn't sound English. His consonants were all switched around and the words seemed to be playing a tune as he spoke them, reminding Dora of her old piano teacher. The prosecution wanted short answers and had done his best to frame his questions accordingly but had reckoned without Dr Green's long-standing love affair with the sound of his own voice.

Had he examined the accused? He had. Was the accused, in his opinion (those words again), of normal intelligence? Dr Green shrugged his shoulders and pouted in a rather showy foreign fashion. The usual *effaluations* were not possible as the subject was unable to either read or write but a long interview and a set of specially devised picture cards had established that the man was borderline Dull. The lawyer suppressed a yawn, 'Dull?' Would he be correct in surmising that the doctor was using the word in a very particular sense? The alienist was all too happy to elaborate. His own personal measure of feeble-mindedness was now favoured by all those who had made a serious study of the subject. It graded intelligence on the following scale: Superior, Normal, Dull, Simple, Idiot, all the way down to Imbecile. In Dr Green's opinion the accused was in the lower reaches of ze Dull spectrum. Not *altogezzer* Simple but definitely not Normal.

There was a frenzied scratch of graphite as the press gallery seized on this appetising cross-headline. And was the psychiatrist of the opinion that the low intelligence of the accused and his overall response to testing was consistent with the criminal type? Yes. Repeated studies had confirmed that there was a causal link between low intelligence and crimes of violence, particularly crimes of a sexual nature.

He then began to expound on the interesting fact that the incidence of the double crime of rape and murder had rocketed during the war. War, in his opinion, had unleashed the slumbering sadistic impulses in ze adult male . . . but the prosecution counsel pulled him down off his hobby horse and brought him back to the matter in hand before the defence could get to his feet. Was the accused, in his opinion, a man capable of extreme violence? The public gallery, like tennis spectators, ticked their heads to the right as he asked this, to take another look at the man in the dock.

Anaemic, undersized with a painfully receding chin; Dora could quite easily imagine Mr Jelly beavering away with his little wood chisel. He was still staring stupidly at his shoes, turning his feet so that the leather caught the light. The only time he had managed to drag his eyes away from them was when he heard the head porter's voice and gazed gormlessly at the witness stand, wondering what the sergeant was doing in this funny place. Dull was definitely the word.

Had Dr Green examined the contents of the cigar box found in the quarters of the accused? Oh yes. In his experience, did this sort of behaviour have any significance? The gallery sat spellbound while the Austrian type spoke of sexual deviation sometimes manifesting itself in a collection of objects – clothing, shoes, stockings – which the sufferer would accumulate so that this 'harem of fetishes' could be used in various acts of self-abuse. The aberration was most commonly found among men who were unable to Function normally.

'Function?'

'The sekssual funkssion.'

Defence's turn. The defence barrister affected a bluff, fifth-form persona with the prosecution's pet alienist, the bewildered *Boy's Own* manner of a man unwilling to accept this ugly continental reading of human behaviour. Could Dr Green please tell the court where he had studied? In Heidelberg. Then at the University of Vienna under Wilhelm Stänker and also a year at the Institut für Sexualwissenschaft in Berlin. The lawyer pulled a bewildered face. Could the jury possibly have that in plain English?

'Sexology.'

'Sex-ology,' the defence counsel gave the jury an old-fashioned look, 'I see.'

And was this Dr *Stänker* he mentioned (he made a special point of pronouncing the name in the German way) the author of a study entitled *Sexual Aberrations*? The hapless alienist seemed pleased to find his mentor's book so widely known. And was it not the case that in this book Professor *Sshhtänker* had concluded that 17 per cent of the male population were suffering from sexual perversion of one kind or another? Did Herr Doktor consider that to be the correct figure? He did. And was it really his contention that *one man in six* – he raised a comradely eyebrow in the direction of the jury benches – was guilty of sexual aberration?

'Stänker's thesis was based on a great deal of research ...' began the Austrian but was cut short by the barrister.

'Professor Stänker's research was conducted where?'

'Berlin.'

'Berlin?'

'Berlin.'

Another puzzled frown for the jury. The alienist must please forgive his ignorance but he wanted to get this whatd'youcallit 'Fet-ish'? business absolutely straight. These fet-ish thingies were what – a lock of hair? A glove? A stolen handkerchief? A comb? A lost button?

Dr Green nodded encouragingly. Yes, ze typical harem of fetishes might contain many such objects. The barrister proceeded with care. And keeping such objects unknown to their previous owner: this was *abnormal* behaviour? He put the suggestion very gently in his best just-clarify-this-for-me-in-layman's-terms manner and the alienist tumbled cleanly into the bear trap that had been dug for him.

'Ze harem of fetishes is a classic symptom of hypersexual aberration.'

'What the man in the street would call abnormal behaviour. A perversion?'

'An abnormal behaviour, yes.'

The defence barrister twirled away from the alienist. A senior colleague had once advised him that one should never despair when defending a case involving any sort of indecency: 'six of the jury won't believe that such things happen and the other six do it themselves'.

'And are you asking the ladies and gentlemen of the jury to accept that a lock of hair, a pocket handkerchief, a faded flower, a favourite pipe, a piece of webbing from a uniform are symptoms of – what was it again? – hypersexual aberration?'

And all of a sudden the air in the court was fragrant and tearful with sacred relics. The barrister lowered his voice to a stage whisper as he turned again to the jury.

'On that basis I suspect that between us we could keep half the alienists in Berlin in business. No further questions.'

There was a satisfied sigh of approval from the lawyers' benches at this first-class piece of boffin-baiting but it made no odds. There was the world of difference between the jury's bottom drawer and a cigar box full of soiled sanitary napkins, as the defence knew perfectly well.

The only character witness called by the defence was the former head of the special school that Jelly had attended, who testified that the accused had been a harmless, gentle, sweet-natured wee lad, very clean and particular in his habits. This, combined with the woman's crocheted fascinator and an equally soft and fluffy lowlands Scottish accent, sowed tiny doubts in the minds of the jury, who began to think forgivingly of harmless idiots in their own families' cupboards.

The prosecution began with infinite gentleness. Might he ask Mrs MacDonald a few general questions about the young men in her charge? Was it or was it not the case that the boys in her care were routinely dosed with medicines? The woman seemed a trifle nonplussed. They gave them castor oil ... And *other* medicines? Bromide, perhaps? She hesitated. The board doctor saw to it that the boys had whatever was right. And was that in order to keep a tight rein on their behaviour? On their *Impulses*? The boys had whatever was right.

The barrister fiddled theatrically with spectacles and leaned across his desk, where a handwritten sheaf of lemon yellow paper had been placed. And yet it was true, was it not, that of the 1,400 feeble-minded boys who had passed through her hands in her five years as directrice of this institution no fewer than 238 had served a term of imprisonment: 102 for acts of violence, 43 for assaults on women? Was it not also the case that no fewer than three of these supposedly harmless imbeciles had subsequently been hanged for murder? Was it not also the case that 57 had fathered illegitimate children and that a further 93 had contracted a loathsome disease as a result of their activities – and this despite a daily dose of medication designed to suppress their revolting appetites?

The lawyer flashed a swift, grateful grin at the pathologist then swooped apologetically toward judge and jury, forestalling the defence, who had begun to fidget at this digression.

'I make these observations merely to establish the extent to which a man such as the accused with severely limited intellectual capacity is subject to urges over which he exercises none of the usual civilised restraints. And I put it to you that this,' pause, '*harmless, dull* man, this man,' another pause, 'who took such *professional* pride,' the jury – a butcher, a baker, a Bakelite moulder – felt themselves warmly enfolded in the lordly, Gray's Inn irony of it, 'such Professional Pride in the state of a few square feet of marmoleum, was in fact a moral imbecile waiting for an opportunity to repay Sergeant Cooper's trust and Mrs MacDonald's kindness with the repulsive deeds we have all heard described.'

The defence, in their desperation, had called a handwriting expert, who testified that the letters scratched in the woman's skin were, in his opinion, formed in the normal way by a left-handed person who knew how to write. The letter E was particularly conclusive, he felt. Unlettered persons copying a capital E tended to draw the top, bottom and left-hand strokes in one go, whereas the E on Mrs Delgado's back had been formed by first writing a capital L – as a literate person would.

The prosecution counsel wasted no time.

' "*Handwriting* expert". Tell me,' he mused, 'is that a full-time position?'

The witness, who looked as if his own handwriting were a trifle on the showy side requiring a broad italic nib and coloured ink, pointed out that he had been retained by Scotland Yard on a number of forgery cases.

Yes. But was this how he earned his living? No, of course it jolly well wasn't how he earned his living. His living, such as it was, was earned as a drawing master at a boys' school in Richmond.

The next three questions practically asked themselves. Was he often called to give evidence in cases where the script to be examined was written on human skin? Had he ever in fact given evidence in such a case before? Had he ever himself tried carving words into human skin with a wood chisel – or a screwdriver, perhaps? The prosecution looked fractionally more awake for this question, as if the handwriting chap with his green tie and soft collar might well be capable of such an outrage.

Any advantage the defence had gained was cancelled out by the recall of Dr Kemble to the stand, who admitted that yes, he had (since you asked) conducted experiments with the pristine quarter-inch wood chisel found in Oswald Jelly's disgusting little glory hole. If anyone wondered where (or on what) these experiments were conducted their curiosity was not to be satisfied.

'Were you able to form letters in the normal way?'

'Not in the normal way, no. Even a sharp instrument has some difficulty etching legible lines in human skin, particularly on the back, where the flesh is quite loose. One forms the letters as best one can but the strokes are not made as one would make them with a pen.'

Chapter 9

The pathologist smiled the smile that had carved the little curve on his cheek when Dora reached the office next morning, the smile that made slaves of Hubbard and Vazard, that had lady jurors eating out of his gloveless hand.

'Don't take off your coat, Mrs Strange. Hubbard has located the portable typewriting machine and we are off to darkest Finchley, where a patient awaits.'

The coroner had sent a car to fetch them. There was a fat, soda-reddened old charlady mopping the red-tiled corridors when they arrived but the only other woman in the building was occupying a porcelain slab.

Kemble was entirely right about the whole 'Mrs' business. The world had undergone a subtle shift since Dora made the spouseless leap from Miss to Mrs. All sorts of unexpected things manifested themselves in everyday situations, as if one suddenly had the power to see people's auras or read their unspoken thoughts. The ring on her finger might spare her the lingering touch of a bus conductor's hand, or the appraising eye of fellow lunchers in the hospital refectory, but the 'Mrs' malarkey made her one of the boys, someone immune to strong language (within reason), a matron who could withstand off-colour stories of travelling salesmen and Egyptologists' daughters (stuffed and made mummies of) without blushing.

The policemen and mortuary officials also took some comfort from the state of her ring finger (as if married life would be ample preparation for dismemberment) but, although the ghost of the late Mr Strange provided Dora with a free pass into their unmaidenly world, she was still welcomed in a faintly mutinous spirit. Miss Parker's advice to the upper sixth on the smooth management of domestic staff was Dora's only guide: 'give orders; don't make requests if you want to assert your authority'.

'Good morning, officer', she addressed one of the policemen in bold, 'I-can-write-my-name-in-the-dust-on-this-piano' tones. 'I shall need a chair and somewhere to set up my typewriting machine. Dr Kemble will begin his post-mortem shortly. And perhaps you could bring us a pot of tea. And some bread and butter if you have it.'

The man looked surprised, annoyed even, but he went away and came back with a chair and table and was later heard snapping instructions to the constable in the corridor, so it was obviously the right tone to take.

Dora concentrated on her typing while Kemble gave his running commentary so the whole business was infinitely less disgusting than the septic theatre demonstration, but she could still match the sounds to the ugly memories: the soft plop of tissue on enamel, the crunch of the rib scissors, the regular whoosh of the cold tap as he carefully catalogued the changes that life and death had effected on the body beneath his blades.

After an hour there was a faint sound of raised voices from outside the door but someone suppressed them and the pathologist worked on, listing his findings in that eerily audible murmur.

'No sign of any pre-existing disease.'

Stomach contents were aspirated into pipettes, slices were taken from kidney and liver, but he took no slice from the subject's well-nourished brain because the female in the case had met her death in a Metropolitan Railway carriage when she was crudely decapitated by a passing train and the head had yet to be recovered. Dora thought of all those unread warning notices.

'Happens far more often than you'd think.' Kemble's voice had taken on the familiar lecturing tone.

'Were this a case of criminal assault' (a little smirk acknowledging his own experience in this area) 'bruising or abrasion of the thighs, hands and wrists should be looked for as well as the presence of stains, blood or secretions on the external organs, and the a-nus', his voice was bored, faintly disgusted, 'should be examined for bruises and lacerations and particular attention paid to the state of the vagina and the hymen (which in our case we have not got).'

The voices outside grew louder, then the door opened and a man with gold-rimmed pince-nez came in.

'Look here, Kemble, the girl's mother is over at the police station. Are you sure all this is strictly pertinent?' (*cutting her about unnecessary*) The man nodded crossly at the growing collection of jars on the steel trolley to the left of the slab. 'It isn't needed for identification. The police here would have been perfectly happy with the stuff in the girl's pockets . . .'

'Any sign of the head?' It was as though he hadn't spoken.

'The men are still searching the line.'

'I have all my samples, Colonel. I should be finished here by the time the next of kin arrives.' Next of kin. The pince-nez man had said 'mother'.

The girl's pretty, white, full-breasted body had been discreetly stitched with twine, orifices plugged and all traces of other matter swabbed away by the time her grief-stricken mother arrived to identify a body she hadn't seen naked since she last bathed it and to be closely questioned regarding abortions she knew nothing about.

The lunchtime editions of the evening papers were full of the charm bracelet case, which had finally run its course that morning. The accused had eventually taken the stand and the transcript of his evidence showed how skilfully the prosecution had exploited Oswald Jelly's habit of echoing the closing words of a sentence. 'It is true, is it not, that you had a long-standing grudge against Mrs Delgado for refusing your advances and that you thought to yourself "I hate this woman and she deserves to die"?' Candy from a baby.

There was only a paragraph on the cigar box and Oswald Jelly would hardly have recognised his beastly little harem of fetishes by the time it had been rendered fit to print. The items of an intimate feminine nature were nowhere to be found, just a few locks of hair and a stocking. It sounded almost romantic.

The defence had been brief. The evidence against his client was entirely circumstantial. It was all very well for Dr Green (looking very, very Austrian and utterly, utterly barmy in his snapshot) to lecture so eloquently on the sexual perversions to be observed among the inhabitants of Berlin but, without wishing to denigrate the work of Herr Stänker, a British jury would know how much weight to attach to his evidence. His learned friend had sought to baffle the jury with a batch of irrelevant statistics but the mental incapacity of the accused was not in itself evidence of criminality. As for the evidence of Dr Kemble regarding the likely size and strength of Miss Delgado's assailant, he begged them to remember that no doctor was infallible, and medics were so often wrong.

There was a verbatim report of the judge's summing up, much of it consisting of a paean of praise to the pathologist, which left the jury in no doubt. The *Evening News* had set some of the more telling phrases in bold type as cross-headlines. Did they remember Dr Kemble, that *incomparable witness*? Did they remember how he stood and the way in which he gave evidence? Had they ever in their puff seen a witness who more thoroughly satisfied them that he was *absolutely impartial*, absolutely fair, absolutely indifferent as to whether his evidence told for one side or the other? Dr Kemble would be the last to make such a claim but his opinion was undoubtedly *the very best opinion* that could be obtained and he was certain they could not have failed to be impressed by the moderation and restraint and fairness, and by the complete *absence of partisanship* displayed by him in the evidence which he gave in the witness box. The defence's observations on Dr Kemble seemed to him to be somewhat less than just 'but of that you are the judges, not I'.

Meanwhile, on an inside page, the Peckham police had arrested Mavis Shirley's uncle, who had taken the opportunity to assault and murder his wife's niece on the pretext of seeing her home safely after the cinema. She had known the man all her life. Had it come as a complete surprise? wondered Dora, or had her teenage years been spent dodging mistletoe and refusing to sit on Uncle Timmy's eager knee?

Dora lunched furtively on a cheese roll she had bought in a baker's shop in Goodge Street, then spent the afternoon typing up the morning's post-mortem before returning to the pile of index cards.

A boy from Dispatch brought a final edition of the *Evening Standard*, which was dominated by the charm bracelet verdict. The jury had required only an hour and a half to decide that Oswald Albert Jelly should be taken to the place from whence he came etc. Meanwhile the stop press column carried the news that Mavis Shirley's Uncle Tim would be spared that particular fate because while alone in his Peckham police cell he had swallowed a two-pint bottle of spirits of salts which he had hidden in the lining of his coat (Poisoning 165B). This succulent news item had been written, typeset and available on street corners a full twenty minutes before the call came from the Peckham coroner asking Kemble to conduct the post-mortem.

Chapter 10

To judge from the chatter Dora overheard on Friday night's omnibus, Saturdays and Sundays were the days when the working world did what it would rather be doing. Instead of adding up someone else's numbers or typing someone else's words or polishing someone else's floor they would be able to watch football matches, fly kites, grow vegetables or pack someone else's dismembered body into a bamboo-banded trunk.

Dora's schoolgirl Saturdays had been mostly spent running up and down cold fields with various items of primitive weaponry (even the typewriting academy had had a lacrosse team). Sundays had been whiled away in freezing churches listening to sere old men bore on about the Lord in the special, badly-translated-from-the-Latin dialect they seemed to reserve for the purpose. Dora had rather relished the thought of a completely blank timetable but her friends and relations seemed to have other ideas.

Local legend had it that Mrs Frith took her Saturday breakfast in bed so Dora was surprised to see her at the head of the table when she came down next day, carefully scraping best butter across a wafer of cold toast.

'Good morning, Theodora. A telegram came for you which I took the liberty of opening. Your aunt expects you for lunch at the Ritz.'

Mrs Frith added hot water to the teapot with a tiny smirk of satisfaction. This was the kind of breakfast dialogue she liked. It set the right tone. She passed the telegram across to Dora. 'I must say I don't think an extra tuppence would have gone amiss.' Dora's family made it a point of honour never to send a telegram of more than a dozen words (address included) but Aunt Jacaranda had excelled herself: 'Lunch Ritzone. Bluefrock. Hatpearls.'

Dora had been given her mother's pearls for her eighteenth birthday and her aunt insisted that she must wear them constantly or they would lose their lustre ('Why do you think the Queen wears hers so often?'). Mrs Frith took a very different view. When she first noticed them on Dora's dressing table the night of her arrival she had made a point of rubbing those stained, greenish teeth against them. She then raised her eyebrows and pursed her lips at the same time: a picture of disapproval.

'*Far* too good to wear every day. But nor can I have them left in your room. Hardly fair on poor Ivy. I think they would be best kept locked away in my bureau.'

Dora caught Mrs Frith sneaking a sidelong glance in the dressing table mirror, imagining the triple string against the neckline of her brown crêpe over tea with her friend Mrs St Keith.

Dora had looked at her own unbobbed, unwaved, lisle-stockinged reflection in the wardrobe door.

'I shouldn't worry, Mrs Frith. No one will dream they're real.'

Although Dora would have preferred a quiet day with her books, a decent lunch was a very welcome thought. Saturday's breakfasts were, if anything, rather less sustaining than the weekday variety. Today's meal consisted of watery scrambled egg and wafer-thin slices of gammon served from a single large dish on the (usually correct) assumption that the PGs would instinctively restrain their appetites in proportion to the food on display, thereby consuming far less than ten separate platefuls would entail (Mrs Frith always imagined that the miracle of the loaves and fishes had operated on a very similar principle).

Mr Stone, who was now openly scanning the personal columns of both *The Times* and the *Morning Post* in search of vacant rooms, wasn't playing nicely and took three slices of ham and two generous spoonfuls of egg, obliging Mrs Frith to send down for extra toast before setting about the morning's household duties.

Having wreaked havoc with the week's domestic economy, Mr Stone then retired to the poky ground-floor back sitting room reserved for the use of guests, where Dora found him lounging ornamentally on the window seat, smoking a Turkish cigarette and gazing out into the stony hole that took up the space between Warwick Square and the garden walls of the next street.

'I know Mother Frith moves in a fairly mysterious way but has anyone the faintest idea what our esteemed hostess is *doing* out there?'

Mrs Frith, wearing a knitted muffler, a pair of sleeve protectors and the familiar holland apron, had suspended an old squirrel coat from a washing line and was beating it repeatedly with a headless Malacca cane.

'Not altogether sure but on past form I should imagine it's something vaguely moth-related.'

Mr Stone tweaked a shred of tobacco from the tip of his tongue and took another long puff of his cigarette.

'Well, she's got a nice day for it.'

'Poor old Frithy,' sighed Aunt Jacaranda when Dora described her morning at Warwick Square. 'What a cruelly disappointing life she's had. I suspect the husband was a brute. He certainly ruined her health. And her looks.' She glanced across at one of the mirrors that lined the room and half-smiled approvingly at her trim, unmarried reflection.

Aunt Jacaranda wore a rather arch brown tailor-made and, despite perilously high heels, she tripped across the floor of the Ritz dining room with the pert pace of a woman half her age. Unfortunately the jaunty effect was sabotaged by thick horn-rimmed spectacles: one pair on her nose (to enable her to see beyond it), the other dangling from a chain round her neck (for reading the menu). She had once tried to do without them and she had the trick ankle to prove it.

Aunt Jacaranda was not, strictly speaking, rich enough for the Ritz nor for the rented chauffeur who had driven her there nor for the smart new coat and skirt she had bought for the purpose, but she economised in other ways and always made the most of her short visits to town. She was registered as Lady Scott. 'No law against it, darling,' she confided in her exasperating stage whisper. 'And they can hardly look it up. Do you know how many Scotts – knights, baronets and barons – there were in the 1920 *Peerage*? *Twenty*, if you count dowagers. The only one even vaguely my age gives her address as a permanent suite at the Savoy so is highly unlikely to "queer my pitch" here. You would be as-tonished, *appalled*, darling, at the difference it makes. Dolly Sherston was here when I stayed last and her room was half the size.'

Dora's aunt was a firm believer in the Parker principle when it came to managing staff and gave a constant string of instructions to any waiter who strayed within bossing distance, demanding anything that wasn't already on the lunch table – black pepper, green onions, white sauce, brown toast, orange marmalade, red biddy – and sending back anything that was.

'No, no, no. *Black* olives. We invalids aren't allowed green. Green ones play havoc with the stomach lining.'

Dora suppressed a faint qualm. It had reached the stage where any mention of a body part was enough to trigger vivid, almost cinematic memories of Alfred Kemble cutting people about.

'The more you fuss the better they like it,' insisted her aunt (a conclusion that flew in the face of all the available evidence).

'Do you know, my dear, it pains me to say it, but there's a man over there in *tweeds*. Dire. What does he save to wear in the country, do you suppose? Corduroys and a smock? And the swine's drinking hock. I expect he'll be wanting a nice *bratwurst* with it. This place isn't what it was.' She drained her sherry glass. 'Now then, what are you doing for this doctor fellow? Agatha Manders tells me he cleans up after all the trunk murders.'

'I'm the departmental secretary. Jolly interesting.'

'Is there a Mrs Kemble?'

'Haven't the faintest.'

Aunt Jacaranda shook her earrings dismissively.

'I think not. Certainly doesn't look like it from what one sees of him in the illustrated papers. Far too dicky-dapper, for a start. One can usually tell. Bachelors come in two basic varieties: the poor-me-lost-dog sort with the missing collar studs and holey hosiery' – Dora thought of Vazard and his inky ankles – 'and the hero-to-his-valet brigade: sharp creases, buttonholes and a glad eye. Married men are seldom either. There's one over there, for example.' Aunt Jacaranda nailed a fellow luncher with a pitying stare. 'Not *grubby* exactly, just slightly shop-soiled. Like all the fight's gone out of them. Like last year's hat.'

There was plenty of fight left in Aunt Jacaranda's ferociously fashionable toque.

'Any female photographs on his desk?'

'Only Mavis.'

'Sister?'

'The Peckham alley person. Strangled with her own stocking.' Funny how they always said that – as if it somehow added insult to injury. As if the murderer should have had the decency to bring his own.

'What a strange girl you are. Of all the jobs to have chosen. Your mother was the same, of course, always fascinated by people's insides. That's how she ended up with your father, only, as we know, he himself wasn't particularly interested in people's insides – or their outsides, for that matter . . .'

Jacaranda and her parents had never really taken to her sister's choice – 'the abominable Dr Strang' as they liked to call him ('Must you marry him, darling? There are bound to be others nicer').

'How is the old fossil?'

'He hasn't written. We agreed that I'd go down next Saturday.' Another weekend stiff with extra-curricular activity.

'I'd offer to join you, darling, but I'm spending a fortnight at that hydro place over at Worthing, "Electric light throughout, separate tables, bathing from our very own tents, no vexatious extras, seawater supplied to all rooms, all the advantages of a sea voyage without the inconvenience of the motion" or so the brochure insists . . .'

Aunt Jacaranda's voice tailed off, implausibly. She lived barely ten miles from her brother-in-law's new Sussex home but had yet to pay a single visit. Her excuses grew ever more colourful but she had never in fact been formally invited.

'Everyone always assumed your father would remarry. He was quite a catch – still is, if you like that sort of thing. No one thought he'd last the year, and people were forever telling him to find a nice sensible woman, but, then again, I suppose that that in itself would have set him against the idea. Pity really. Much nicer for you than all those agency nurses and poor old Frithy. Men do remarry, as a rule, and those French watering places are an obvious hunting ground. He must be in great demand down in Sussex. He's barely sixty. Still takes an interest in such things, I expect.'

Chapter 11

A new boy had mixed up the Sunday newspaper orders for his entire Pimlico patch and delivered everything one house wrong. Had Mrs Frith divined this she would have taken great delight in sailing next door, *News of the World* between finger and thumb, and demanding the release of her *Sunday Times*. As it was, she spread the offending newspaper across her *escritoire* and began devouring it in a state of righteous disgust.

A badly decomposed body had been washed up off the north coast of Cornwall. The hands were severely worn but the resourceful police doctor had peeled away the rotting skin and revealed the reverse fingerprints. Unfortunately, by the time the local constabulary reached the lodgings of the missing Cornishwoman who best fitted the corpse's description they discovered that her relations, not wanting to pay funeral expenses, had scrubbed clean every inch of the floor and walls, every stick of furniture and every item in the kitchen dresser so that not a trace of her existence remained. Happily, their cunning plans had come to naught because the brother had been overheard boasting of their cleverness in his local public house by an off-duty police officer.

Mrs Frith wondered whether they would now be obliged to pay for the funeral. A cardboard coffin and 'no flowers by request', no doubt. She thought, not for the first time, of the paltry spectacle her own obsequies would generate. One could settle all the arrangements in advance, of course (people did), but no amount of flame mahogany would make up for a poor turnout at the graveside. Hard to imagine who would trek out to Highgate. The odd Frith? A PG or two? It was enough to make a person leave their body to science.

Messrs Stone and Haddon were walking past the door on their way out for a morning stroll when Stone spotted Mrs Frith's sensational reading matter.

'Delivered in error,' explained the landlady hastily, 'astonishing what filth people read.'

'How delicious. May we?'

Mr Haddon flopped decoratively on to a little yellow velvet *canapé* and immediately lighted on a story about a West London cinema organist.

'*Gross interference* with a small boy.'

'Twelve,' said Stone, reading over his shoulder, 'not *that* small.'

'Lived with his parents in Camden Town and was of good character.'

'The organist?'

'No. His young friend. "Good character" . . . *Peculiar* thing to say. Are they not, as a rule?'

'Twelve-year-old boys? Not if my prep school was any guide.'

'It seems the offending organist stopped his car in a street near the boy's home and the obliging young cove agreed to ride with him and give directions to Portland Place. They then appear to have driven around various streets and the whole of Hyde Park . . . *twice* round Hyde Park – at which point the accused was struck by a "sudden insane impulse" and the offence (unspecified) occurred. Six months' hard labour without the option and lucky to get it, apparently. The judge went easy on him because it was a first offence.'

'Or the first time anyone complained,' said Stone, reaching for his cigarette case but immediately re-pocketing it after a glacial glance from Mrs Frith.

'The judge was very much in favour of the guilty plea. Spared the boy a spell in the witness box.'

A snort from Mr Stone.

'Not to mention sparing the defence counsel the unpleasant necessity of pointing out that Hyde Park is hardly *en route* to Portland Place. Sighs of relief all round in Camden Town, I should have thought.'

'Well, you can say what you like but Justice Whatsit thought the guilty plea was "manly". Says so in the summing up.'

Manly indeed. Mrs Frith made a show of placing the newspaper in the waste-paper basket as her two lodgers left the room but retrieved it when she heard the street door slam shut behind them and settled back down at the writing desk.

A 48-year-old mother of six from Dundee was being prosecuted for the wilful murder of a 19-year-old girl on whom she had performed an illegal operation. The boyfriend, Italian-looking name, had broken down in the witness box. He had begged her to keep the child. He had wanted to marry her, he said. Had he?

There was an entire page of pictures and background devoted to the Peckham alley murder, including a photograph of murderous Uncle Tim taken at a local fancy dress pageant at which he had won third prize for his Richard the Third costume (unfortunate to say the least). The two-column photograph of his niece (alias 'Alley girl') had obviously been taken from one of those colourised High Street portraits that had brushed away bad skin and given a cherubic flush to her plump, puppy-fattened cheeks. No teeth in the smile, which probably meant they weren't very good. That class. And blonde.

No one would have called Mrs Frith's frozen yellow waves blonde. She was too old to be a blonde now in any case, dead or alive. Or a brunette, or a redhead, come to that. Should she ever be mercilessly clubbed to death with a blunt instrument by person or persons unknown it would be 'war widow slain,' not even 'Captain's widow' (not if they checked properly). Her murder, her whole life would be described in terms of someone already dead. But if she hadn't said yes to Archibald Frith that sunny August afternoon she'd still only be 'St Albans spinster' or 'Harley Street typist', which would surely be worse.

There would be photographs below the headline, of course. They always had to have a photograph, sometimes more than one, to help people decide whether or not they gave a damn. To see whether your looks – too pretty? too stony-faced? – might help explain or even excuse your sudden, violent end. Mrs Frith gazed crossly across at her sternly polished sideboard, wondering which image the maid would pick to please some smooth-talking reporter. The only one she had ever really liked was fifteen years old now, a hand-coloured head and shoulders taken in a studio in St Albans just after her engagement to Lt. Archibald Frith, only son of nobody of the slightest interest.

Mrs Frith stood on tiptoe, tilted her chin and raised her eyebrows fractionally as she peered up into the heavy gilt overmantel then looked again at the photograph. She ought really to have something more recent on show, murdered or not. The landlady turned her head to throw a shadow across her double chin. They could do anything in their darkrooms, those boys – one had only to look at the Duchess of York, whom she had once seen coming out of a house in Harley Street. The princess's stout, unimpressive figure bore scant resemblance to the fashionable beauty in the society pages. Mrs Frith checked her reflection once more. Not really worth the expense of a cabinet portrait just for her own drawing room. She was hardly about to start sending picture postcards of herself to the surviving Friths and if her own people thought she had money to waste on such things the begging letters would start up again. Best not.

Mrs Frith's neighbour, Mrs St Keith, had had herself 'done' quite recently by a Bond Street man and the result was a delightful portrait of a pretty young matron with a firm jaw line, a peaches and cream complexion and a head of glistening golden curls – hardly a speaking likeness but should she ever be found dead among the cretonnes in that vulgar morning room of hers, strangled with one of those arty scarves she affected, her murder and dismemberment would make a fine showing in the early editions. 'Belgravia widow'? Mrs St Keith did have 'Lower Belgravia' on her writing paper but any lower than St George's Square and you'd be in the river.

The St Keith portrait showed her seated at a fruitwood bureau, toying with an alabaster paper knife, and the clever photographer had managed to rejuvenate her spotty old claws, smoothing away the knotted knuckles with a tiny sable brush and giving her tawdry little topaz the starry twinkle of a sapphire. Mrs Frith looked complacently down at her own soft, white paws and the handsome emerald on her third finger. Not the ring that the late lieutenant had placed there but an altogether larger, smarter stone she had bought for herself after the war when unconsummated engagement rings could be had for a couple of guineas a piece.

St Keith. There was no saint of that name in Mrs Frith's almanac and she suspected that the canonisation had been a snobbish little fiction on the Keith family's part – a fiction of quite recent origin to judge from the contents of Hermione's house, which was Waring and Gillow from scullery to attics. At least Mrs Frith had a few decent pieces. She ran a finger along the marble top of the chiffonier, noting, with something like disappointment, that the surface was entirely free from dust.

Theodora's pathologist person seemed to take a leading role in the charm bracelet business, which was splashed across two entire pages with pictures of the murderer, the prosecuting barrister and the victim: 'a vivacious blonde fond of society' (a description that made 'Pimlico spinster' seem positively desirable). The left-hand page also carried the inevitable two snapshots of Kemble: one skipping jauntily down the courtroom steps, the other in a white coat standing next to a rack of glass tubes, looking as if he were about to break the bad news about your latest Wasserman test results.

The newspaper's proprietor had supplemented the court coverage with a leading article on the pernicious concept of the 'harmless lunatic' and pressing the case for the sterilisation of the unfit. The article alleged that the convicted man had fathered three illegitimate children while still supposedly in the care of an institution for the feeble-minded, and these very children were themselves confined in various London asylums thus creating a further drain on national efficiency. Wouldn't harm a fly, kept himself to himself, good as gold, right as ninepence and very clean in his habits? Hardly.

Mrs Frith refolded the newspaper and placed it resolutely in the waste basket. The *News of the World* was one of life's despondent voices, she felt. Mrs Frith's beloved penny shelf had yielded a pamphlet on The Power of New Thought. 'Never,' insisted the writer, 'stay closely and continuously in the atmosphere of a despondent voice. If you find anyone determined to talk failure and sickness and misfortune and disaster: walk away. Their despondent voice is a slow poison, their complaints are slow poisons which will paralyse your courage and kill your ambition. Shun the despondent voice. Rise up and realise your strength. Inhale deeply and imagine that you breathe in love, health, wisdom, usefulness, success, opulence or any other qualities you might like to possess.'

Sound enough advice, but what if the despondent voice were your own?

Chapter 12

PGs were not encouraged to receive visitors but Mrs Frith made an exception for Theodora, she said, for her father's sake. Dora's first visitor was to be Lettice Roberts, an old school chum who had written that she would be between trains on Sunday afternoon and might she call in to see her at Warwick Square before catching the express to Canterbury? Unfortunately, she sent this cheery news on a penny postcard. This meant that Mrs Frith was able to mobilise her forces before Dora could carry out her original plan of simply meeting her friend at the street door in her hat and coat and whisking her off for a proper tea at an hotel somewhere.

Lettice. Which was Lettice? Who were her people? During the Harley-Street-to-Paddington years Mrs Frith had maintained an unhealthily close, *in-loco-parentis* interest in Dora's friends, firmly convinced that it was her duty to ensure that the child associated with the Right Sort. Her encyclopaedic grasp of unimportant detail – aunts or uncles in Debrett, houses in town, favoured hockey position – had led Dora to conflate her whole acquaintance to two composite (and entirely imaginary) schoolgirls with curly dark hair, a strong forehand and a secret passion for Douglas Fairbanks.

'Lettice Roberts.'

'Lettice Roberts? Saw *The Thief of Baghdad* six times? Senior tennis captain?' What a crashing bore the girl sounded.

'No, Mrs Frith. You've got the wrong girl.'

'What does her father do?'

'Doctor. In Canterbury – St Alphage Lane.' Why had she said that? Why had she bothered with the address? More information to be slotted away and cross-referenced in that voracious, smoked-oak card index of a brain.

'Large family?'

'Just her brother.'

'Older? Younger?' The woman was relentless, determined to worry the subject to death like a cat with a particularly intractable piece of fancy knitting.

'Older.'

'Medic?'

Dora wished she could say that no, he was a sanitary inspector or a tailor or a trombonist or a piano tuner or night watchman for a lock hospital in Limehouse but Mrs Frith was right, confound her. Medicine did seem to run in families. The landlady smiled with satisfaction when her guess proved correct.

'And the practice will fall to him, of course.' Everyone in Frithland glided toward the grave on smoothly oiled tracks of precedence and convenience and the fatuous fatalism of it irritated Dora into betraying yet more information.

'Not at all. Lettice writes that he hopes to specialise.'

Mrs Frith pulled a face. The don't-tell-me-I'm-a-student-of-human-nature face.

'With a nice, fat Canterbury practice all ready and waiting? I'd be *very* surprised.'

'Quentin is very determined.'

'Lettice and *Quentin*?' A twitch of Frith lips. 'And this Lettice is one of your bluestocking friends, I take it?' Mrs Frith contrived to infuse 'bluestocking' with the pitying tone she would have used for 'crippled' or 'Welsh'.

'She's training to be a schoolmistress,' admitted Dora, grudgingly.

As she helped her off with her coat Dora managed to warn Lettice to expect the third degree from the landlady, certain that Mrs Frith would join them at the tea table.

'My lips are sealed,' hissed Lettice gamely.

Mrs Frith's drawing room was an elegantly proportioned chamber with a rather fine marble chimneypiece but its beautiful bones were obscured by the landlady's apparent determination to amass the ugliest collection of furniture in captivity. Mrs Frith had it on the highest authority (i.e. yet another Victoria Street book bargain) that a room's fitments should never exceed more than one-fifth of its overall volume. Unfortunately, while Mrs Frith had never had the slightest difficulty with anything to do with pounds, shillings and pence, her arithmetic was less reliable when it came to the cubic footage taken up by a half-pantechnicon of furniture. The spatial mathematics of the calculation had utterly defeated her. Did the ceiling height go beyond the picture rails? Did one include alcoves?

As a result, the room was filled with a convivial gathering of machine-veneered eponyms: two Chesterfields, a Recamier, a Davenport, an Ottoman, a Sutherland table, a Wellington chest and a Tantalus all jostled aggressively for space at supposedly voguish angles. The sense of claustrophobia this induced was intensified by Mrs Frith's fondness for fabrics with bird and flower designs so large that not a single specimen could be seen in its entirety. The chair backs and cushions were a riot of headless, wingless doves and broken blossoms.

Mrs Frith's homemaking bible (not actually called 'Beautiful Rooms and How to Disguise Them', but it ought to have been) also insisted that pairs of pictures were 'shoppy'. This was unfortunate as Mrs Frith's late mother-in-law had acquired all her prints in sets of two. Mrs Frith had tried to mitigate this by divorcing them from each other so that the Bridge of Sighs was beside the window and the Rialto skulked behind the door, but this simply invited guests to play a kind of pictorial pellmanism as they wondered whether Rosetti's *Ophelia* was matched in some godforsaken attic by David's *Death of Marat*.

Lettice had very little natural interest in Douglas Fairbanks. Tall, loose-limbed and trimly sheathed in grey flannel, she was assistant chemistry mistress at a newly founded girls' boarding school in Buckinghamshire: West Amersham Ladies College (motto: Follow the Gleam). The building and grounds were, if anything, a good half mile east of Amersham but 'West' had more tone (or so the founder had felt). Nearer to Cheltenham, at any rate.

Mrs Frith wasted no time and immediately began probing Lettice on the subject of family doctoring in general and doctoring families in particular. Quentin, confirmed Lettice, had no wish to compost quietly down in a ready-made practice in Canterbury. His interests lay very largely in the field of surgery.

'A *sur*-geon?' As if it were not a seemly profession to aspire to over tea, as if anyone with an ounce of breeding would have said 'solicitor' or 'librarian' or 'feather curler' out of sheer common politeness. Mrs Frith's recent run-in with New Thought had given her a precious insight into the evils of the operating theatre. Surgery, in her newly opened eyes, was an unwarranted experiment on the part of a cabal of medics determined to put their godless hands where man had no business going.

Tea was hardly worth the name: two spoons in the pot (what the grocer dubbed 'domestic blend') and kitchen butter on paper-thin bread supplemented by four very small, very dry sponge cakes. Mrs Frith had made these with her own fair hand, fearing (rightly) that the cook would not take kindly to a recipe which could just about furnish a cake plate while using only half an egg.

There had already been a dangerous difference of opinion that morning about the need for milk (rather than milk-and-water) in a batter pudding, and Mrs Frith had no desire to provoke a further confrontation. Even bad cooks were very thin on the ground. Theodora's guest didn't even eat her cake in the end. Mrs Frith made a remark about Sunday timetables and Lettice (rather enterprisingly) looked at her wristwatch in alarm and sprang from her chair.

'Thank goodness you reminded me, Mrs Frith. It's nearly four now! I must dash or I shall lose my train. Are you sure you want to brave the walk to the station, Dora? It's jolly cold.'

Mrs Frith looked reproachfully at the four cakes but her resentment went unnoticed in the flurry of hats, coats and umbrellas and, after a few hasty politenesses, both girls had melted from the room.

They bumped into Miss Digby by the door. She was reading a copy of the previous evening's paper that had been left on the hall table.

'Blonde spinster found drowned' said the Stop Press.

This was more than enough to arouse the suffragette in Lettice. 'Blonde spinster,' she hissed. 'One doesn't get blond bachelors, does one?'

'No,' agreed Miss Digby, almost regretfully. 'No. One doesn't.'

Lettice took Dora's gloved hand and tucked it under her arm as they walked to the station.

'We could have some *tea*.' She made the suggestion as if Mrs Frith's miserable spread had simply never taken place. 'Poor you. Was there ever a Mr Frith?'

'Captain Frith. Killed in action, apparently. Or missing presumed killed at any rate. Although there's no picture in the parlour, which is odd. Mr Stone thinks he might be a polite fiction . . .'

Lettice was very taken by the idea of a polite fiction. *East Lynne*, perhaps, and then began to speculate about the impolite sort, concluding at last that modern fiction was essentially impolite if it was to be worth reading. All very witty but you could almost hear the wax cylinder going round in her brain as she warmed to her theme, recording her *bons mots* for use in the staff common room after the Easter hols.

'Ridiculous woman.'

'I've known her half my life.'

'Poor you,' repeated Lettice, squeezing her arm. 'The *look* on her face when I mentioned surgery. As if someone had broken wind.'

Within twenty minutes the pair were tucked cosily around a table at a nearby hotel ordering one and sixpenny teas. Sunday supper *chez* Frith was to be the best fish pie the embattled cook could concoct with three small fillets of coley, and an apple pudding made with watery batter, and Dora was glad to stoke up with crumpets and meat paste sandwiches and iced fancy cakes.

'What are the other PGs like?'

'The Stone chap's really quite amusing. Teases the Frith rather but that's all to the good. Otherwise it's jolly hard to know. La Frith tends to regard any conversational gambit the way anyone else would view a live coal on the hearth rug and pours cold water on it before it can do any lasting damage, so apart from a spot of precision salt-passing we've had few chances to bond. We aren't allowed health or politics and she gets decidedly shirty if anyone mentions the food (and the less said about it the better, quite honestly).'

Oh dear. Dora had completely forgotten that Lettice had an entire bonnetful of bees and that domestic science was one of her absolute favourites. All home cooking, she reminded Dora, was an utter waste of time. The remedy for the country's appalling level of nutrition was not to teach every woman to cook but to forbid the vast majority of women from ever setting foot in the kitchen. Why should every woman learn cookery any more than every man should learn tailoring? In a terrace of twenty houses one found twenty kitchens. Fraught little frights fretting over their burnt offerings, and the next day it began all over again. A waste of food. A criminal waste of female energy. Far better to leave these things to experts: communal canteens, wholemeal sandwiches, nourishing salads.

But even Lettice couldn't talk nutrition indefinitely.

'So. How is the infamous Dr Whatsit? Is he as dashing as his photographs?' It was a bit like being pumped by Mrs Frith. Dora was suddenly evasive.

'I don't really know.'

'Was he ever a *doctor* doctor, do you suppose?'

'Dunno. He definitely did some regular doctoring in the war . . . You could look him up.'

'And is filing as deadly as it sounds? Not exactly one of the Careers for Enterprising Young Ladies the old school had in mind. Did you let old Nosey Parker know what you were up to? There was certainly no mention of you in the old girls' newsletter. Ursula Fox got two paragraphs. She's at the Stepney School for Mothers, heaven help them, training to be a health visitor for the Health and Cleanliness Council. I had a letter. Foxy tried showing one of their hygiene lecture films at the local picture palace. She and the other Cleanliness bods had to pass round leaflets warning about Dirty Bertie and Clean Eugene and remind everyone to turn their socks inside out overnight and wash hands before meals. *Very* popular in the sixpenny seats but only because the leaflets could be compacted into paper pellets and flicked at the screen. Mary Bingham – remember her? Always in goal – is now private governess to a diplomat in Bombay, and *all three* Horne sisters are apparently enjoying the challenges of married life – what were the odds? I doubt Theodora Strang's adventures as a lowly clerical drudge would merit a mention.' Was Lettice gloating? Sounded jolly like it.

'I didn't write.'

'Miss Parker won't acknowledge it if you do. She didn't cram you for Oxford only to see you reduced to putting the dead of greater London into alphabetical order.' She jolly well was gloating. 'A is for Asphyxiation, B is for Blunt Instrument, C is for Cholera, D is for Dismemberment … "*In-des-CRI-bably vul-gar*" ' – words that their headmistress applied to anything from Angela Brazil to ear piercing.

'Our high mistress at Amersham has a grand piano in her study covered with a velvet cloth and dozens of photographs of any old girls who make the cut: coming out portraits, graduation pictures. The limited space means that competition among the alumnae is quite fierce, but a really smart marriage seems to cancel out a mere bachelor of arts just the same. Preposterous female.'

'Hellish. How are you finding it otherwise?'

'Mmm. "Lettice Roberts is *relishing* her new life as assistant chemistry mistress of a Buckinghamshire girls school," according to the Cirencester newsletter. No, she jolly well isn't. I was told off for being hatless in the high street the other morning. You'd think the staff might be exempt at least; it's a miracle I wasn't punished. Girls caught in town without their hats are made to wear them indoors all day for a week. Or used to be until Gertrude Trubshaw of the lower fourth started a craze for it. Jolly hard keeping a straight face with the whole of your stinks class wearing panamas with their white coats, I can tell you. Nothing changes. Talking of "polite fiction" they still ban "unsuitable" books: Warwick Deeping is the latest anathema. A girl was caught with *Sorrel and Son* and the under mistress actually burned it in the refectory fire – made rather a merry blaze. And there's a fantastically complicated list of things that can and can't be worn from the third Sunday after Septuagesima, which I must say I have yet to master.'

Dora wasn't listening. She was thinking of the stupid little newsletter, wondering what she would have wanted them to print. 'Theodora Strang has graduated with a first in medicine from Somerville' or 'Theodora Kemble (née Strang) writes to say that she is relishing the challenges of married life . . .' She pulled herself clear of her reverie with a guilty start.

'Papa was so mortified by the filing business he just tells people I'm working at the university.'

'Should have come to Amersham with me. We could have roomed together.' Another keen squeeze of the arm. 'Even your pa wouldn't have minded teaching.'

'Yes, he would. The female teaching profession robs the national gene pool of valuable material, I'll have you know. Healthy, intelligent, well-motivated females should be mothers of six, not schoolmistresses.' Dora's voice had tightened into a button-backed Oxford drawl. 'If the daughters of the middle class don't keep the numbers up then we'll be outbred by the under man, apparently. Somerville and Girton are mere accessories in a long-term programme of racial suicide did they but know it.'

'Even supposing one wanted to be mother of six – and speaking as deputy house mother of twenty-eight I have to say that the prospect is uniquely unalluring – where does Dr Strang propose to find the fathers of six? Fairly thin on the ground, I should have thought.'

'Lord knows. Polygamy probably. I wouldn't put it past him. Anyhow, I should hate teaching: not the teaching part so much but the whole staff common room business. Sounds like school all over again. And the pathology lark isn't so bad – much more than just boring old filing. When I got there on Monday the secretary had left under something of a cloud – I did ask why but no one would utter – so they've let me try my hand at typing and once they found I could spell "haemorrhage" the Kemble personage agreed to take me on as a sort of assistant.'

The one and sixpenny teas were now a few buttery dishes and cake crumbs but Lettice boldly ordered more hot water and managed to stretch the pot to another two cups.

'So. Have you got a good murder yet?'

'I'll say. Heaps. Don't you read the newspapers?'

'We have the *Morning Post* in the common room but nothing yellow. Filthy muck.'

'Nothing near as filthy as the real thing. They can't print most of it but it's amazing what they do get away with. Mrs F was sent *The News of the World* this morning by mistake. All in code, of course: "fond of society, intimacy, items of a personal nature, private parts" – all that. Ghastly.'

'Ghastly,' echoed Lettice.

Dora looked towards Lettice but focused beyond her: seeing the picture painted by Kemble's eight index cards; hearing the soft voice in her ear telling tales of violent early death.

'If anyone were to write a little impolite fiction on the same subject it would be stopped at Calais and yet there it is on a million breakfast tables. You can't imagine what it's like typing it all up.'

Lettice took her arm again and pressed her gloved hand. She didn't let go.

'Chin up. Beats feather-curling.'

Chapter 13

Monday morning was spent at Holborn mortuary. Either the building was subsiding or there was something wrong with the design of the slab, because a good half of the fluids drained on to the floor as the pathologist worked and gathered in a noxious puddle to the side of Dora's typewriting table. Dora raised her feet and placed them on the crossrails of the rickety bentwood chair, not daring to interrupt. It was only when the mortuary assistant was swabbing, stuffing and stitching the corpse (which had been found with its head in the kitchen stove and which might reasonably have expected a simple verdict of suicide) that Dr Kemble noticed the foetid little moat that had formed around her.

'I can't put my feet down.'

'Stand on your chair and I'll come and get you.'

Easier said than done. She hitched up her skirt and carefully climbed up while the pathologist, having removed gloves, apron and overalls, paddled into the mess with his white rubber galoshes, grimacing cheerfully.

'Put your arms around my neck.'

Later that night, the mortuary assistant had already wheeled away the corpse and washed down the slab. Later that night, the pathologist laid Dora down on the chilly white porcelain and cut away her clothes with his icy rib scissors, cataloguing each mark on her body as he painstakingly inflicted it.

The following day dawned so crisp and bright that Dora walked all the way to Whitehall before hailing an omnibus, her head filled with her dark, delicious dream. She was eager to see Kemble again while the memory was still hot and fresh but the office was deserted with nothing but a note from Hubbard smugly explaining that he (not Mrs Strange) would be accompanying the chief as he went about his business at Hackney and Islington mortuaries, so there.

When they returned an hour later Hubbard immediately sat down at his desk and slowly began translating his Pitman jottings into longhand so that Dora could have the privilege of typing them all up in triplicate on the pre-printed post-mortem forms. Dora had tried pointing out that it was far quicker for her to just type up the lot *in situ* with her portable machine but Hubbard clearly preferred the old, haphazard system.

Dora banged away at her typewriter all morning, doggedly filing and cross-referencing index cards while she waited for each fresh sheet from the scribbling Hubbard. She was getting through cards at a terrific rate but would only take a dozen or so at a time from a packet, thereby necessitating frequent trips to the store cupboard. Frequent opportunities of imagining Kemble sneaking in from the other side. It was rather a shock when she finally did bump into him. He put a hand on her shoulder.

'Well? How are you getting on, Mrs Strange?' His voice was wrongly soft – as if he didn't want it to be heard in the office outside. The hand slid down her back to her waist and she could feel the bony warmth of his fingers through the fabric of her blouse. Except that it wasn't her blouse. Mrs Frith was in dispute with the steam laundry company and the only thing not hopelessly soiled had been the victim's pink artificial silk. Dora assumed that the pathologist had come into the cupboard for a fresh supply of green ink, but that wasn't all he wanted.

The telephone was blaring away in the office but although Kemble's hand released her, he still didn't move out of the way and she had to press tight against him to get to the door. It was the telephone on her own desk that was ringing and she felt that Hubbard was looking at her suspiciously as she dashed across the room to answer it. Her hand shook and she had to fight to keep the kisses out of her voice as she transferred the call to the lab.

After a few minutes the pathologist surfaced from behind the scratched green door.

'I'm afraid I told both coroners that their men could collect today's PM reports from the porter first thing tomorrow, Mrs Strange. Do you have any engagements this evening?'

'They serve dinner at eight at my lodgings.'

He smiled. He remembered landladies. 'And what does dinner consist of in lodging houses these days?'

'I've only been there a week but the list in the hall says that Tuesday will be toad and tapioca.'

'Is it Welsh warebit and waffles on Wednesdays?'

He lowered his chin and looked very straight-faced over the top of his steel-rimmed reading glasses.

'Well, Mrs Strange, I have a great many slides to prepare but we should both be finished by seven and I think the kitty might run to something a mite more digestible than toads. There's a place nearby that does a fairly edible mixed grill.'

Dora could feel the excitement tingling through her chest as she pictured herself smiling shyly at him over the rim of her wine glass, other diners turning to look as he held forth wittily on slow poisoning or sudden death.

He was heading back to the lab as he made his thrilling invitation and turned his head as he reached the doorway. 'Oh and telephone to my wife, would you? Kensington 2829. Make my apologies and say that I shan't be home for dinner.'

Chapter 14

Hubbard's tadpole eyes were monitoring Dora from the far corner of the room. She struggled to appear composed as her fumbling fingers took a sheet of white paper from the drawer and threaded it blindly into the machine. She began typing as fast as she possibly could. 'I must try not to be so feeble I must try not to be so feeble I must try not to be so feeble', filling the page with the stupid sentence, restarting it over and over so that the staggered words and spaces crystallised into a typographic wallpaper.

Her right hand removed the telephone receiver from its cradle while her left carefully unwound the typing from the machine and fed in another sheet. Only then did she make the call.

The wife, this blasted wife that no one had ever seen fit to mention, that no reporter ever alluded to, answered the telephone herself. She had a breathy, actressy sort of voice for telephone purposes undercut somewhat by the sound of two children enthusiastically skinning each other alive in the background.

'Hello? Mrs Kemble? This is Mrs Strange at Dr Kemble's office.' The words sounded guarded and unnatural, as if a masked man in a jewelled turban were holding a knife to her throat. 'Dr Kemble asked me to telephone to say that he has been detained in the laboratory and will not be home for dinner this evening.'

There must have been wives in the world who would have greeted such news by dancing a buck and wing in the breakfast room before spending a happy evening tucked up with a barrel of biscuits, a thermos of cocoa and the latest Warwick Deeping, but Constance Kemble was clearly not one of them. The breathy tone was now firmly back in its box and a well-bred whine took its place.

'But he promised he'd be home in time to hear little Alfred's new piece and the Phippses are dining with us . . .' No they jolly well weren't. She was fibbing. You could tell.

'I am frightfully sorry, Mrs Kemble. The doctor is back in the laboratory now but I will pass on your message.'

Mrs Frith was equally annoyed at having her scrupulously portioned dinner disrupted.

'But it's lamb cutlets,' she lied, 'and chocolate pudding.' Why not *fillets mignon* and *fraises de bois* while she was at it? 'Will they be paying you for the extra hours?' she added, in a sudden show of secretarial solidarity. 'Don't let yourself be taken advantage of.'

Dora's fingers carried on working the keys while her head was filled with a mental recording of the whining woman on the telephone and the hearty screams of sundry little Kembles in the background. How many little Kembles? Two? Three? It could have been a dozen from the noise level. So much for Aunt Jacaranda's insistence that married men were easy to spot. Kemble displayed none of the usual symptoms. No hand-coloured studio shots of peach-complexioned wives and chubby cherubic children on his desk. No bachelor holes in his socks but the brightly buttonholed Dr Kemble was also far too well turned-out for a husband according to her aunt's personal scale (immaculate, superior, normal, dull, *dire*). And, more crucially, married men with children didn't, wouldn't, shouldn't kiss defenceless girls in cupboards. *Happily* married men didn't, anyway . . .

Dora clutched guiltily at this consoling fantasy as she adjusted the post-mortem form into the spool and continued the business of decoding Hubbard's notes. She was finished by a quarter to seven. Plenty of time for the omnibus to get her home to Warwick Square and the waiting toad. Plenty of time for Dr Kemble to motor back to Kensington and dine with Mrs Kemble and her phantom Phippses. Time for goodnight kisses in the nursery. She tried to picture the children: skinny, green-eyed inquisitive little boys with sideways smiles, picking their scabs with tweezers and bringing home dead birds to dissect in the scullery sink.

The mixed grill place was more an inn than a restaurant with an upstairs dining room furnished with red plush where clubless men washed down large steaks with old burgundy. Dora and Kemble were shown to a corner booth and two pink gins and a bottle of claret appeared the instant they sat down. The pathologist didn't even glance at the menu.

'A couple of mixed grills please, Frank, not too well done but not rare either – I plan to eat it, not dissect it – and a few of your nice roasted tomatoes.'

He placed a gasper between his lips, cupping his hands around the flame to shield it from invisible winds and hide its light from watchful enemy eyes.

'People usually ask me how I became a pathologist. "How did you become a pathologist, Dr Kemble".' He swallowed half the contents of his gin glass and stared hard at her face.

'How did you become a pathologist, Dr Kemble?' She repeated the question in the same carefully toneless tone she had used on the telephone, almost relieved to have her lines fed to her.

'I'm glad you asked me that. It's been weeks, days, *hours* since anyone asked. It certainly wasn't the career my family would have chosen. My mother had three boys: me and the Berties. Bertram and Cuthbert. Twins.' He flashed a quick, weary smile at the waiting barman, who read this as a signal for another pink gin.

'Mother wasn't too keen when I went in for medicine. I think she thought it vulgar. Which it is, of course.'

'I qualified in '13 and the very next day I received a letter from a Savile Row tailor – my father's old tailor, as a matter of fact – inviting me to be fitted for a morning coat and striped trousers. The next post brought a note from Locks saying that my silk hat was awaiting collection (which it may still be, for all I know to the contrary). Mother had it all mapped out: Royce motor (they have clearance for the topper, don't you know), house in Manchester Square and a knighthood by fifty. But regular doctoring has never interested me. I was cutting up dead bodies for a living before I'd even properly qualified. Sir Arthur roped me in as his assistant demonstrator and I went in for pathology as soon as my preliminary studies were over. Dear mama could just about have borne Harley Street but she never appreciated the importance of my work: that dead men tell tales even when there's no crime involved (which there isn't the vast majority of the time).' He sounded disappointed.

'I think Mama originally had some woolly, old world plan that the Berties and I would all three share out the great professions: law, army, church. Doctoring simply wasn't on the list. In the event, of course, we all went into the army. The whole bloody world went into the army.'

'The Berties could hardly wait. We were all lunching with mother one stupid, stupid afternoon when the solicitor's wife mentioned that Miss Vesta Tilley was to be making an appearance at the local theatre and were they all going? I certainly wasn't. Made my excuses after lunch. Fast train back to Paddington and hot foot to Holborn mortuary. Chronic lead poisoning. It was two days before I received a cheery, sneery little postcard from the Berties. To hell with the 'varsity. Hadn't even waited for a commission.

'Four furious pages from mama by the same post. Her last hope was that her big, strong, beautiful sons would fall at the next hurdle when they turned up at the recruiting office for their physical exam to get the whole thing signed and sealed. A good half of the patriots who joined Miss Tilley on stage never saw action: rickets, short sight, bad teeth, exactly like that pathetic specimen we had in the septic theatre last week. Fat chance of him being passed fit. But not the Berties: Bertie and Bertie were fit as blasted fleas: A1 tip-top cannon fodder. As if *fitness* were ever going to come into it. The boat could drop them at Boulogne. A day on a train to Béthune and a two-hour limp to the front. They'd die as neatly. *Tests.*' He spat the word. 'All so that they could be blown to bits defending godforgotten corners of foreign fields that had bugger all to do with them. Dead at nineteen, same age as that charm bracelet tick.' He stared furiously into his gin. 'On my first leave I could hardly bear to look at any man under seventy not in uniform. Flat feet? What difference would that have made when they were crawling through the ooze of Flanders? But all of the asthmatics and rheumatics, all the slack-winded and feeble-minded, were spared. Spared, what's more, to carry on the race while those who passed the all-important "test" died like cattle as the poet has it . . . Exactly the same at the dressing station. Hours of precious doctoring wasted ministering to hopeless amputees. French triage worked on an entirely different principle, of course . . .'

The whole narrative had the suspicious fluency of a twice-told tale and Dora found it surprisingly hard to feel sympathetic. How had Mrs Culvey reacted?

'I remember feeling a complete fraud as I headed off to France – what possible earthly use was a morbid anatomist going to be in the trenches? – but then I discovered that I would be teamed up with one of Wimpole Street's finest gynaecologists. Cocaine addict but a pleasant enough sort. *Not,*' another gulp of gin, 'that France was entirely without interest from the morbid anatomy side. *Extraordinary* wounds.

A blow from an entrenching tool could cut a man clean in half, like something from a Leonardo codex or those models of ocean liners they have at the booking offices. A post-mortem is positively surreptitious in comparison: neat little taxidermist's holes sewn up tidily afterwards. The wounds made a nonsense of all the medicine I'd ever learned.'

'The war reconciled mother to medicine for a while. I think she imagined that I would be travelling to Flanders as some kind of medical retainer to the other two, as if the whole filthy business were a heavily armed grand tour, and that I would somehow be keeping the pair of them *safe*. But of course I couldn't bloody well keep them safe.' Something happened to his voice at this point, like a change of key.

'Ran across brother Bertram entirely by chance one muddy afternoon. Said his batman was keeping a stock of undated letters to be posted home at intervals in the not-very-unlikely event he was hit or went missing. Save the old girl from fretting, he felt. As it turned out, the CO's letter arrived first and his own cheery fictions thanking mater for unreceived parcels carried on for several weeks to come. "Died of his wounds," the CO wrote.' The green eyes jabbed resentfully at Dora. 'Doesn't sound so very bad, does it? "Wounds"? You think of a gunshot or two, a stabbing, a garden fork carelessly jabbed through the foot: tidy, manageable, treatable horrors, not a torso turned out like a schoolboy's suitcase.'

Dora looked back at her chops and kidneys.

'And then Cuthbert. Cuthbert wasn't kept safe either. Cuthbert was shot crossing into no-man's land, four stretcher bearers were killed trying to fetch him back, so in the end they left him there and by dawn there was nothing left to stretcher off, he'd been hit so many times. Not what the telegram said, of course.' He checked her face for a reaction in a way that made her wonder if the story was even true.

'And so with both of them gone it fell to me to keep myself safe and set about making some more Berties. PDQ. I still have the letter she wrote. You'd think a war would put people off marriage but the whole of Europe was ringing with the Wedding March in a great, mad dash to the altar as if the race knew that it had to perpetuate itself. In Paris they were hitched in batches of twenty – posthumously in some cases. Making honest widows of the mistresses. Safeguarding the pension.' He gave Dora an almost guilty glance as if waiting for her reproaches. 'I managed to hold out until '21. Young Alfred was born the same year. We must hurry up and have another, and another, said mama. Too much of a hurry, as it turned out.' Again he looked at Dora as if she had missed her cue. 'She died. Then four years later I met Constance.'

Two wives.

'This will sound silly to you but it's a great relief to discuss it at all. I can never talk about these things to Constance. We were actually on the train on the way to the honeymoon when she suggested that I might consider "branching out" from pathology. Ten solid days of hints and pleas and sulks.' Those bottle-green eyes, boyish suddenly, nailed her with a look as if begging her to understand 'She said', the lips flickered into a smile, 'she said it wasn't res*pec*table.' He really was a very talented mimic and struck exactly the querulous, meticulously elocuted tones that Dora had heard on the telephone that afternoon. She smiled in spite of herself.

'You've gone very *very* quiet, Mrs Strange.' He waggled his head very, very reproachfully and ever so slightly tipsily from side to side.

Dora sipped primly at her drink. 'I don't know what to do next.'

'Next?'

She looked over his shoulder as she spoke. The room was almost empty of diners and the waiter had stationed himself at the far end out of earshot and was screwing the silver tops off all the salt pots and filling them with a little spoon, carefully posting a few grains of rice into each.

'I don't know where to send my letter of resignation. Do I write to the bursar? Or the bureau? Or does Hubbard have to do it?'

'Resignation? Don't be silly.'

'Nothing silly about it. I only agreed to come with you this evening to say that I really must give notice. You simply can't,' she imagined herself firing a housemaid. Very grown-up. Absolutely no nonsense, '*behave* like that.'

'Mmm. If that's the case why didn't you resign yesterday when I carried you in my arms or last Tuesday when you gave us your,' another soft growl, '*assistance* in the laboratory?'

The caress in his voice and the second glass of claret were making her head swim.

'You can't resign. Please don't resign. The department needs you. I need you. Damn it, even Hubbard probably needs you.'

His charm was drying up her resolve like sunshine on a wet lawn.

'Mrs Kemble,' she couldn't bring herself to say 'wife', 'Mrs Kemble said that you were having Phippses for dinner.' Even as she said it she could feel the laughter dangerously rising, feel the warmth ebbing seductively back across the space between them. He seemed to sense it and leaned back in his chair, laughing softly.

'*Phipp-ses* for dinner. Probably beats toad and tapioca. Fillet of Phipps. Only not, of course. The Phippses are fictional – or at least they are this evening. I'd have known. Phippses for dinner means *major* domestic upheaval: a whole week debating the relative merits of potted shrimps and *foie gras*; a complete audit of linen and crystal; a written warning to the cook; the whole bedroom decked with prospective gowns; enough flowers for a small funeral; children crated up in cold storage for the duration and *what* a pity we couldn't have beef or venison as you carve *so* beautifully, darling. I *do* carve beautifully.' He stroked a dissecting fingernail down the back of Dora's hand, leaving a fleeting white trace across the skin. '*So* beautifully but my skill has unfortunate associations. *Such* bad taste.' Another contemptuous echo of that mansion block miaow.

'You took me completely by surprise the other day. We get through an astonishing number of clerical bods in the department. Prim little typewriters who want to work in a hospital but who can't spell diphtheria and who faint at the sight of a kidney dish, let alone a kidney.'

Dora's own kidney was curled up between her cabbage and potatoes. She swallowed hard.

He suddenly seemed to become aware of the meat on his own plate and attacked it ravenously: a morsel of sirloin: an inky little mushroom, a diagnostic slice of kidney (*one clean sweep of the belly of the knife; draw, never press the blade*).

'You aren't eating, Mrs Strange.'

There was blood oozing from the steak on her plate.

'I'm not very hungry.'

'Nonsense. Eat up.' His voice had taken on a faintly fatherly tone. 'Don't think about it. Just eat it. Never think about meat. That way madness lies: and vegetarianism.'

'My father says that vegetarianism is the unspeakable in pursuit of the uneatable.' She smiled faintly at the memory. 'A neighbour of his in Sussex once brought their spinster sister to dine one evening. Papa was given advance warning of the poor lady's vegetarian views but proceeded to order a meal composed entirely of whole animals: oysters, freshwater trout, grouse – there was even mincemeat in the pudding – and gave instructions that every dish was to be offered to her. Her whole supper consisted of garnish: three triangles of wholewheat toast, a wedge of lemon, two leaves of lettuce, game chips and *crème anglaise*. Papa showed absolutely no mercy. He says it's just a dietary fad and that if the good Lord had meant us to subsist on nuts we'd each have a fluffy red tail.'

'For once I have to agree with him.'

'For once?'

'Yes.' A faint twinge of discomfort as he pushed away his plate and lit a gasper. 'We crossed swords a few years ago. Served on the same committee. Remind me, did the good Dr Strang have a specialty?'

She hesitated. 'Father never talked to me about his work.' A mite Jesuitical but perfectly true (he didn't ever actually *talk* about it). 'Particularly once he learned of my interest in medicine. He didn't approve. It was just general doctoring, I think.'

'No pet ailments?'

Dora thought of the anxious-looking men in her father's Harley Street waiting room, the therapeutic material to be found in the lower reaches of his bookshelves. Specialised, certainly, but hardly the sort of thing one put on a brass plate. Did Kemble know about it?

He mashed his cigarette stub against the side of the ashtray and looked down at his unnaturally bleached white fingernails, at his long, handsome hands. Hands that had spent the morning excavating the gangrenous uterus of a sixteen-year-old girl from Bethnal Green. (*Cervical scarring suggests previous pregnancies not carried to term.*) He drained his glass and changed the subject with the same deft carelessness he'd shown when he tossed the scalpel to his left hand.

'She doesn't want ... my wife doesn't want to *be married*,' he gave an unnatural weight to the words, 'to a pathologist.'

He stroked Dora's hand again with the back of those clever fingers before she could pull her arm away. His touch was very, very gentle this time, almost a tickle. Like the man on the train.

'I'm being a cad.' His voice grew deeper and softer as he spoke until it was practically a purr. 'One shouldn't tell the truth about such things just as one shouldn't kiss lovely young girls in cupboards.' He sat back, savouring the tint of the blush he had made and Dora felt the memory of the two kisses well up inside her like sick.

'Let's go, shall we? I'll put you in a taxi.'

He left ten shillings without waiting for the bill and she followed him down the dark panelled stairway into the cobbled entry that joined the inn to the street. He turned to look at her under the light of a lamp.

'I recognise that.' He peered down at Mavis Shirley's blouse. 'If I were to reach out right now, put my hand inside the collar and *pull*.' The fingers clenched into a fist. 'I can predict exactly how the fibres would shear, exactly which buttonholes would yield.' Dora's hand moved protectively to her throat. 'And then I should have another glimpse of that neat little row of – six, was it? – blue forget-me-nots. Probably just as well we had Hubbard with us.'

Or what? Dora fished in her coat pocket for her gloves, trying in vain to douse the image of her body lying on the floor of the lab: bitten, bruised, hitherto *intacta*.

A cab passed and he hailed it, but later that night, between chilly Warwick Square sheets, the taxi was slower to appear. Alfred Kemble's arm was around her, pulling her towards him, his voice an urgent whisper, the words puffing softly against the skin of her neck. She couldn't leave, she mustn't leave, he *needed* her. The only good thing to happen in ten years.

Chapter 15

'A *man*,' Mrs Frith was always fanatical about the distinction between *man* and *gentleman*, 'a man by the name of Hubbard has telephoned to say that your Dr Kemble has been called to Brighton on a case and that you are to meet them at Victoria Station at half-past eight and that he will bring the typewriting machine. You will just have time to change.' Mrs Frith looked pointedly at Dora's everyday blouse and skirt. 'And the other hat, I think.'

Hubbard was waiting reproachfully by the Brighton platform clutching a wallet of post-mortem forms and the portable typewriter, which hung heavily from the end of his arm as he was convinced it would be stolen the moment it left his grasp.

'Has Dr Kemble not arrived?' Dora glanced from Hubbard to the destination board. 'There's a train in five minutes.'

This struck some sort of nerve. Hubbard appeared to know the *ABC* by heart. Five minutes? A snort. Only if by 'train' she meant a third-rate suburban service that stopped at every station and enjoyed an eight-minute halt at East Croydon. The 9.05 did the journey in seventy-six minutes flat. Restaurant car and everything.

'And if we missed that one?'

Hubbard didn't hear the tease in her voice and gave chapter and verse on the 9.20 and the slow one after that (108 minutes and no dining car).

The pathologist arrived with his bag just as Hubbard delivered this riveting bulletin.

'You missed your vocation, Hubbard. Nice little job on the railways would just suit you.'

Hubbard, not wanted on voyage, retired hurt to the lab and the pathologist recklessly entrusted Dora's machine to a passing porter, who led them to an empty compartment in a Pullman carriage.

'A wise woman once taught me,' confided Kemble as he deposited their coats on the rack, 'a sure-fire method for ensuring a compartment to oneself.'

A furred and feathered matron sailed along the corridor as he spoke (Mrs Frith's instincts had been entirely correct, hatwise) and peered at the empty seats around them. The pathologist immediately moved his hat one seat along, patted the plush beside him and beckoned to the woman with an ingratiating grin.

'Never fails. Although there is another fairly reliable technique.' The hand on Dora's knee felt warm through the light wool of her dress. 'You're looking very nice today, Mrs Strange.' He leaned forward and gazed approvingly at the hat and frock. Another seatless passenger thought better of chaperoning them. 'Very nice.'

'Now then, I have a bone to pick with you.' He slid the compartment door across and very deliberately drew down the blinds on the corridor side as the train pulled out of the station. 'I've been doing a tiny bit of digging. Are you quite sure your papa didn't have a special area of expertise?'

The blush was an answer in itself.

'He had a number of patients, soldiers, who couldn't . . .'

'Couldn't?' He moved closer and slipped a hand inside her cardigan.

'Couldn't. You know. Shell-shocked. He prescribed sleeping draughts for them.'

'Ah. The restoration of manly vigour. Yes.'

'I found some books he used to give to them.'

'Did you, by Jove, dirty old Dr Strange.'

Dora pulled a face at the thought of her father making personal use of the fascinating shelf behind the collection of Staffordshire flatback figures. She had never imagined him reading any of them, any more than she had imagined him taking any of the medicines in the surgery cabinet.

'The books helped, apparently. Sometimes he used to give them an anaesthetic, make an incision, then simply sew it up again. Quite a good success rate. He wrote a paper about it. There was a copy of it inside one of the books.'

'Was there now? And how did you discover that, might one enquire?' He didn't wait for an answer. His removed his hand and stared across the carriage, suddenly back in military memoir mode.

'Funny to think of a soldier not being able to get it up. They used to queue up outside the brothels with their trousers at half-mast, all primed and ready with ten-franc notes in their hands waiting for girls – girls who'd be too young to kiss back on civvy street – propped up on torn and grimy pillows getting through half a dozen men an hour. Kept the medics pretty busy: constant tail parades, umpteen tubes of ointment, endless lectures on basic hygiene – lectures that no one ever listened to. Disease didn't frighten them. They were all going to die tomorrow. Of something.

'The other ranks thought of nothing else. I remember once in the trenches coming across a group of Tommies standing in a circle round a corporal who was giving a no-holds-barred account of his wedding night – doing all the voices, as you might say. Should have been on the stage. "Oh Bill, you mustn't. Oh Bill, it's too big," all done in this frightened falsetto and his whole audience working away in unison and the ground under them all glazed and muddy with spunk . . .'

His voice tailed off. Dora opened her mouth very slightly and rested her head against the seat cushion. The guard would be along the corridor to inspect the tickets at any moment. It wouldn't be more than a peck. She closed her eyes, pictured the swift lunge forward, pictured the dark head tilting to the right as his mouth closed over hers, but the kiss never came.

'Good plan. I might have a short nap myself,' said Kemble, putting his *Morning Post* on the opposite seat beneath his outstretched feet. He was asleep in moments.

Chapter 16

It was a fine bright day and the dark blue strip of the sea and the light blue of the wrought-iron promenade visible from the top of West Street station looked strangely flat and unconvincing at the bottom of the grey, commonplace street, like a piece of music hall scenery.

It was a short walk to the mortuary – Alfred Kemble could find his way to virtually every mortuary in the South of England, rather as Aunt Jacaranda knew the whereabouts of all the smart hotels. Various policemen and a bluff, avuncular chap with military moustaches greeted the pathologist and were introduced to Mrs Strange.

The badly mutilated body of a balding, bespectacled middle-aged man had been found in a Southern Railway tunnel on the approach to Brighton between the rails and the tunnel wall, subject presumed fallen from moving train.

'Looks like another Peeping Tom case, sir.'

There was no warning about this particular practice pinned inside the train doors next to the one about sticking your head out, and yet it too was surprisingly common if the number of cases in Hubbard's miraculous index was anything to go by (175A steam railroads, traumatisation by).

And that was only the *un*successful ones. Like the half-dressed bodies found trussed and gagged in cupboards or the naked men found hanging from the backs of bedroom doors they were probably just the tip of the iceberg, the unlucky ones, the stupid ones who hadn't studied the route to establish when and where the tunnels came (Hubbard could probably advise).

The mortuary was as cold as its slab and the assistant had to bring bowls of hot water for the pathologist to warm his gloved hands in as he worked. The white rubber galoshes were kept free of the icy floor by a series of duckboards, bleached pale with constant scrubbing. One of the constables kindly fetched an old railway timetable to go under Mrs Strange's freezing feet.

Colliding with a brick railway tunnel at speed made a considerable mess of the human body. The skull was shattered and there were numerous other injuries including a dislocated wrist, multiple leg fractures, broken pelvis, broken neck, extensive lacerations and a severed arm. Cause of death was hardly a mystery but the blades probed on: Hutchinson's teeth and sabre shins indicative of congenital syphilis, tubercular lesions on both lungs. The deceased suffered from corns from tight-fitting shoes and had not kept his feet very clean. The capacity of the brain cavity suggested mental deficiency.

A policeman brought two plates of sandwiches and the pathologist held his with a fresh pair of bone forceps so that he wouldn't have to re-sterilise his gloves before getting back to work. No forceps for Dora who held her sandwich inside her pocket handkerchief.

The light was already fading by the time the necropsy was finished. The mortuary man disinfected and powdered the pathologist's gloves while Dr Kemble washed and dried his hands and packed away his tools and specimens.

'Thank you, Jenkins, always a pleasure working with you. You run a very tight ship.' Jenkins wriggled with pleasure, happily trousering his ten-shilling tip.

'There seems little point in returning to town this evening, Mrs Strange, as I shall be giving evidence at Lewes tomorrow. I have all my notes here.'

A careful cough from the mortuary-keeper. If the doctor was planning to remain overnight he wouldn't find a room in Lewes what with the biscuit tin business starting yesterday: lawyers, journalists, sightseers. Better off getting an early taxi from Brighton.

'Sound advice, Jenkins.'

The air outside seemed clean and almost warm compared to the acid chill of the dissecting room.

'No reason for you to head home either, Mrs Strange. I shall need you to take notes during my evidence tomorrow. They know me at the Metropole. We should be able to find rooms there.' *Rooms*, not room. '"English home comforts without ostentation" as it always claims in the *ABC*. That all right with you?'

He bought them both toothbrushes in a chemist's shop and waited outside a draper's while she chose a nightgown (an absurdly complicated procedure. Did madam want lawn, cotton or flannelette? Did madam prefer a long or a short sleeve? Did madam require a plain or figured material? Where was the widow Frith when you needed her?). They walked along the promenade to the hotel, carefully maintaining an unwritten distance between them: together but not together. There were little lights strung between the street lamps on the esplanade that twinkled on the water where the beaches had been.

The typewriter and the leather case full of knives and bottled flesh did duty for overnight bags. Mrs Strange was allocated a nice spacious sea view with bath. Kemble's room was on another floor. A telegram was dispatched to Warwick Square while Dora scurried upstairs to take off her hat and run a damp comb through her hair: 'Detained Brighton Dr and Mrs Kemble. Return Friday PM' (the truth would have saved three halfpence).

The Metropole dining room had the dead, beefy smell of rancid dripping. White aproned men patrolled the room with domed silver-plated gurneys and an array of knives (*butchers' knives*). A sommelier uniformed in a dark red jacket like a refugee from a comic opera came to talk to them about wines. He had only one arm. Had the other been left in France? Or had it simply been torn off while clinging to the outside of a second-class railway carriage?

The really great wines were of course no longer available (Dora remembered from her father's table the automatic sic transit glorification of all exhausted vintages) but the red-coated man found them a rather fine Bordeaux – far too good for a meal of almost Frith-like awfulness. Their food was served with Byzantine flummery by a baffling succession of busboys and waiters, each of them bred for one, very specific task: tweezing bread rolls on to side plates or transferring nameless vegetables from dish to plate with a peculiar rib-scissory device.

The pathologist was scrupulously careful to maintain the proprieties – it was an hotel dining room not the upstairs parlour of a Fitzrovia inn. Mrs Strange was having *gigot d'agneau* and Mrs Strange would like *pommes vapeur* with that and Mrs Strange was also rather partial to something that looked suspiciously like cabbage mould. Their talk was dull, domestic, small – did she often stay at the Metropole? – every word clearly audible at the next table, as if they had agreed beforehand that they must assure the waiters that their relationship was entirely above board. No whispering of war. No coded messages of desire. But Dora made up for it when the pathologist slipped away from the table to be replaced by his daydream twin, who lowered his voice and told her when he would come to her room, what he would do when he arrived and what she would do when he did it. She felt as if someone had poured a jug of gravy into her lap.

'Everything all right?' He was back at the table, bluff and brotherly, not a bit like his dream self. Dora pushed away her strawberry ice and resigned herself to the charade.

'I *do* hope you'll forgive me, Dr Kemble,' smarmed Dora, her voice playing a stupid little tune with the words, 'but I have an early start tomorrow.'

A waiting waiter instinctively materialised to pull out her chair as the pathologist rose to his feet. They shook hands as he left for the smoking room.

'Thank you so much for joining me this evening, Mrs Strange, and please do give Roger my regards when he returns.' *Roger.* Dora tried to picture him: balding, bespectacled, well-nourished . . .

The large, comfortable room and its large, comfortable bed were already crowded with lovers by the time Dora had climbed the stairs. All the characters in the stories in that forgotten cache of Harley Street books were acting out their saucy little scenes the only way they knew how. The parlour maid and the guards officer on all fours over by the fireplace; the master's daughter sitting astride the gamekeeper on the large chintz armchair ('the tight folds of her warm sheath throbbing on the column of his straining shaft') and the sheikh 'stroking his enormous pulsating member as he surveyed his naked prize, her pear-white body spread-eagled on the satin counterpane'.

In her mind's eye the pathologist snaked a clean, warm hand around Dora's waist. He wanted her, he had wanted her from the moment he first came upon her in that darkened office. He could have taken her then, strange frightened little creature, panting with excitement as he told the police inspector of the bitten nipples of the Peckham alley victim. Wanted her again today in the railway carriage, wanted her as she sat sipping her wine, fingering her pearls and looking at him with those wet, hungry eyes.

The storytelling voice murmured on while the ambidextrous fingers undressed her in moments (*like he was peeling his breakfast egg*). And the pair of them joined the cast of characters that had lived in her head since she was in the lower fifth 'as he plucked the flower of her maidenhood with his big tool as stiff as a rod of iron and poured his boiling essence into her cleft, deluging her with his hot discharge, raising her to the seventh heaven of bliss'.

The corridor floorboards creaked and Dora's heart raced at every passing footfall but the door never opened.

Chapter 17

Dora was woken by the agonised screams of the gulls on the esplanade and lay bewildered for a moment in the big, soft bed. A girl brought the breakfast he had ordered for her from his room two floors away: big, soft eggs, strong Indian tea.

Probably just as well. Even Mrs Strange, unflappable, sophisticated woman of mystery, couldn't have carried off eggs and bacon in the palm court under the gaze of all those Aunt Jacarandas. Miss Parker's last-minute life lessons had been fairly sketchy on major social taboos but Dora was fairly confident that breakfasting with a gentleman who is not one's husband, like unchaperoned gin-drinking in public houses, would come fairly high up in the league table of Things That Are Not Done. Breakfast in bed was altogether more prudent. He was probably a bear in the mornings in any case. Her father barely uttered before noon and would spend his breakfast hour tutting behind *The Times*. Perhaps Kemble was the same. Besides, what did one say to a girl you had just opted not to seduce? Even 'Did you sleep well?' would be indes-*cri*-bably vulgar in the circumstances.

The bedside telephone rang as she was pinning up her hair. They were sending a car at eight thirty. He would meet her downstairs. Mrs Strange should settle her own bill. He would reimburse her in due course.

'What notes will you need me to take?' asked Dora, her tone cold and secretarial.

'Notes?'

She had imagined that that crack about taking notes in Lewes was merely a blind for the benefit of the Brighton mortuary assistant but it was clear that he really did have no other use for her. It was hard to keep the disappointment out of her voice.

'You said yesterday that you wanted me to remain with you in Lewes to take notes.'

'Ah, yes, notes. Yes. Slight change of plan. I'm sure the clerk's transcript will be adequate.'

There was a click as he replaced the receiver.

Kemble tipped his way out of the hotel (*they know me at the Metropole*) and spent the leisurely coastal drive reading through the portfolio Hubbard had so presciently provided.

The two-week treasure hunt for the mortal remains of Mrs Florence Gibbon had begun in the umbrella stand of the ladies' waiting room at Lewes railway station, where her right leg had been found on Christmas Eve. Three days later Mr and Mrs Reginald Holledge (the Portslade couple whose biscuit tin had given the case its name) returned from a Yuletide visit to his sister (though *why* they had to go all the way up there every year to be preached at and patronised, Mrs Holledge would never understand). Their first thought on arriving home had been a cup of tea and a nice piece of shortbread . . .

A protracted search of the Sussex coast with a team of bloodhounds eventually led the police to the crime scene: a rented cottage ('Bellevue') whose gory contents were to be catalogued and reassembled by Alfred Kemble. The famous London pathologist, together with his doughty assistants, had worked round the clock in the bloodstained sitting room. For the next month any body part found anywhere (and there were a depressing number) was assumed to belong to the late Mrs Gibbon.

An arrest was made fairly swiftly. A charred dustbin containing the partially burned remains of a man's suit and heavily bloodstained shirt had been discovered behind Bellevue's tumbledown garden shed. Laundry marks (the policeman's friend) led them to a party who rejoiced in the entirely fictitious name of James Fitzjames. Mr Fitzjames had had the good sense to wear a trilby hat and fawn raincoat on his visit to the steam laundry. These magic garments would normally render their wearer invisible and the police might never have found the owner of the shirt had it not been for his 'well-groomed and athletic appearance,' which made him surprisingly easy to trace even though his name was not James Fitzjames, as advertised, but John Flynn of Sebastopol Terrace, West Ealing, where he shared the first floor with a woman known to the neighbours as Mrs Flynn.

This mouth-watering case had earned three whole pages in the *Sunday Pictorial* when it first came to light (all of them lovingly stuck down in one of Hubbard's scrapbooks). The gory and gripping details were rendered all the tastier by Flynn's striking good looks, which had caused the story to capture the public imagination (although this seemed a fairly easy beast to catch if the newspapers were any guide).

Dora and Kemble had a smooth enough ride along the coast and up through New heaven, but Lewes High Street was so clogged with motorcars that they were obliged to cover the last two hundred yards on foot. The courthouse wasn't due to open its doors until nine o'clock but the queue of would-be spectators had begun forming at six. The peculiarly revolting nature of the evidence had prompted the judge to invoke the Sex Disqualification Removal Act so that the jury in the case was entirely male, but his lordship's jurisdiction didn't extend to the public gallery, which was wearing its doggiest hat and toxic quantities of scent.

The pathologist was greeted with the usual deferential handshakes by the prosecution counsel while a clerk gave Dora her pick of the gallery benches just as the hour struck and the waiting crowd was let slip.

The woman next to Dora had acquired her front row seat by the simple expedient of having her maid join the growing queue at six fifteen. She was pressed so close that when she leaned forward to get a closer look at the court below, Dora's cheek was tickled by the two sleeping foxes draped affectionately across her shoulders. The legal team were packed so tightly on to their bench that Mr Anthony Granger, appearing for the prosecution, was perched on a mere three inches of mahogany and in constant danger of dropping off the end of the row.

When the defendant was led to the dock, Dora's neighbour produced a set of mother of pearl opera glasses from her muff to see whether his manly beauty lived up to the newspaper descriptions. He was handsome, certainly. Handsome enough to seduce his West London mistress and to tempt Mrs Gibbon to spend her savings on renting the draughty seaside rendezvous which formed a base for his card-sharping activities in the nearby coastal hotels. Coastal hotels with large, comfortable beds. Whenever Dora shut her eyes she was back in her Metropole bedroom feeling the slippery chill of the counterpane on her back as the imaginary kisses cascaded across her pear-white skin. 'The floodgates of sexual sap were unleashed and the shower of virile elixir brought peace to her womb.'

When called to the stand to plead the previous day, Mr Flynn had freely admitted portioning the late Mrs Gibbon into forty-nine separate pieces but denied all knowledge of her actual death (pick the bones out of that, as one of the crime reporters remarked, unprintably, to a colleague).

A fair amount of time had been spent establishing the identity of the victim with the questionable help of a succession of vague and unsatisfactory witnesses. With no head, no hands and no handbag it became surprisingly hard to put a name to a person. Mrs Gibbon was, like all dead blondes of her age, somewhat fond of society, but society had never looked very hard at Mrs Gibbon. Nice enough sort: tallish, blondish. But none of her extensive acquaintance was sufficiently observant to be able to identify her forearm let alone the big toe found in Mr Holledge's scrimshaw cigarette box.

Alfred Kemble didn't need head or hands to form a picture of the victim. Judging from the length of the thigh bone, the dead woman was not less than five feet six inches in height. The armpits had been shaved. The genital passage and the organs of generation had not been found but a portion of the mons Veneris attached to the leg found in the waiting room umbrella stand showed the hair to have been naturally light in colour (a little shimmy of surprise from Dora's foxy neighbour). The five toenails had been expertly lacquered with scarlet varnish. The victim had a very well-developed bust. These striking physical features were sufficient to narrow the search and the close fit between the medical records of Mrs Florence Gibbon and the condition of the mortal remains found at Bellevue – smallpox vaccination, an appendectomy, scarring of the urethra consistent with some species of chronic infection – were, in Dr Kemble's opinion, sufficient grounds for believing those remains to be hers.

Having given the victim a name, they could now (after the early lunch recess) turn their attention to how she met her fate. Had Dr Kemble examined the items found in the home of the Holledges at Portslade? He had. Had he found a scrimshaw cigarette box on the mantelpiece? You bet. And what did it contain? It contained a big toe from a right foot. Anything he wanted to say about that? The big toe had worn well-fitting shoes and the nail was painted the same shade of red as the foot attached to the leg found in the railway umbrella stand (it was a popular shade but the odds on said digit belonging elsewhere were, to say the least, minuscule). The rest of the leg had yet to be found.

Had Dr Kemble also found at Portslade a biscuit tin? Indeed he had. And could he describe this *biscuit tin*? The barrister spoke the words in the puzzled tones of a man whose biscuits (if any) were freshly baked daily. There was a pause while everyone else in court formed a mental picture of a biscuit tin, Scottie dogs, thatched cottages, Windsor Castle.

'It contained several portions of organ tissue: the bulk of the liver, a small piece of the spleen, the heart and both kidneys.' (*and a few of your nice roasted tomatoes*)

'On examination of all these organs which you found in the tin box was there any condition of disease about any of them?'

'No active disease at all.'

Perhaps he could now turn to the material found at the rented cottage. Could the pathologist tell the court in his own language what he found in the grate? Perhaps he could.

'I saw a saw described as a tenon saw.'

'You saw a saw?'

'I saw a saw.'

'E saw Esau,' muttered an old woman behind Dora, unstoppably.

'It was rusty and greasy and had a piece of flesh adhering to it.'

'Was there a saucer on the floor?'

'There was.'

Could he tell the court about that saucer? Go on, be a sport.

'It contained solidified fat.'

'Was there also a large two-gallon saucepan?' Funny he should ask that . . .

'And its contents?'

The two-gallon saucepan contained a great deal of reddish fluid with a thick layer of grease on the surface and a portion of flesh in the bottom and yes, since you ask, there was an Army and Navy stores hatbox containing several more items of interest. Do tell.

'I found a large number of pieces of flesh in the hatbox. Thirty-seven in all.'

'Thirty-seven *separate* pieces?' wondered the judge. Lord alone knew what he meant by it.

'Thirty-seven separate pieces. One piece had been cut from the back of the right shoulder and included the shoulder blade and part of the collar bone and part of the bone of the upper arm. Both of these bones had been sawn across. The second piece consisted of skin, fat and muscle from the region of the navel.'

'And the other thirty-five?' (sums were obviously a strong point).

'The other thirty-five pieces consisted of skin, most of them having fat upon them and many of them also muscle.'

'Upon five of the pieces of flesh what did you find?'

'On five pieces I found hair resembling that from the private part – pubic hair.'

'Fair or dark?' There was a studied casualness in the way the lawyer put the question, as if he'd placed a large bet on the outcome and didn't want the odds to change.

'Fair.'

'And what was the condition of the thirty-seven pieces of flesh found in the hatbox? Had they too been boiled?'

'All boiled. May I add that, of course, they were all human' (just in case anyone thought they were dealing with the dismemberment of a well-nourished blonde chimpanzee).

'And in the tin trunk, Exhibit 8, what did you find?'

'Four large pieces of a human body.'

'Boiled?' Again the casual tone, as if they might very well have been fried, or baked in a mould with kitchen butter and white pepper.

'They were not boiled and there were portions of certain organs attached to the trunk.'

'The trunk?' The judge had become confused.

'The trunk of the body in the trunk, m'lord. One of the sections consisted of the right half of the chest together with the spinal column from the level of the sixth cervical bone from the neck to a point at which the pelvis had been sawn off.'

A woman in the row in front was touching her body as if doing a personal inventory of each part as the pathologist mentioned it.

'The breast bone was attached to this piece and portions of most of the left ribs.'

'Was the right breast present on that piece?'

'It was.' Teasing.

'Is there *anything* you want to tell us about that?'

'When I pressed it milky fluid escaped from the nipple.'

The woman with the friendly furs had obviously spent the recess on an impromptu shopping expedition. Something – something fairly small and light by the look of it – had obviously caught her eye because there was a smart little candy-striped carrier bag on her lap with 'Chez Delphine' written on it in a showy italic script. She whipped the fancy tissue paper package from the bag and was surreptitiously sick into it.

The judged gazed out at the court with an air of resigned revulsion.

'You had better say at once what that indicates.'

There were knowing nods of disgust from Dora's bench as the pathologist stated the obvious.

'And have you been able to find at all … anywhere … the *uterus?*'

'No.'

'Perhaps you would like to summarise your findings for the court?'

The pathologist spoke clearly but very quickly, as if his audience had an important lecture to get to.

'All the material which I have examined from the station waiting room, the bungalow at Portslade and the cottage at Pevensey Bay: portions of the trunk, the organs, pieces of boiled flesh, are all of them human and correspond with parts of a single body – no duplicates at all.'

Dora could see one of the jurors frown slightly, as if wondering what the pathologist would have done if a rogue organ had turned up, like finding a corner of the Tower of London in a jigsaw puzzle of *The Laughing Cavalier*.

'The dismemberment of the parts had been performed after death and did not suggest an experienced slaughterman. The body was that of an adult female of big build and fair hair. She was pregnant, in my opinion, at the time of her death. There was no indication of any previous pregnancy which had run its full term ...'

The unspoken hint was unmistakable. No *evidence*. No lacerations. No actual lesions. Not even a uterus to play with. Just Alfred Kemble's assumption that a big, fair woman alone with a south coast card-sharp in a seaside cottage would not exactly be a stranger to expectations of motherhood.

The cross-questioning was brief, to the point and entirely ineffectual. No, admitted Kemble, none of the grisly *disjecta membra* found in the cottage or bungalow had enabled him to determine the cause of death and yes, the time of death was also something of a mystery. Was there any evidence that would give some clue to the identity of the murderer? No. Were there any traces of blood or other material not belonging to the deceased which might help identify her killer? No. Did any of this cut any ice with the twelve men of the jury? Not a hope.

Innocent men did not hack pregnant corpses into forty-nine separate pieces, parboil them and distribute them around the East Sussex coast.

No further questions.

Kemble looked at his fob watch as he stood down and signalled to Dora to meet him outside. Dora, who had rather wanted to stay and hear the summing up, pocketed her unused notebook and pencil and scooted downstairs while the clerk found a taxi to rush them to Lewes station in time for the 5.26. A gleaming first-class Pullman was waiting at the far end of the platform but instead Kemble bundled Dora into a second class no-corridor compartment as the whistle sounded and the porter slammed the door shut.

'You haven't spoken to me all day.' (As if she'd had an opportunity.)

His newspaper slithered from his grasp, conveniently carpeting the floor as he knelt at her feet. Hubbard could have told them that there were nineteen minutes between Lewes and Haywards Heath. Dora leaned back in her seat, rigid with disbelief. It was very, very different from the kiss she had been expecting. There was a scene like this in *Cranford* but it was one she seldom read. It had seemed so far-fetched ... She watched the flicker of passing telegraph poles, constantly expecting a bald bespectacled head to loom up against the window only to be swept clear as the train steamed into the Clayton tunnel.

By the time the train stopped they were each back in their corner seats as if butter wouldn't melt, Dora's heartbeat in synch with the rattle of the train. Three excursion passengers clambered aboard just as the train was pulling out. They had an early edition of the *Evening News*.

' "Thirty-seven separate pieces ..." Wouldn't think it to look at him.'

'Look at who?'

'The Brighton biscuit tin bloke. That trial that started yesterday. "Dressed, in a grey suit and a striped necktie he strode into the court with unwonted briskness".'

'Unwanted what?'

'Biscuits,' said the third, decisively.

'I'd ruddy well think it to look at him. Looks a nasty piece of work to me, striped necktie or no striped necktie.'

The jury knew only what it was told but the police, the prosecution (and their pet pathologist) knew a great deal more about the defendant, and the evening newspapermen had only to go to their cuttings libraries to find a slim but chunky bundle of newsprint which told them that John Flynn was not the unfortunate victim of circumstances that his natty grey suit might suggest. John Flynn, alias James Fitzjames, had served a five-year sentence for brutally attacking a woman while robbing a bank manager's house. There had also been an extremely colourful juvenile episode in which he had indecently assaulted no fewer than seven girl guides on the pier at Southend (Dora found it hard to imagine how he got through so many. Why hadn't they warned each other? Had they all sent each other to Coventry?). This inside knowledge coloured everything the reporters wrote.

It was already growing dark as the train pulled into the terminus.

'Don't be surprised when you get a postcard from Constance thanking you for keeping her company in Brighton.' The pathologist stroked her cheek absently. 'A little circumstantial evidence for that demon landlady.' Dora managed a grateful smile. Such foresight.

Chapter 18

'This crime of yours was all over yesterday's evening papers,' said Mrs Frith, accusingly, as she refilled Dora's breakfast teacup, as if Dora herself had dismembered the body and left the bits all over the dining room. 'The headlines talk of nothing but biscuit tins.'

'Gosh,' gushed Miss Digby 'I haven't seen anything about it. Is it an interesting case?'

Mr Haddon patted Mr Stone on the back while Dora struggled to think of a single element of her day in Lewes that wouldn't cause Mrs Frith and the PGs to rush retching for the exits.

'The public gallery was packed. Like a first night at the theatre. Lots of society people – or so the newspapers said.'

'How perfectly thrilling,' gushed Miss Andrews. 'Anyone one might know?'

'Ghouls,' ruled Mrs Frith.

After breakfast Mr Stone took up his favourite Saturday morning perch on the window seat in the PGs parlour. He peered out into the yard disappointedly.

'I thought Saturday was Frithy's regular day for squirrel-smacking but not a sign, sadly.' Mr Stone blew a ring of smoke at a print of Renoir's *Umbrellas*.

'I told her I saw a mouse on the stairs.'

'You *didn't*.'

'Worked like a charm. Found her on hands and knees in the dining room blowing cayenne pepper into cracks in the skirting board. At least I think it was cayenne pepper. Might have been rouge, I suppose.'

Mr Stone had developed a charladylike passion for yellow journalism. He had devoured two editions of Friday's *Evening Standard* and had already dashed out to buy the morning's *Mirror*. He flounced open his newspaper and glanced at the masthead.

'Twenty-third of March. Perhaps the squirrel season has closed. Open season on big blondes, though. Poor Mrs Gibbon. And poor baby Gibbon, apparently. What prudes they all are. The *Mirror* is perfectly happy to tell us that the victim had "expectations of motherhood" but that "certain portions were missing," unlike yesterday's *Standard*, which drew the line at "an interesting condition". Interesting? Very much a matter of opinion, I should have thought. A *psychic trance* would be a jolly interesting condition, ditto catalepsy, and religious ecstasy sounds positively fascinating, but *pregnancy*? Hardly.'

Miss Digby couldn't decide how best to respond to Mr Stone. She'd already confessed as much to Dora. Mr Stone was obviously rather *smart*. Most gentlemen, especially quizzical ones like Roderick Stone, liked it if you laughed at all their jokes. But how could one be sure that a joke had been made? Miss Digby had devised a special face to be worn while he read from the newspapers. A hungry half-smile like someone desperate to be picked for a netball team.

'A young woman has been found dead in a house in Dundee,' he continued. ' "Stripped of clothing except for one stocking and mutilated in a manner only to be described in a medical text book." The body, you'll be happy to learn, "had not been *interfered* with". One never reads any of this stuff in *The Times*. It's like another universe.' He carried on reading delightedly. ' "A demented Armenian named Titus . . ." sounds like a limerick. "A demented Armenian named Titus . . ." '

'Was plagued with a case of arthritis?' suggested Mr Haddon.

'It improved very slightly if massaged twice nightly,' volunteered Dora (very much to everyone's surprise).

'A thought that is sure to excite us.'

'Anyhow,' said Mr Stone, 'returning to the matter in hand. "A demented Armenian named Titus has shot and killed the manageress of the Horseshoe Hotel in the Tottenham Court Road" – and can one honestly blame him? Landladies being what they are. Practically an occupational hazard I should have thought.'

Yet more uncertain laughter from Miss Digby. Her face was mildewed with a light dusting of face powder.

'And we get two whole pages on the biscuit tin beast: "When Miss Minter, one of the most tragic figures in this grim drama, entered the court it was seen at the very outset that she was deeply affected." Come on, Haddon, you do the actions.'

Mr Haddon rose to his feet and held his hands in front of him as if clutching a handbag as Mr Stone continued his recital.

' "Her gait as she made her way to the witness box contrasted with the very smart nigger-brown costume and black cloche hat and veil which she wore" – fashion tips for the well-dressed murder witness – "Water was fetched." ' (Mr Haddon sipped prettily at an imaginary tumbler) ' "Miss Minter then recovered a little, raised her veil and dabbed at her face with a snowy scrap of Valenciennes lace." Don't pad your part, Hadders.'

'It seems you had a nice day for your Sussex jaunt, Miss Strang.

' "The sunshine came fitfully through the windows but the habitual gloom of the courtroom remained. A door in the dull mahogany wall had opened and in the tall, narrow opening stood Flynn. He might have been a painted picture, he stood so motionless, his very light grey suit being in striking contrast to the dark brown wood in which he was framed. He then gazed around the court and when a chair was placed for him, sat down, carefully pulling up his trousers to preserve their crease."

'Tut tut. Man's obviously a bounder but the reporter certainly seems smitten. "There is something amazingly handsome and electric about the clean-cut almost classical features: a long, thin nose, a firm cleft chin, eyes dark, flashing and deep set and the most fascinating head of hair. If there is such a thing as masculine beauty, then this man has been very generously endowed." I say, steady on. Mind you, there's quite a lot of competition by the sound of it. They had a new witness in the afternoon: Savage of the Yard. "Clean-shaven, alert and looking more like a Varsity athlete than a detective, Chief Inspector Percy Savage entered the witness box with a firm, manly tread." ' Mr Stone gave an approving whistle. 'Percy sounds very much the thing, certainly pulls the crowds. "Women who had sat hour after hour through the long, sensational trial came with flushed and eager faces to its last dread chapter" – that'll be you, Miss Strang.'

' "Dr Alfred Kemble had not proceeded far with the sickening details of the boiled and burned fragments of flesh and bone," sounds like Thursday's supper, "When Flynn's amazing calm and apparent unconcern deserted him. His delicate hand covered his eyes, his head was bowed and he had every appearance of a man passing through severe mental torture or bodily pain. He may have wept, but if so his right hand hid the tears." Stirring stuff. "For one moment Flynn stood gazing at the judge with the light of fierce resentment in those dark, fascinating eyes." '

Mr Stone broke off at the sound of the front door latch. Mrs Frith had just returned from posting a letter and the rattle of the coat stand could be heard as she hung her hat in the vestibule.

Stone slid another cigarette from its tin, raised his knees to his chest and placed his feet under him on the window seat.

'Stand on that chair,' he whispered. 'Quick.' Dora climbed uncertainly on to a spoon-backed chair just as Mrs Frith swept into the room.

'What are you doing, Miss Strang?'

'I wouldn't swear to it,' drawled Mr Stone, winking the other eye at Mr Haddon, 'but I'm almost certain I saw something run under the bureau.'

Dora escaped to her room and packed her overnight bag. Mrs Frith greeted her approvingly when she returned to the front hall. There was a fresh tin of pepper in her hand.

It was one of the many frugal dreams of Mrs Frith's life to have a houseful of lodgers so well-stocked with provincial relations (or personal charm) that they would spend every weekend running someone else's hot water, using someone else's electricity and eating someone else's dainty dishes. The reluctant landlady had always done her best to keep the weekend numbers down by shaming her guests into lunching and dining elsewhere, reminiscing about their (entirely fictional) predecessors who had the good grace to spend Saturday to Mondays with friends or family in the shires. If one didn't count Christmas and Easter her best score to date had been one Saturday the previous spring when all but one of her PGs had decamped to the country. She herself had dined with Mrs St Keith (Dover sole, lamb cutlets, strawberry fool) while Miss Digby (who clearly had no friends whatever) had had to make do with something cold on a tray left over from Friday night's excesses thus reducing the day's catering costs to a nice, round zero.

'*So* important to get out of town if one can,' cooed Mrs Frith, levering the lid off the pepper tin with a halfpenny. 'Please send the doctor my warmest regards.' The initial flurry of neighbourly interest that had attended Dr Strang's arrival in a small Sussex town two years earlier had died down somewhat but he still.

* * *

The initial flurry of neighbourly interest that had attended Dr Strang's arrival in a small Sussex town two years earlier had died down somewhat but he still maintained a polite level of intercourse. How his wife would have relished it all. She had never liked Harley Street although it turned out to be the perfect address for a woman of her inexplicably delicate state.

The diagnoses had varied: anaemia, thin blood, debility. Various colleagues ministered to her with foul-tasting tonics or sent her off for hydrotherapy and radium mud baths but her appetite never rallied and she grew weaker by the month. Finally, after a year of sofa-bound decline the charming Mrs Leopold Strang caught a cold and died. Not even influenza (which he could have forgiven) but a common or garden cold that any normal constitution could easily have withstood.

Dora's knock was answered by Minnie, the house-cum-parlour maid (her title varied from apron to apron). Minnie had been acquired locally together with an old man called Sproat, who limped around the garden burbling under his breath, snipping the blooms off herbaceous perennials in the name of dead-heading. The rest of the staff – Cole the butler and a large ginger-haired, floury-fingered woman who answered to the name of Mrs Bartlett – had been imported from Harley Street. (No one had seen or heard tell of any Mr Bartlett but it seemed that cooks, like pathologists' assistants, came complete with invisible husbands.)

'Dr Strang is in the library, Miss,' murmured Minnie. A warning, not an invitation. Her father emerged on the stroke of four.

'I didn't think you'd want the bother of dinner *and* luncheon. I've invited some neighbours this evening. The Bamptons and the Markhams – who are both bringing their Elsies. Major Kerr Stanley is also joining us and an Honourable Mrs Fish. Lavinia Fish. She has taken the Hartleys' old place for the twelvemonth.'

The Markhams arrived in a state of mildly belligerent contrition with a different child from the one advertised. Elsie's visit to a friend had been extended another week and meanwhile Rick (or Dick or Nick) had arrived home unexpectedly that afternoon. They had tried to telephone to give notice of the substitution but had until that moment been unaware of Dr Strang's Luddite resistance to the usual twentieth-century amenities. Colonel Markham was still seething.

'Never dawned on me. No one expected old Mrs Castle to have a line installed – the old girl was deaf as a post – but it was only when I called the exchange that I realised you'd done nothing about it. Easy enough. Telegraph pole's only across the road.'

The company gathered by the drawing-room window to join the Colonel in squinting out into the blackness at the spot beyond the yew hedges where the maypole of wires clustered on the corner of the street.

Leopold Strang had regarded the telephone as a necessary evil for a practising physician but he had seldom made personal use of the instrument and saw absolutely no need for it in retirement. Cole could run any urgent errands and there was a perfectly good pillar box by his front gate. Even with a reduced Saturday service the Markhams could easily have let him know their change of plan by postcard – or by telegram, come to that. Dr Strang was very comfortably off in retirement but still remained convinced that there were few tales that couldn't be told in six words – a belief he shared (did he but know it) with the sub-editors of the *Daily Mirror* – 'Nicholas substitute Elsie. Trust forgive inconvenience' or (more truthfully) 'Nicholas rusticated drunkenness. Bringing Strangwards. Mortified'.

The prodigal seemed entirely unrepentant in his made-up tie and mauve socks and made a beeline for Cole and his salver of sherry glasses.

Dora had braced herself for the usual lecture on the telephone as a force for evil in contemporary discourse and was surprised by her father's mild-mannered, almost cheery response. Not-at-all-not-at-all. Always happy to see young er ... er ... Sorry to be such a dinosaur but the postal service in Sussex had always seemed excellent. One could, after all, always fire off a telegram *in extremis*. (He was not to know that the war had given Perdita Markham a horror of telegrams and, as with all her likes and dislikes – cheese, rhododendrons, sweet vermouth, the Irish – she assumed it to be universal.)

'Oh no, Dr Strang, *not* the telegraph. *So* anxious-making. Particularly with dear Theodora away by herself in town.'

Dora wondered what terrible scenario Mrs Markham envisaged? 'Sussex girl found headless in train. Abortionist named.'

They were still ten for dinner and Dr Strang, with no wife to fret about such matters, made no effort to make pigeon pairs of his guests: 'They are dining, not mating, Theodora.'

Elsie Markham's absence was actually a great comfort to her parents, sustaining them through the shock of her brother's indiscretions. Something Else's winter in London with her cousin had yielded an invitation to an immensely grand estate in the north of England. To the utter astonishment of her entire acquaintance, her stay had been extended by another week. She danced badly (having had so very little practice) and her interest in cocktails and mixed doubles and spiritualism and all the other Sussex fads was minimal but she wore tweeds with conviction, had a handicap of six and exercised a peculiar fascination over horses, dogs and small children. These qualities, miserably under-exploited on her home turf, had borne spectacular fruit during her winter in town, where she caught the fancy of a sporty, good-natured young man (tall *and* titled). An announcement was expected imminently. Precious Little Else could hardly powder her nose for pique and her bad temper was proving hard to contain. She stared rather crossly at Dora's frock.

'You look frightfully smart.' With a sharp, almost suspicious note of surprise, Little Else managed to turn the compliment into an insult. And Dora did look smart – even her father had remarked on it when she came down for dinner but only to point out that something a little more *jeune fille* would have pleased him better.

'Aunt Jacaranda got it for me.'

'I doubt that an old maid like Jacaranda is the best judge of what's suitable.' 'Suitable' in this particular instance presumably meaning something fluffy in a pastel shade.

'Blue is always so flattering.' Mrs Fish was determined to make a conquest of her young hostess.

Augusta Bampton was slightly dubious about Mrs Fish. Her only copy of *Debrett* had been bought when her own mama had been taking a close interest in eligible young men. There *were* honourable Fishes in the book and it was not impossible that Lavinia Fish had married one of them, or that the ennoblement of some long-lost Fish had somehow dragged her up to a higher social level (eldest sons went down like ninepins during the war) but Mrs Bampton was not altogether convinced. Hons always confused her. Wasn't there supposed to be a Christian name? The Hon. Mrs Ebenezer Fish or what-have-you? She was keeping her doubts to herself until she had a chance to motor in to Hastings and trawl for Fishes in the lending library. Meanwhile she seethed inwardly as the Fish female applied the starting handle to the conversation and steered it to some of her favourite spots.

Honourable or not, their new neighbour was a remarkably handsome woman. Leopold Strang had spoken with her only briefly at some purgatorial gathering convened by the Bampton female but his first impression was extremely favourable. She had once had a brush with Christian Science and although an operation for appendicitis had seen off that particular fad, she remained firmly of the opinion that disease was, by and large, a matter the mind could control. As a result she never spoke of her own health and took a firm, Frith-like line with anyone who sought to introduce the subject. In her view the only proper response to 'How are you?' was a hearty 'Never better'. This had immediately recommended her to Dr Strang and he was surprised how keenly he had looked forward to their second meeting.

The doctor had previously always thought of widows as a breed of dangerous pest, an opinion he had formed during his annual fortnight at Biarritz. It had grown easier to avoid them lately but there were still a terrifying number of overdressed ladies of thirty-nine smouldering unwillingly on the nation's sacrificial pyre and very glad indeed to make the acquaintance of a well-preserved widower of sixty. *Please* pardon the intrusion but had they not met the previous summer at her brother's place in Harrogate? Or, more brazen still, that they were *sure* that the doctor would forgive the liberty but ... could he *possibly* take a look at a mosquito bite or a sunburn or at a swollen wrist or ankle?

They were all there for the taking had he any appetite whatsoever for their overripe charms and they weren't necessarily holding out for a second trip up the aisle, either, to judge by their dress and behaviour. Indeed, an unwanted acquaintance (there was seldom any other kind for Dr Strang) who had inconsiderately taken to summering in the same hotel, once confided, after suicidal quantities of a very indifferent cognac, that most of them were so grateful for a few flowers and a bit of attention that a good-looking man like himself could enjoy all the matrimonial *rights* he wanted without the *rites* ever being mentioned (if you got his drift).

The man, a retired major in the Dragoon Guards (or so he claimed) had tapped the side of his sunburned nose conspiratorially. Dr Strang had given him a mercilessly diagnostic stare through his gold pince-nez: hypertension, bile, gout probably, haemorrhoids almost certainly, arteriosclerosis and incipient liver disease. His teeth were none too good either. A miracle he was still in any condition to go corridor-creeping with the winsome widows of Biarritz.

Dr Strang had managed perfectly well without feminine companionship since his wife's death. Twenty grains of bromide in his morning tea took care of any unwelcome urges and the very thought of exchanging more than the briefest civilities with these sagging, beaded bolsters of womanhood filled him with utter disgust. His female patients (of whom he had very few) were quite bad enough with their floodings and flushings and irregularities. Even today, in retirement, he wasn't to be spared their bleatings. They were forever buttonholing him at tea parties. They knew they shouldn't ask, really *oughtn't* to pester him now that he had retired from practice but Dr Napier was so indecently *young*. Was it quite *normal* for whatever it was to stop, or fail to start, or go on so long, or swell up quite so much, or go that peculiar colour, or give off that disgusting smell? Doctoring was a life sentence. Sussex, it seemed, was in danger of yielding the same old filthy catalogue of woe – and no blasted fee to show for it. He took to recommending cold baths and a strict diet of dry toast and soda water and gradually Dr Napier with his Edinburgh pedigree and his little roentgen apparatus began to look a great deal more appealing.

This sudden, positively youthful interest in Lavinia Fish had caught Dr Strang entirely unawares. She had an unusually fine figure. Most women of her age seemed more upholstered than dressed, in clothes cunningly fashioned to obliterate their shape (or whatever was left of it). Mrs Fish's dark red frock, though clearly of recent make, made one very pleasantly aware of the sumptuous lines beneath.

Mrs Fish, who had taken careful stock of Dr Strang's exquisitely furnished drawing room through her lorgnette when the others were squabbling about the distance to the telegraph pole, had decided to set the dial to 'fascinate'.

She leaned confidingly towards Dora.

'Your work sounds thrilling, Miss Strang. You must tell us all about this charm bracelet business.'

'Which business is this?' wondered Dr Strang.

'They call it the charm bracelet case.' Mrs Fish's diamond earrings twinkled in the candlelight. 'A woman murdered by one of the porters in her block of flats, man called Jelly. He was half-witted, apparently.'

'Indeed? There was nothing about it in my paper.'

The *Mirror*-reading Mrs Fish, anxious to get back on to a higher intellectual plane, observed that it was more than likely that both of the horrid man's parents had been similarly mentally afflicted and what a pity it was that society punished people who should never have been born in the first place. Very true, agreed Dr Strang, cautiously.

Colonel Markham had read several pamphlets on the subject and happily parroted a raft of cherished (and largely inaccurate) statistics. The latest report by the Mental Deficiency Committee had apparently found 300,000 – or was it 3 million? – mental deficients in England and Wales alone (the implication being that the loonies of Scotland were simply too numerous to count). Only one in five men volunteering for the army was able to pass the physical examination – and they were the ones fit enough to limp as far as the recruiting office ... Didn't seem to stop them reproducing, mind you. Criminals and halfwits breeding like rabbits while the spat-wearing classes could barely fill a pew.

Dora groaned inwardly as her father waded in.

'Very true, Colonel. This selfish vogue for small families is entirely deplorable. The middle classes have a duty to the empire.'

Dr Strang disliked children but he had at one time wanted a large family. He looked again at Mrs Fish, at the firm, white skin of her neck. Still of childbearing age? He rather thought so. His almost ruttish reverie was broken by the sound of the conversation suddenly catching fire.

'Three hundred thousand feeble-minded?' fretted Mrs Bampton.

'Horrid,' nodded Elsie.

'And lunatics,' chimed in Mrs Markham, who had taken rather a fancy to the Sauternes.

'And lunatics what?' snapped Dr Strang. Really this sort of conversation was far better conducted over the port.

'Far *more* lunatics,' Mother Markham swallowed a hiccup, 'all having lots of baby lunatics.'

'Epileptics,' shuddered Mrs Bampton.

'Mongolian imbeciles,' suggested Elsie.

'Aments,' trumped young Nicholas, keen, as always, not to be left out of any debate.

'Alcoholics,' countered Mr Bampton mischievously, eyeing Nicholas's wine glass.

Colonel Markham's fury at his son's university disgrace had finally been given an outlet. Asylums and special schools springing up everywhere you looked. Utter madness. The history of civilisation was a series of racial tragedies. The more you cosseted these evolutionary failures the faster they would breed and the more physical, mental and moral cripples there would be perpetuating their kind without let or hindrance with the result that educated, law-abiding, taxpayers – gentlefolk, as he was not ashamed to call them – would be out-bred by the under man and the yellow races would triumph.

'But surely, if it really is all in the blood, then banging them up in bins will be a saving in the long term?' It seemed the Markham boy had been to school after all. 'I mean to say confinement will eventually mean there are fewer of them.'

'Why will it?' Little Else was sadly out of her depth.

The youth fumbled for a response suitable for mixed company. 'Well, you know. *Separate dorms.*'

'No no no no no. Cheaper to send a boy to Oxford than keep him in a special school for morons.' Colonel Markham looked wistfully in the direction of his son, as if it might have been worth the extra.

Mrs Fish was having none of it. Incarceration was an entirely unnecessary expense and actually (a saintly little nod at this point) wasn't it rather inhumane to keep them confined? If the, ahem, *procedure* were performed on a purely voluntary basis it posed no threat whatsoever to the so-called rights of the individual.

Mrs Fish's voice was unexpectedly deep and there was a slight huskiness to it that gave a whispery intimacy to anything she said – provided of course that one paid no mind to the words themselves . . .

'Properly administered social surgery will amputate the gangrenous appendage which endangers the life and health of the entire social organism.'

It was, Dora realised, a verbatim quote from the Hektographed speech in Mrs Culvey's middle drawer. It had looked far more persuasive on the page. Infinitely more persuasive if you imagined Alfred Kemble in witty, world-weary lecture-room mode. She could almost see the teasing twitch of the lips as he titillated his audience with that deliberately florid turn of phrase. *Gangrenous.* It just sounded disgusting when the Fish woman said it. Meanwhile Mrs Bampton's doubts increased. An honest-to-goodness honourable would never discuss gangrene at the dinner table.

Dora noticed her father growing alarmingly pale.

'I *beg* your pardon, *what* did you say?'

Mrs Fish sensed at once that she had not struck the right note but soldiered on regardless.

'The Americans have the right idea. Quite a simple procedure, apparently. And it can be done with x-rays nowadays. Completely painless.'

The lovely castle that Dr Strang had built in the air for himself and the voluptuous, soft-voiced Mrs Fish was tumbling into ruins before the soup had even been cleared. But the honourable widow's modest proposal had struck a chord with the rest of Dr Strang's dinner guests. Little Else's papa saw an opportunity to take one of his pet subjects out for an airing.

'Look at dogs,' barked Mr Bampton, determined to get a word in edgeways.

'Oh papa, must we? *Again?*' yapped Elsie, who turned her attention to the state of her prettily buffed fingernails. There probably wouldn't even be dancing afterwards. Did Dr boring old Strang even *have* a gramophone?

Mrs Fish returned to the fray. 'A properly planned programme . . .' such pretty words for the lips that she paused and said them again '. . . a properly planned programme of sterilisation means that feeble-mindedness or any other undesirable traits can simply be bred out and the racial stream will gradually purify itself. The Americans have the right idea. Terribly progressive.'

Was it indeed. Dr Strang's misery was complete. His loathing for amateur biologists was matched only by his contempt for Americans. Had Mrs Fish made a close study of the subject? No of course she jolly well hadn't. Feeble-mindedness was no more hereditary than a liking for Dickens or a weakness for Sauternes. Malnourished, uneducated women were self-evidently less likely to raise healthy intelligent children but that had nothing whatever to do with their genetic inheritance.

He warmed to his theme. Was she aware that among the candidates for this 'progressive' American policy were any deemed to be suffering from an hereditary taint? The blind? The deaf? The deformed? Sufferers from cretinism? Anyone subject to fits or seizures? Anyone of abnormally low intelligence? Alcoholics? He too had noted that the Markham boy, like his mother, was finding the Sauternes very much to his taste.

'I doubt many of us would be sitting at this table if these criteria had been applied to our ancestors. I know that I should not.'

'I suppose a social problem group only exists when it actually becomes a social problem,' piped Nicholas, almost brightly, 'which doesn't really include Aunt Edwina, whatever one might say about her.'

Colonel Markham looked cross and rather confused, as if he'd just lost his wallet to a conjuror.

'Seemed to me you were on the side of the angels a moment ago, Strang old chap. All in favour of curbing the fecundity of the under man and all that.'

'I fail to see how a concern for the falling birth rate and a sincere wish that the breeding and raising of children be undertaken by the likes of Elsie and Dora rather than some illiterate drunk can have led you to assume that I share your enthusiasm for the wholesale sterilisation of the unfit, let alone – what is that fatuous expression that Kemble and his people like to use? – the purification of the blessed germ plasm.'

'Still a drain on the state,' persisted Colonel Markham, exasperated and by now extremely bored by the shoppy, scientific turn the conversation had taken, but his host was relentless.

'If social inadequates actually *request* sterilisation then by all means change the law and sterilise them. But don't pretend that this is an exercise in selective breeding. The very idea that a notion as wishy-washy as "feeble-mindedness" or "criminality" can have a simple genetic character … Amateur social biology is riddled with expressions that simply have no place in a proper scientific discussion. These are matters of taste, not science. This whole human betterment nonsense is nothing more than bogus biology peddled by a bunch of snobs and racist cranks.'

Dora, ready to cry with embarrassment and infuriated by her father's determination to contradict everyone, tried to get the debate back on track.

'But papa, you have to admit that if we sterilised anyone with a genuine hereditary taint the bad blood could be bred out of the gene pool in a matter of generations.' No one actually said 'Hear hear' or pinged the side of their glass with a butter knife, but Dora sensed she had the room on her side.

Her father bowled her a look of almost corrosive disdain.

'Would we indeed?' Dr Strang swallowed a fortifying forkful of fish. 'I was always brought up to refrain from comment on subjects of which I was entirely ignorant but that fashion seems now to have waned.' He took a sip of water like a judge about to pass sentence.

Mrs Fish felt that the conversation was sliding out of her control. The doctor had clearly lost any sense of decorum.

'How tall is he?' Dr Strang inspected Markham Minor over his spectacles.

'Er. Just under five ten.'

'Do you imagine for a moment he'd be anything like that size if you'd had to feed him on bread and margarine? Barely half the population has a diet adequate for basic health. Of course they're short. Of course they're stupid. Of course they're diseased. But I say again' (Nicholas Markham, who had spent his young manhood being bored by some of the best in the business, expertly stifled a yawn) 'Do any of you seriously imagine that stupidity or moral imbecility are carried in the genes like red hair or left-handedness or short sight?' Leopold Strang flashed a sudden look at Mrs Fish, who was still gazing mildly towards him from the far end of the table. 'Even if it were, have you any inkling how many hundreds of years of viciously selective breeding it would take to weed out any taint you deemed undesirable? And how wide will you cast your net? The lame? The epileptic? The partially sighted?' He addressed this last to Mrs Fish herself and as he did so stuck out his tongue and waggled it from side to side.

The rest of his guests were too stunned to react to this extraordinary display but all turned their heads to see how the Fish would take it. The same vague, slightly patronising smile continued in place and remained there for Dr Strang's next question, an apparent change of subject that convinced her that her host knew when he was beaten.

'They tell me you drive your own motor car, Mrs Fish. How do you find the roads hereabouts? Well signposted?'

Leopold Strang's family crystal chimed alarmingly as Mrs Bampton aimed a restraining kick at Precious Little Else, who was making a noise like an asthmatic Pekingese.

All in all, Mrs Fish was pleased with her performance at the dinner. The doctor had proved tiresome in the end, but the conversation had been stimulating and she had, she felt, given excellent value. She turned her blurry blue gaze to the daughter. Strange girl.

'This Kemble cove is quite a celebrity. I see you've had the business with the biscuit tin all week,' thrilled Mrs Fish, past caring what the insufferable Dr Strang thought of her reading matter. 'Did they ever find the other leg?' Her host noted the wet click of her dental plate as she prattled unstoppably on.

Mrs Bampton and Elsie had leaned towards them, equally fascinated by the grisly details but Dr Strang shut down all discussion of matters pathological like someone covering a parrot for the night.

'I may say. I may say' – the whole world was a public meeting to Dr Strang. He simply had no other register. You could all but hear the tetchy tap of the gavel. 'I may sa-ay,' brayed the doctor inexorably, 'that I contrived to conduct a Harley Street practice for thirty years without once resorting to the vulgarity of discussing the human body, dead or alive, when dining in mixed company.'

Almost sick with disappointment, he turned with studied effect to Dora, leaving Mrs Fish for ever on the dark side of his favour

'Your mother had more taste.'

'I'm a woman of the world, Dr Strang.'

'I'm extremely sorry to hear it.'

Which pretty much put the tin hat on it. Mrs Fish, surprised but, Dora suspected, rather amused by the doctor's rudeness, had obviously decided to give the old fool up as a bad job and simply laughed her pretty porcelain and vulcanite laugh. She adjusted her position so that Colonel Markham, her immediate neighbour, would receive the full force of that velvety embonpoint.

'He's very handsome, isn't he? Miss Strang's pathologist?' She looked across to Dora for confirmation.

Was he hers? And how did Mrs Fish know? As if she could see the very handsome man in question on his knees in a second-class railway carriage taking full advantage of a signal failure just outside East Grinstead.

'*So* handsome.'

Chapter 19

'I would be grateful if you could instruct these pathology people to make their arrangements with you during office hours. It is made quite clear in my terms: "No use of the telephone except in cases of genuine emergency". I cannot be seen to make exceptions,' hissed Mrs Frith, passing Dora the receiver as she ran a yellow duster across the hall table. 'It's that rude Hubbard person.'

'But it *is* a genuine emergency,' said the disembodied voice on the telephone. It wasn't Hubbard. Dora pressed the Bakelite hard against her ear so that Mrs Frith couldn't hear the words

'I need you here, Lexham Gardens. Can't come to the office today. Indisposed. Hubbard knows all about it. A few reports to write.'

The waiting landlady dusted the receiver with automatic hand as she replaced it.

'Sorry, Mrs Frith. They want me to go straight to Kensington mortuary. They never know until the last minute and it does save so much time.'

He answered the door himself, informally dressed in grey flannels and a soft-collared shirt. He looked much younger suddenly. He didn't look indisposed.

There was little sign of the Phipps-feeding Constance in the ground-floor furnishings. The drawing room was done in the taste of a much older woman. A thin, dry, self-consciously stylish older woman for whom Rennie Mackintosh and William Morris were obviously minor deities and who could no more lounge on a sofa than pay a call before luncheon. The cheerless good taste of this arty, rush-bottomed parlour would have made it a perfect waiting room.

'Arts and crafts,' sighed Dora.

He looked almost uncomprehending.

'Is it? I'm afraid I don't go in for that sort of thing. Leave it to the experts. Mother bought it all when Ottilie and I were married. It isn't to Constance's taste, apparently.'

He gazed around the room as if wondering for the umpteenth time what it was his second wife could possibly find to dislike. He turned to straighten a photograph perched on one of the punishingly plain, light oak side tables: a young but very serious-looking Alfred Kemble flanked by two dashing blond boys smiling wide, crack-shooting, *victor ludorum* smiles. All three were in uniform.

'My brothers. The blessed Berties. My late mother had some mad, old world idea that the three of us should be law, army and church but of course we all ended up in the army. The whole bloody world went into the army.'

'So you said the other evening.'

'Did I?' He sat down on a fumed oak settee, took a long gulp from what looked a lot like a pink gin and replaced the glass on the table beside him. There was a slice of lemon in the glass and one of its pips began rising and falling with the bubbles of soda. He gazed at it, fascinated.

'There was a shell crater bang alongside our dressing station and it had a corpse in it: great big dead German. One of the boys had all but drowned trying to fish the thing out so there Fritz lay. One morning he disappeared then the following day he was back again. All to do with which stage of decomposition the body had reached: methane, hydrogen sulphide, carbon dioxide. And atmospheric pressure, obviously. Like a barometer. Better than hanging a bit of seaweed on the back door.'

His eyes were focused far off, as if deliberately re-viewing each atrocity while his long index finger wagged comically up and down at the memory of the floating corpse.

'When we were stationed at Ypres a fresh bombardment unearthed a corpse impacted in the wall of a trench. Just the boot, sticking out of the mud. The tommies used to polish it for luck. See your face in it.'

The black tide of reminiscence seemed unstoppable.

'We were moved after that to a clearing station in some girls' school or other. Quite a useful building for a field hospital but the Germans had been using it before us. Instead of burying the amputated limbs they simply used to throw them out of a back window. Huge great pile of them. Hubbard cleared it. Good old Hubbard. Even took stock (as only Hubbard could). 187 German arms (74 of them tattooed) and 239 German legs. Enough for half a battalion. Had a nightmare about it once. Like a huge centipede ...'

It probably made him feel better to talk about it. Dora hoped so. But she was starting to get that bored, guilty feeling she always got when men began talking of their war experiences. Strange how similar they were. Had they all, by some hideous coincidence, shared the same trench? Had they all had a booted corpse in their mud? Or had they all simply read the same memoirs and absorbed the anecdotes into one big collective memory? Dora's own war was a jumble of recollections: tiny coloured flags on a schoolroom map; badly knitted socks; tired young men with grey faces and empty sleeves tucked tidily into coat pockets as if they were forever counting their change.

He drained his glass.

'I thought we could work upstairs. There's something I need you to help me with.'

He headed on up without waiting for her to take off her coat and hat and she saw him disappear into a room on the right of the first-floor landing. She trotted up after him. Only one flight but her heart was racing.

'Come in here, could you?'

The room was a mass of pink organza and gilding. Nothing arts and crafts about it.

'Constance's room,' he explained.

A second bedroom could be glimpsed through the half-open connecting doors, a smaller double-bedded version of the downstairs drawing room (the room he had shared with his late wife). Separate bedrooms for this woman who didn't want to be *married* to a pathologist. Dora found herself hugging the thought.

There was a picture of two small, blazered boys on a table just outside the bedroom but nothing in the room itself. Also quite a good sign.

The first child, Alfred, had been conceived on the honeymoon and the second, Bertram (after his late uncle), began life exactly three days after his mother returned from the maternity home. Another son (Cuthbert) had been due to arrive in time to celebrate his parents' third wedding anniversary but that toast was never drunk.

Alfred Kemble had worn a black armband for the statutory two months but this widower's weed didn't seem to discourage the busy hostesses of Kensington. The increasingly eminent Dr Kemble was regularly pestered with invitations to dinners, luncheons – even Saturday to Mondays (although his sons – still only three and two – were very obvious flies in the social ointment).

Either the boys were inconsolable or they were a great deal more badly behaved than he had ever realised. When their original nursemaid had decamped (without notice: such a *fuss*, honestly) he had applied to an employment agency, throwing himself on the mercy of the (extremely susceptible) proprietor, who duly unearthed Nanny Lynch, whose bittersweet blend of discipline and devotion had worked wonders within days of her arrival.

Nanny had no complaints about the domestic arrangements – so much simpler when there was no mother to spoil the poor orphaned lambs or disrupt her tidy routines. Nanny ordered and supervised their meals, bought their clothes, combed their hair, even chose their schools, but this really very satisfactory state of affairs was not to last. There were women everywhere.

Much to everyone's surprise and pique, the eligible Dr Kemble's fancy eventually lighted on Miss Valentine, the departmental typist. Miss Valentine (unlike a surprising percentage of her immediate competition) had held out firmly for matrimony. Alfred Kemble, tempted daily by sleek ankles, a neat figure and a vague but not unpleasant smell of suburban flower gardens and thwarted constantly in his attempts to ambush her in the supplies cupboard, eventually decided that she would serve as well as any.

Nanny had been reluctant to yield her newly gained empire, and her charges, taking their cue from her starchy sniffs and evasions, resolved to dislike their new mama. While this was not in itself a condemnation – they disliked all sorts of perfectly nice, wholesome things: kippers, strawberries, *baths* – it made a slight nonsense of the idea of a second wife. Certain areas of the doctor's life were greatly simplified, to be sure, and the exhausting run of dinner invitations fell off sharply, but Constance's well-nourished young body was not really adequate compensation for the very doubtful pleasure of her company.

He had told Dora half the truth. She really had, for an irritating while, tried to persuade him to move to another branch of medicine – re-train if you please – but had eventually admitted defeat. Without the department in common their conversation was miserably diminished. She continued to take a polite (if not particularly intelligent) interest in his daily doings but he found it hard to return the compliment when she cut the crusts off her conversation and parried with news of a morning at the stores or a dress fitting or an afternoon's bridge at her mother's. Worse still, after the first dutiful surrenderings, she became less and less willing to pass through his expert hands.

This increasing distaste for her husband's profession, combined with his habit of waking up screaming about 'rats as big as fucking cats get 'em off me Hubbard!' was what had caused her to decamp to the adjoining room, which she had done up in pink satin and parcel gilt like a behind-the-lines knocking shop. It was, apparently, an exact replica of the bedroom of a Mrs Van Rooden which she had seen pictured in one of the idiotic magazines she was forever buying.

Lady Mary Kemble, by then installed in the Berkshire nursing home where she spent her last agonising year, had been merciless. The first daughter-in-law was not all she might have hoped but the second had remained in a resolutely uninteresting condition for three whole years of marriage despite transforming the marital bedroom into a perfumed tart's boudoir of in-des-*cri*-ba-ble vulgarity. Why Constance would want to ape the tastes of anyone déclassée enough to have their own home photographed in the public prints was an enduring mystery to her mother-in-law.

The whole beastly room reeked of scent, noted Dora. Ghastly. Alfred Kemble sat on a pink velvet piano stool thingy in front of the dressing table. He lit a cigarette and placed the spent match in one of the crystal dishes on the glass top. Dora spied a brown glass medicine bottle tucked behind the dressing set: Veronal. Kemble picked up a scent spray.

'Shalimar. It means "temple of love" in Sanskrit – or so Constance keeps telling me.'

There was a small pile of index cards and a fountain pen on the glass top of the dressing table and his bag – the big, bad bag full of blades and jars – was on the floor at his side. He leaned down and pulled something out: a black or brown something about eighteen inches long with a sort of loopy thing at one end.

'I wondered if you might help me with another little experiment. You were such a *sport* the other day. Hubbard has always been very accommodating but I suspect this is slightly beyond the call of duty. All entirely above board. Constance is visiting her mother in Surrey and Nanny and the boys are infesting the Science Museum but Mrs Bateman our cook is within screaming distance if you're worried about a chaperone.'

He rose from the stool and pushed it against the wall to clear a space in front of the dressing table.

'It's in connection with a case.' Unlike him not to say which. The index cards on the dressing table were blank. 'My, er, associate over in the hospital found me an amputated limb to play with but I need to see the effect on living tissue to decide whether injuries are *pre* or *post mortem*.' His thumb stroked the plaited leather. 'Strangely enough, it is well-nigh impossible to whip oneself – surprisingly difficult to bring the necessary force to bear. Won't take a moment, I promise. I'm sure you must be itching to get back to Hubbard and the whole A to Z business. Do we have anything filed under Z? Attacks by zebras? Or Zoster? Nasty condition but I don't think anyone ever died of it.'

He handed Dora the whip while he removed his shirt. The handle still had a fine dusting of mercury powder where Scotland Yard had once tested it for fingerprints. It gave the leather a dry, silky, rosin-y feel like the bow of the violin her father had so very badly wanted her to play (and that she had played so very badly). Her trembling fingers automatically spread out along the leather – quite the wrong grip. She switched to a firm forehand hold – *an absolute flat unspun stroke is the ideal to aim at* – and raised her arm uncertainly. It was all faintly reminiscent of one of the racier scenes from *The Sermons of John Donne*.

'Hard as you like. Probably best to surprise me.'

He certainly looked surprised. Jolly surprised – but not unpleasantly so. His pupils blossomed with shock as the plaited leather cracked down on his shoulder.

'Not there, you fool. Where I can see.'

Again the sharp whistle as the whip sliced through the air, the satisfying *thwack* as it hit its aim.

The marks on the skin appeared almost instantaneously. He didn't cry out and his first thought was to take note of the impact made by well-oiled hide on living tissue. The green scribble was accompanied by a quick sketch of the red chevron design already emerging on his skin. Only then did he look at her.

'Hard to judge from the scars but the pattern from the tip is better defined, suggesting that the attacker in the case was standing and the victim lying on her back.'

He winced noticeably as he bent his legs to kneel at Dora's feet and she was suddenly reminded of Vazard's pub story of Hubbard's heroics and smiled as she tried to picture the weedy young corporal carrying his wounded boss to safety, like the engraving of Aeneas and Anchises in her Latin primer.

Kemble lay down, his flesh very white against the sugary pink of Constance's carpet. The even melody of his voice was, as always, peculiarly at odds with his subject matter.

'Just a few more strokes just *here*, if you would. I need to see the effect on the areola.'

Dora imagined herself swatting a large, pinkish-brown fly and brought her arm down harder and faster than before.

His gasp was drowned out by the piercing cry of the smart white telephone on the bedside table. His hand, which was poised over the waistband of his flannels, reached across for the receiver. Was there indeed? Was Sir Godfrey not available?

Was he, by Jove. Yes, he supposed so, Dr Vazard could meet him there. Kemble got into his shirt with soldierly speed while Dora retreated to the landing.

'Thank you, Mrs Strange'. His voice was the last thing to recover. 'That will have to do for today. You can find your own way out, can't you? I need to make some more sketches while the marks are still fresh.'

The omnibus was practically empty at that time of day. Dora sat at the front and closed her eyes, losing herself in a very different version of events. She imagined Kemble ushering her up the stairs and then leaning against the bolted bedroom door, flannels unbuttoned, imagined his surprise and delight as she fell to her knees on the carpet and showed him all she had learned from *The Tenant of Wildfell Hall Volume II* ('manly elixir,' all that malarkey). How surprised he would have been. Oh Mrs Strange. Whatever were girls taught in school these days. And as he rebuttoned his flannels she would notice the handle of the whip sticking out of his bag but this time it would be she who grasped it, she who decided which patterns should be made.

Chapter 20

'Hubbard knows all about it'? No, he jolly well didn't. Hubbard knew precisely nothing of Dora's morning trip to Lexham Gardens. What time did she call this?

'Dr Kemble was working at home this morning. He telephoned to my diggings to ask for my help with an experiment.'

'What experiment? What case was he working on?'

'He didn't say.'

Thankfully Mrs A's trolley crashed through the door before he could question her further.

Dora spent the hour before lunch mechanically cross-referencing case cards, a fiddly but undemanding task that allowed her mind free rein. Constance, vulgar, perfumed, undeserving little Constance, didn't want to be married to a pathologist so she was unlikely to demur at divorcing one. The boys could decently be packed off to some high security prep school somewhere – far better for them. She hadn't got as far as doing up the house. She wasn't really all that fussed about curtains and what have you although the putrid pink boudoir would have to go. And the whole separate bedrooms nonsense. She felt another sudden charge of desire remembering him lying shirtless on the carpet. Had they really been collecting evidence for a case? None of the necropsies in her filing piles had mentioned whips and there was nothing in the papers . . .

Vazard, who was spending more and more of his time over in the main hospital, paid them a visit after lunch. He had ostensibly come to collect a file but stayed hovering around Dora's desk, complimenting her on the progress she'd made with the filing, stammering slightly.

'I was wondering . . .'

Dora's telephone rang. It was Kemble.

'I trust you've made full notes on this morning's experiment.' Hubbard glanced over at the telephone suspiciously, waiting for her to transfer the call to someone more qualified to deal with it. She held the receiver close against her ear so that Kemble's smutty whispers couldn't be heard. 'Later, more careful examination revealed that there was also a series of herringbone abrasions on the chest and marks of a similar pattern discernible on the silky white skin of the urinary meatus which had been inflicted some time after the marks on the torso.'

Vazard was still yammering on. Now that the weather was growing milder he wondered if Miss, er, Strang might, er, care to join him on a little Saturday outing. The other voice continued in her ear.

'The marks of the whip suggested that the original assailant had been standing over the victim.'

She cupped her hand over the mouthpiece.

'Saturday? I can't, I'm afraid.'

She turned back to the telephone.

'No. No. I'm afraid Dr Kemble is not to be disturbed.'

Vazard was still there.

'Quite sure? Healing blast of Surrey air? Guard against sunlight starvation?'

'Yes. I've made a full note of your findings'.

She shot him a busy smile.

'I can't. My aunt is in town. Another time?'

'Right-ho. Maybe next Saturday? I shan't forget.'

The telephone had gone dead. She could sense Hubbard watching her.

Chapter 21

Nanny had not been in favour of the boys' outing to the pathology department. Nanny hated travelling of any kind and only really approved of journeys that were within walking distance of Kensington Gardens. Born and brought up in King's Lynn, her London was even smaller than Dora's: the park to the north, Ranelagh to the south and no further east than Drury Lane (and then only at Christmas). She had a particular aversion to the underground railway. Taximeter cabs were bad enough but *anyone* could use the 'Tube': never knew who you might sit next to, what you might catch. The Circle Line to Euston Square took Nanny through places that simply weren't on her personal map of the world. Supposing the locomotive were to break down and they had to get out? Where *was* the Edgware Road?

Despite her fears, Nanny delivered her charges safely to the Willcox Wing. The smaller (supposedly more endearing) child was not his usual self, apparently.

'We've got another of our nasty little rashes, haven't we?' The child glared at her as if to say 'speak for yourself.' 'And we've been off our food today, haven't we?' Which wasn't at all like us according to Nanny, who was mistakenly convinced that everyone found her charges' insides as gripping as she obviously did. 'Not *at all* like us. Best mince and then rice pudding and jam? And we hardly touched it.'

Which was not strictly true, as Kemble major swiftly made plain.

'*I* would have eaten his pudding,' confided his brother, 'but *she* wouldn't let me.'

'That's quite enough of that, Alfred.'

'*She* ate it. *All* the pudding. And the mince. I *loathe* mince.' New word: Loathe. Using it showed his tongue, all brown from his last stick of liquorice.

'*Do* stop it, you two!' whined Bertram in an unconscious parody of his stepmother's incessant refrain. 'I've got a splitting headache'.

'Don't be silly, Bertram. Little boys don't get headaches,' decreed Nanny, unanswerably.

'Would you like to see Lindberg? He's in here.' The elder child proudly produced a matchbox from his blazer pocket.

'I'm sure Mrs Strange doesn't want to see your caterpillar.' Nanny's loyal soul was secretly convinced that she would really (but Nanny was, of course, right the first time).

Alfred stared pointedly at Dora's desk.

'Can we have some of your sweets?'

'What sweets?'

'In your drawer. In a little tin. Mrs Whatsit always let us.'

'There aren't any.'

'Greedy.'

Nanny pretended to rebuke him then reminded him to tell the assembled company how the three of them had spent the last hour and Alfred took the floor with a speech that broke all previous records for tedium. He rocked back and forth on his Nanny-polished lace-up shoes as he spoke, like someone reciting 'Gunga Din'.

'We-eeee.'

He had a particularly irritating voice. It was self-consciously childlike, as if he were reading every word aloud from a book with small words and big pictures. With difficulty.

'We went. We went to the muuuseeeum. We went to the museum and I saw *bones*.' He seemed to be incapable of closing his mouth.

Their father patted them both warily on the head and gave them each a shilling. Two fine sons, people always said (safe in the knowledge that they would never have to spend more than fifteen consecutive minutes in their company).

'Come along, Alfred. The lady and gentlemen are very busy.'

Happily, a recent unscheduled arrival from one of the operating theatres had placed the lab itself squarely out of bounds. The older boy was disappointed but not entirely surprised.

'Swizz. I *knew* we wouldn't be seeing anything decent. Can't I just have one look at the *cadaver*?' A word so new and special it had its own private matchbox in his brain to keep it in. 'I am nine.'

'Say goodbye to your father, boys.'

The nine-year-old shook hands and grunted at his father, who was sunning his back at the office window in the two-minute blast of daylight that visited the third floor each afternoon. He was quite obviously itching for the pair of them to clear off. What had he been thinking of? The younger boy was pushed towards him but winced unattractively as the afternoon sun streamed across his face and he retreated back to the skirts of Nanny's navy gaberdine raincoat.

'Don't sulk, Bertram, please. Off you go. Mind Nanny.'

The nursery party filed out into the green gloom of the corridor. The air in the room was spiked deliciously with sulphur the moment the door closed as three cigarettes were simultaneously lit.

'Fine boys, sir,' mumbled Vazard (someone had had to say it and he seemed to have drawn the short straw). 'Shame about the little chap's headache. Does he suffer from them a lot?'

Kemble absently lit a second cigarette (although his first was still smouldering in the ashtray), completely forgetting to answer.

Chapter 22

The funeral was as bad as it could possibly have been. Worse. It was held in Bournemouth where the parents of the first Mrs Kemble had unaccountably decided to retire, making the ceremony a monumental inconvenience for everyone but themselves.

Mrs Moulton, little Bertram's grandmama, had not particularly wanted to take charge of the arrangements but it was not the type of thing you could trust a man like Kemble to carry out decently, and it was hardly a stepmother's place to bury her predecessor's children. Not at all The Thing. The Thing (whatever it may have been) loomed very large in Mrs Moulton's life: dictating her menus, selecting her gowns, drawing up her guest lists. She and Mr Moulton had their Position to think of and she thought of hers a very great deal. In the end poor Hubbard had done most of the legwork, putting in the announcements, getting the body down from London and so forth (no picnic during the Easter holiday).

Dorothy Moulton had actually seen very little of the child but he'd seemed a nice enough boy. She had never been 'grandmama'. That particular title had been nabbed by the other side but she hadn't especially wanted it. When Alfred had first begun to talk (*disgracefully* late, the child was nearly three before anyone got a word of sense out of him) she and her husband were still only in their mid forties and in no hurry for grand-anything. They had tried to get the boys to call them Dottie and Tonto. The children, confused and congenitally bloody-minded, called them both 'Sir'.

The service had been timed to finish at half past two (tea was cheaper than luncheon). It had rained heavily the entire morning, which was rather pleasing (spring sunshine would have set quite the wrong tone). The mourners had shambled about with umbrellas at the graveside then crawled back to the house in a series of large unheated cars for a frugal and unappetising collation of curling sandwiches (salmon paste or tongue), cut at the crack of dawn from loaves bought the previous day, and lukewarm China tea in cold white china cups borrowed from the vicarage. Mrs Moulton's largest tea set only had twenty-one cups (and twenty-three saucers) and although she wasn't expecting a huge turn-out you never quite knew with funerals. In the event, there would have been more than enough of the Royal Worcester to go round.

Anyone in hopes of anything stronger than Lapsang Suchong was in for a disappointment, but Kemble, who had known the Moultons for the best part of a decade, had come prepared. As soon as they arrived back at the house he had cornered Dora by the huge bay window with his back to the family group and silently poured brown liquid into his cup and hers from a sizeable silver flask. It made the tea taste jolly peculiar but it was the first time she had felt warm all day. The in-laws had no fires after Good Friday and had trusted that the crush of people would take the chill off their icy front parlour.

Little Alfred was wearing a worryingly tight Eton suit and had stationed himself at the far end of the tea table where he could work his way through the plate of chocolate wafer biscuits unobserved by Nanny, who was, once again, savouring the sudden decline of young Bertram with one of the Moultons' golf club friends: 'Bright as a button at the museum that morning and dead on the playroom floor by suppertime.'

'How dreadful for young Alfred,' mused Dora aloud to the pathologist, 'to lose his brother.'

'I lost both of mine.' As if he were playing a private game of bereavement lotto whereby the loss of brothers, wife, son effortlessly trumped Alfred's loss of Bertram. He had insisted that Dora come with him to the funeral – 'I shall need to get some reports written up on the train' – but there had been no Cranford-style kisses, no words even, just the occasional rustle of newspaper, the regular hiss of a lighted match.

'Have you come far?' The late mother-in-law had buttonholed Dora during her careful circuit of the room. 'I'm Dorothy Moulton, Bertram's grandmother.' The (bone-dry) lace handkerchief she was holding between her pinky-blue fingertips fluttered a little at the grandson's name. 'And you must be . . . ?'

'Dora Strang. I work for Dr Kemble at the hospital. He felt that someone should come along to represent the department.'

'Secretary, I suppose?' She gave the word all four syllables and flared her lips away from her mouth as she pronounced it, like someone eating something messy and afraid to smudge the rouge on their lips. 'Constance, the present Mrs Kemble, was Alfred's secretary too. Ye-es,' she pronounced it to rhyme with 'race'. 'She was Alfred's secretary. But that was *after* Ottilie died,' she conceded.

Meanwhile the other mourners were transfixed by the arrival of an old woman painstakingly lagged in sundry shades and textures of black. Her body was like a vast embroidered cushion of jet, bombazine, grosgrain and moiré embellished with wormy tubes of silk, interlaced in a Celtic design of faggoting and what may well have been Mountmellick work: a walking sample book of fashionable Dickensian mourning wear.

Dora wondered at first whether the old crone had simply lurked in the church during the funeral, all dressed up for a spot of tea and sympathy, and bagged a ride in one of the cars going back to the house.

Mrs Moulton stopped pretending to talk to Dora, grabbed her husband's sleeve as he passed and nodded her sharp, powdery nose in the old lady's direction.

'Excuse me a moment, Mrs er.'

The two of them moved away and began whispering together. Dora thought for one glorious moment that the old lady would be asked to leave or stretchered off by a gang of pall-bearers but it turned out she had a perfect right to be there.

'Hello, Nellie, old girl. Bad business this.' The pathologist poured a large slug of his brandy into the old lady's teacup.

'I had to come on the train. Long way, Bournemouth. Three hours not including the cab up to Waterloo. I come in a car the only other time. They don't ask me down much.' She nodded accusingly in the direction of Mrs Moulton. 'No skin off my bleedin' nose.' She looked sharply at the prettily pleated fan of coloured paper in the empty grate. 'Wouldn't have hurt to light a fire on a day like this but that's her all over: tight as arseholes.'

Nellie had a rather loud, deliciously penetrating voice and her last word detonated very nicely in the pious hush of the room. Everyone had turned to look at poor Dorothy's secret aunt-in-law in her absurd fancy dress mourning get-up, but the pathologist seemed cheered by the sight of the strange old lady, her funereal largesse so out of place among the niggardly black armbands and glumly smart gowns. A good half of Nellie's big walnut wardrobe was taken up with bodices and spencers and tippets that never saw daylight at any other time (she liked cheerful colours as a rule) as well as a big old cigar box full of black-edged handkerchiefs and a vast collection of mourning jewellery made from the plaited hair of the long-forgotten dead trapped in isinglass lockets – her own particular harem of fetishes.

Nellie's determination to attend the funeral hadn't a great deal to do with her feelings for her great-nephew (whom she had hardly met) but she seemed indignant at his early death nonetheless.

'It's a rotten shame. Little kid like that. Rotten bloody shame. Men-in-gi-tis? You didn't look after him proper. What's the good of having a doctor in the family if they don't look after their own?'

Dora turned to watch the pathologist's face, watch his reaction to the question that everyone else had left unspoken.

'You can doctor him now all right, I suppose? Now he's dead.'

Nellie took a long, consoling sip of tea. 'Only saw him twice, of course. Once at the christening and then again at his mum's funeral.'

She looked down at the sooty carapace of beads and brocade, like bubbles of pitch on the side of a barrel. Her hastily-drawn brown eyebrows scribbled a little ripple of befuddlement across her forehead, as if surprised that she should, by some peculiar coincidence, be wearing precisely the same outfit today.

'Your new Mrs Kemble looks very smart.' An accusation, not an observation. Dora turned to the door where a pretty, business-like woman in a black coat and skirt was carefully putting up her veil. Kemble spotted her entrance and immediately ushered the old lady to the refreshment table on the far side of the room, wheeling his back to the door like a waltzer changing tack.

The second Mrs Kemble had dressed the part but seemed puzzled and slightly resentful: surrounded by the basic ingredients of grief and wondering how on earth to assemble them into something other people might recognise as maternal feeling (*cold fish and how to disguise it*).

She was particularly disappointed not to find a glass of sherry waiting for her. Constance Kemble liked sherry and she'd had nothing since the train. A very accommodating salesmen in the wines and spirits department at one of the big stores had taught her that Madam could get a really very drinkable amontillado (*un*drinkable amontillado didn't bear thinking about) for only thirty shillings a dozen. He was also kind enough to mark it up as 'sundries' in the monthly accounts – not that Freddie even bothered to glance at the bills any more.

Constance had been delighted to hand over the funeral arrangements to old Mother Moulton – what did one call the woman? Aboriginal tribesmen apparently had a separate word for every grade of family relationship: younger brother's wife's sister, the lot. There had been an article in *The Listener* about it. 'My husband's first mother-in-law' ought to be a piece of cake. Anyway, the two women had agreed (for once) that it really wouldn't, really *really* wouldn't be fitting for Constance to take charge. It was sad. Very sad. Poor little boy. Poor dozy, spotty, dreary, humourless, philatelic, numismatic, adenoidal little boy. In any case, Constance had hardly been well placed to direct operations as she had been spending the last two weeks in her old bedroom at her mother's house in Guildford and had only returned when Nanny telephoned with the news.

She'd only met the Moultons themselves twice but she must have had a suspiciously smart, second wifely look about her because everyone in the room seemed to have deduced who she was. They were positively queuing up to lavish her with condolences. Yes, it was sad. *Veh, veh* sad. Like Mrs Moulton she had a little scrap of lawn to play with (also bone dry). The sickly vanilla scent of Shalimar on the fabric was so strong and evoked the morning in the Lexham Gardens bedroom so vividly that Dora almost heaved. She took a deep breath.

'Mrs Kemble? I work in your husband's department.'

Constance Kemble looked Dora up and down without ceremony, a sneery glance taking in the drab clothes, the uncoiffed hair.

'It's Strange, isn't it? *Mrs* Strange, presumably. We spoke on the telephone. Your husband was in the navy, I believe?' A queer look in her eye; a knowing glance at Dora's gold band; an even sicker feeling in Dora's stomach. She could feel her muscles trying to iron the misery out of her face, out of her voice.

'A very sad occasion. It must have been a terrible shock to you all,' recited Dora. 'Such a nice little chap.'

But Constance Kemble was in no mood for funereal small talk.

'I very nearly didn't come at all. I was hardly "mummy", was I? He'd only just learned to stop calling me Mrs Valentine.'

Mrs Valentine. Had Mrs Valentine been a good sport?

'I could probably have got out of it.' There was an actressy trace of kohl pencil round those angry brown eyes. 'No one would blame me, would they? "In *her* condition …" I can just imagine them saying it. They'd already let me off arranging the funeral. I couldn't have done it from Guildford in any case. I had to go up to town yesterday, dig out something suitable to wear but I'm going back tonight. I'm not going back there. Let Nanny sort it out.'

Her breath smelled of Parma violets. Dora wondered whether she had been drinking although the glazed expression didn't look much like tipsiness. She thought of the Veronal bottle on the Lexham Gardens dressing table.

The angry eyes skewered Dora once again.

'Do you know how the first Mrs Kemble met her end?' She lowered her voice. 'Not even old Mother Moulton knows the real answer to this one. I only know because the cook told me. She bled to death by the hall telephone *making a fuss*, trying to drag him away from an interesting little necropsy.' She puffed sharply on her absurdly smart ebony cigarette holder. 'Not a risk I plan to take.'

She made a dutiful (if rather unsteady) circuit of the room, being coldly consoled, then kissed Dorothy Moulton's chilly cheek, announcing that she had a taxi waiting. She made a point of saying goodbye to Dora.

'My doctor tells me I'm in no condition to make the journey twice in one day so I'm staying at the Royal Bath, which is proving rather a disappointment for an hotel whose telegraphic address is "Luxuriate". I think if I had a telegraphic address of my own I should like it to be "Enchantment" – don't you think? What about you, Mrs Strange, what would yours be?'

'What was she saying to you?' Kemble emptied the last of his flask into his cold tea.

'Nothing. She didn't say anything.'

Kemble drained his cup and took his watch from his pocket.

'I have some reports to write back at the lab, Mrs Strange. Sorry, Dorothy. Can't stay, I'm afraid. Thank you for all you've done. Very sad business.'

The room rumbled with tuttings of sympathy at the great man laid low by his loss but Dora could hear the kindly coos rising to a scandalised buzz as she fidgeted into her galoshes in the front hall – 'Not so much as one word to each other. Very bad form.'

Kemble took her hand once they were seated in the back of the motor and pushed it into his lap. Like a stone in his pocket.

They had first-class tickets but he pinched tight hold of her arm and once again hurried her on past the Pullman carriages to the second-class coaches. The guard's signal was sounding loud and shrill through the open window but, just as they were pulling away, Dora reached out for the handle and somehow tumbled out of the compartment and in again through the next door along. The stationmaster's whistle drowned out the guard's reproachful shouts.

It was the fashion for the Upper Third and Lower Fourth forms to cry buckets on the school train at the start of each term. The younger girls would carry snapshots of loved ones (mostly four-legged) as an aid to ululation. But the tears dried up abruptly at the start of the Upper Fourth when the girls made the thrilling switch from panamas to boaters and weeping was decreed 'Early Victorian' unless a pet had actually died (or a younger brother, obviously). Dora lay full length on the seat, feeling the tears drizzling down the side of her head and tickling their way into her ears as she thought of Constance. Constance, who supposedly hadn't wanted to be married to a pathologist. Constance and her interesting blasted condition. Living proof that she had, on at least one occasion relatively recently, wanted to be married to a pathologist after all.

Chapter 23

There must have been a hundred letters of condolence. Every coroner, every prosecuting counsel, every police superintendent, every mortuary keeper felt obliged to write, mourning the passing of this small boy they had never met. The sensible ones kept it short but a surprising number felt the need to match the death with some loss of their own.

The pathologist had debated having a card printed thanking them for their thoughts at this time, but those ghostly victims of long illnesses bravely borne or cut down like flowers by everything from Spanish flu to Clapham omnibuses made a uniform response impossible – or so Nanny Lynch said. Nanny Lynch's long career in childcare had left her extremely well informed on the subject of sudden infant death and Nanny Lynch said all letters must be answered personally, handwritten with one's newest nib.

Nanny Lynch was too busy with the remaining child to offer her own services as amanuensis. Young Alfred had been invited to spend the rest of the Easter vac in rainy Bournemouth but had kicked up a stink at the thought of being walled up on the South coast with Dottie and rotten old Tonto. 'Can't I stay with Nanny? Can't I? There's *lots* to sort out' (his brother's stamp collection to start with: there was a Penny Red plate number he had his eye on).

When his first wife had died Alfred Kemble's mother had supplied him with a ream of cream laid headed paper printed with a thick black border, but although he had received a flood of letters telling him what a marvellous woman his wife had been and how they themselves had felt when their wives, husbands, parents, sweethearts, Airedales etc. had crossed the great divide, the mourning stationery had remained untouched.

The pathologist placed all 480 sheets of it on Dora's desk on Tuesday morning together with a vast bundle of envelopes (many of them not even opened).

He gazed at the pile with evident distaste.

'Mrs Strange, I wonder if you would be kind enough to deal with this for me.'

'Couldn't Mrs Kemble reply on your behalf?'

'Mrs Kemble is no longer in residence. No need to do them by hand. Whatever you think appropriate. Sign them pp.'

The letters of form were easy enough. Just another typing exercise: 'I must try not to be so mournful I must try not to be so mournful.'

There was just one used sheet scrunched into the top of the open packet – the widower's sole attempt at replying to the first bereavement. It was easy to see why he hadn't sent it. More like a case history than a letter: 'sudden placental abruption resulting in haemorrhage and death'.

Wives did die, reflected Dora. Wives died all the time. Especially pregnant wives. Especially tipsy pregnant wives with Veronal bottles on their dressing tables. Dora had a whole drawerful of case cards to prove it. 'Twenty-six years old, hitherto excellent health, no evidence of pre-existing disease' etc. She held this cruelly comforting thought as her fingers carried out the task. 'Dear Sir Godfrey, I write to thank you for your letter of condolence on the death of my wife Constance.' Whoops. Dora had actually typed the words. She crushed the sheet in her hand and stuffed it into her coat pocket.

Hubbard was looking at her dumbly from behind his corner desk. He had arrived that morning wearing a black armband on his sleeve but had removed it when he realised that he was alone in his show of grief.

'Many left to do?' It was almost human.

'Dr Kemble has asked me to pp these but I can't possibly, can I? Bad enough having them typed.'

And so, after Dora had banged out the first few dozen, the pair of them sat either side of Dora's desk with the bottle of green ink between them and forged their way guiltily through the pile of near-identical letters. Then Hubbard produced a saucer of water and a scrap of sponge and Dora folded while he stuffed and sealed the envelopes.

'Nice little chap.'

'Well this is all very cosy,' breezed Kemble when he arrived back from his morning's rummage among the entrails of the dead.

Hubbard sprang away from Dora's desk like a dog caught sharing the cat's chaise longue. Dr Kemble had been offered a few days' leave but had preferred to soldier on with post-mortems at Ealing and St Pancras. He had again borrowed Vazard from the obstetrics department to take notes as he worked (Hubbard's long face was a continual reproach). The rather wan-looking houseman entered the office just as the lab door closed behind the pathologist – had he hung back on purpose? Vazard's smile seemed like an afterthought as he placed the chief's Gladstone bag on the floor and fished a small sheaf of papers from his overcoat pocket.

'Coronary aneurism and a ten-year-old girl with diphtheria. Open and shut (or so the coroner thought). All in my very best copperplate.'

Dora finished the letter she was typing ('I was so very sorry that Bertram's passing should have awakened such sad memories for you'), then fed a post-mortem form into the machine and began tap-tapping her way through the death of another child. Open and shut? Open and shut the abdomen. Open and shut the ribcage. Open and shut the skull. Samples of every organ. Vaginal swabs . . .

There was no one in the lab when Dora took the typed forms through and it was another hour before she heard the pathologist return from a long, lawyerly lunch (brown soup, white fish, red meat). She ploughed on with cross-reffing the case notes, forever shunting the existing cards from drawer to drawer as more and still more asphyxiations and brain haemorrhages and carcinomas took their proper place in Hubbard's almighty system. Syphilis cross-references now took up two whole drawers. A box of cards was soon used up.

Dora took care to turn the handle of the supplies cupboard door as slowly and quietly as she could, but opening it somehow sucked at the entrance on the laboratory side, producing a telltale click.

'Hello again.'

Was it France that had taught him to whisper so very, very quietly? His face and hair added a strong saloon-bar smell to the double chemistry flavour of the room. His mouth tasted of cigars and the hands that tore open the buttons under her camiknickers had been chilled by the long walk back from Fleet Street. In less time than it took to unzip an abdomen, her skirt had been bunched round her waist and she had been lifted bodily and perched on the sill of the sightless supplies cupboard window. Kemble looked down at her as he tucked a sheet of pale green blotting paper between her tail end and the painted wood. A cursory, diagnostic glance, as if checking for any sign of assault or pre-existing disease then suddenly, without a kiss, without a caress, he unbuttoned his trousers and began work, the cold fingers pinching the backs of her knees as his pelvis rolled sulkily back and forth against hers. 'She learned the mystery of love between two souls and her maiden's secrets were opened to his straining shaft as he poured his boiling essence into Alice.' Nothing about pain. Nothing about the beastly look on his face. Dora threw her head back to keep the tears from falling and bit her lip to keep in the scream. The door wasn't even properly shut.

When it was over he reached behind him and tweaked a piece of cotton wool from one of the blue paper packets on the shelf then, one-handed, uncorked a small brown bottle, tipped a few drops of purple liquid on to the white wadding and deftly polished himself for luck – 'good old pinky-panky' – before re-buttoning his fly.

'We're getting low on report forms, Mrs Strange. Remind me to order some.'

The man of her dreams.

Dora screwed up the stained sheet of blotting paper and tamped it between her legs before dropping down on to the linoleum and fumbling together the buttons of her blouse. Her skirt fell back into place. No telltale creases scarred the pleated box of thornproof tweed. The sated ghosts of the ravished heroines of *Cranford* and *Wildfell Hall* tiptoed from the room, embarrassed by the gulf that had opened up between fantasy and reality.

She was still resting the crown of her head against the icy glass of the window when the door on the office side opened behind her.

'We ought to move your desk in here.'

Dora tilted her head back to upright and some of her tears fell out. She sniffed and straightened her shaking shoulders, taking care to keep the scratchy pledget of blotting paper in place (*orifices plugged and all traces of other matter swabbed away. As if you and your instruments had never been . . .*).

'Sorry. Very early Victorian.'

Vazard's arms folded around her very, very tightly, pressing her wet face against his chest. He seemed to be kissing her hair.

'Bit thick of him to make you do all those letters. Wouldn't be quite so bad if we hadn't all met the kid.'

Dora pulled away slightly and he began dabbing her face very, very gently with another boll of cotton from the dark blue packet.

'There.' Another gentle dab. 'I blame myself in a way. I mean it's been nearly twenty years since the chief gave any thought to clinical symptoms but the headache and the photophobia are classic second-year stuff. Poor little chap.'

'Dr Kemble didn't look at him at all. You really mustn't blame yourself. "Doctors are not infallible and are so often wrong" as the defence bods always say.'

'Most encouraging.'

He still wasn't letting go. What made him kiss her? Had what Kemble had done somehow made her kissable? Or was it the room itself? The grey-green six-by-four cell probably stank of stolen embraces. The silk-stockinged Mrs Culvey. Or Miss Harris, Dora's immediate predecessor, who had left without notice after only a week – although not before typing herself a glowing reference. Dora had found it (filed in a folder tartly labelled 'Departmental resignations 1929 to date'): 'Miss Harris has been a real boon to the department and remained admirably focused on her work regardless of the many distractions of this busy laboratory and would be an asset to any clerical sphere.' Well played, Miss Harris.

'Have you many more letters to do?'

'Only a few. I broke off to do some cross-referencing for a bit of light relief. I've reached the Epping Forest case.'

'Oh dear me yes: "Injuries too revolting to describe" – not that that stopped Kemble. Good for nearly a dozen cards I should think. Very nasty.' But he was smiling at her. As if he were pleased at the thought of her weak stomach, as if he actually rather wanted her to be early Victorian.

'Chin up, old thing. I sometimes wonder whether you're cut out for anything quite as morbid as Morbid Anatomy. Which reminds me, the mother-and-baby people are short a typist. We lose the odd one but far less gruesome on the whole. You might apply . . .'

His hand carried on absently smoothing her hair until he suddenly caught sight of his wristwatch. He was due back at Obstetrics at three . . . Look here, talking of early Victorian, would she like to spend Saturday at the Crystal Palace? Had she ever been? His landlady would cut them a few sandwiches. The train went from Victoria. He could pick her up from her diggings – or meet under the clock if she'd rather. So eager. Like a spaniel with its lead in its mouth.

Dora didn't want Vazard to take her to Crystal Palace. She didn't especially want him to kiss her but the whispery voice and the kindly embrace were so strange, so sweet, so soft . . . She nodded dumbly.

'Splendid. And what should Mrs Tottle put in the sandwiches?'

'Not meat.'

Chapter 24

A long, quietly tearful bath at bedtime had enabled Dora to get to sleep surprisingly easily but she woke before four and lay listening to the distant ping of the ormolu clock in the drawing room. As it inaccurately struck the hours, she relived the hateful few minutes in the supplies cupboard and drafted endless letters of resignation. Letters written in the same kind of code the papers used when reporting crimes too revolting to describe.

A dull grey light was struggling through the gap in the curtains at six and she thought of Oswald Jelly eating his hearty breakfast as the clock chimed. His execution merited barely a paragraph in the morning papers, crowded off the crime pages by the forthcoming trial of a woman charged with murdering her newborn baby: 'Kemble to speak for the prosecution'.

He was already in his hat and overcoat when Dora arrived at the office and was tetchily winding his watch and staring crossly at Hubbard's empty desk. The pathologist was preparing a paper on abortion and infanticide for one of his leagues and he had wanted Hubbard to tag along and take notes from the gallery but he still hadn't materialised by nine thirty.

'Perhaps Mrs Strange will oblige.' He didn't look at her as he said it. 'I need to leave at once to consult with the legal chaps. Mrs Strange can follow by taxi.'

'Should be mildly fascinating,' said Vazard, as Kemble swept from the room. 'Only wish I could join you but it could be a shade awkward – a conflict of interest, you might say. Mr Steen, my present boss over in tots and bots, is down as an expert witness for the alleged baby killer – actually telephoned to the defence and offered his services. He and the chief have locked horns before. Similar case to this: dead baby, unmarried mother, squalid two-roomed tenement. Steen always gives the benefit of the doubt in baby cases – as does the law, pretty much – but the chief sees abortioners everywhere. All highly explosive.'

'And the tenement woman – last time – was she found guilty?'

'Oh Lord, yes. The chief really threw all his weight behind it. Showed no mercy: clear case of antenatal infanticide – pretty strong given the remains weren't discovered for nearly a year – but the judge was with him – "no name in Britain, no name in Europe, on medico-legal questions is on the same plane as the name of Kemble", all that guff – and the jury were powerless to resist. Mind you, it didn't take in the end: verdict overturned on appeal. He was hopping mad. Funny really, him being so anti. He'd be the first person to argue for sterilisation.'

When Dora arrived at the court entrance Kemble and the prosecution lawyer were just finishing their conference.

'Shouldn't keep you too long,' smiled the lawyer. 'Looks pretty open and shut.' (Those words again.)

Dora took her place in the gallery. There were only a handful of spectators. A few rather down-at-heel women (presumably friends or family of the accused) plus the merest sprinkling of ghoulish old crones too poor to seek shelter in a picture palace. She felt a mouse run over her shoe as she peered down at the court.

The woman's lawyer, the best the state could do under the Poor Prisoner's Defence Act, looked very young and very bogus in his crisp new wig, like a chorus boy in a sixth-form production of *Trial by Jury*. He had been in close conference with a dark-haired man in faultless morning dress who left the room as they were all called to order.

The pathologist had taken his seat in the body of the court but proceedings had hardly begun before the defence bod approached the bench and rubbed wigs with the judge and the next thing they all knew, his honour was asking his opposite number if he would object to his witness sitting outside on the bench with the others there's-a-good-chap.

Dora watched as Kemble rose to his feet with an air of studied unconcern and, without looking at the lawyer or the judge, make his way to the door of the court, his left foot dragging slightly as he crossed the polished floor.

A chair was brought for the accused, a young, slatternly creature in a cheap black dress and coat. Her hair had been hennaed (in an earlier life) and there was a wide mousy band either side of the parting. Her cheeks and lips had been hastily rouged and made a ghoulish contrast with the tripe-white skin of her face.

Could she describe the events of the fourth of January last? Apparently not. Her eyes stared blankly back at him like someone peeping through holes cut in a badly painted picture. Too simple-minded to understand the question? Too drunk on the night in question? Or was she merely surprised to be asked the same bloody thing all over a-bloody-gain? They wanted her to tell them what happened in her own words but she continued staring dumbly at the lawyer, who was nudged by the judge about contempt. Then the lawyer spotted a handwritten note on his desk and his voice was different when he spoke again, as if the stage directions had changed.

She had been expecting a child? She could only nod. And had everything been going well? She shook her head. She began to rock to and fro in her chair as she told them about the pains and the bleeding. The boy in the wig said he *understood* that it must be very painful and distressing for her to relive that terrible afternoon but he carried on with his questions just the same. Understood? Understood what it was to feel your baby hurting and have it fall out of you white and wet and silent on the oilcloth floor. *Understood?*

'It was twisted round and round. I pulled it away to make it tidy and I wrapped it – wrapped *him* – in the shawl I made and held his hand.'

Her own hand had released its grip on the rail of the dock and was held close in front of her face as she said it, the finger and thumb barely an inch apart.

This play-acting was all very well, sneered the prosecution counsel, but was it not in fact the case that *Miss* Waite, unwilling to be burdened by an illegitimate child, had in fact strangled the infant moments after its birth before it had so much as drawn its first breath?

The gallery all but hissed and booed. No further questions.

It was time to bring in the big guns (or gun, anyway) but Alfred Kemble, alone on a bench in the corridor, had not been in court for the defendant's evidence, and he began in entirely the wrong key.

Had he examined the body of the infant found at 72 Blenheim Buildings?

He had.

And was he able to state whether the infant had met its death from natural causes?

'In my opinion it had not.'

'That is your definite opinion?'

'That is my definite opinion. *Others* . . .' the mere tone of his voice immediately conjured an inferior tribe of shifty, unreliable little men: back-street pathologists who didn't know their business. 'Others,' he repeated, 'may take a different view.'

He stood down and Dora saw him begin walking to his usual ringside seat by sheer force of habit until an usher deferentially cupped his elbow and guided him back to the bench outside.

The next witness was a doctor with a practice near the woman's flat who had been summoned to the scene. Was the child born dead or had it, in his opinion, met its death shortly after birth? He wasn't qualified to say.

'Never stopped anyone before,' grumbled an old gallery regular in a fantastically feathered hat.

They were on the point of decanting the doctor back into the corridor but he asked to point out that he had seen the accused on an earlier occasion. Everyone sat up and took notice – the prosecution practically licked his lips. And why was that? The accused had called at his surgery in some distress just before Christmas in the belief that she was having a miscarriage. He had examined her and assured her that that was not the case (to her apparent relief). The prosecution lawyer looked as though he had lost a shilling and found sixpence.

It was time for Vazard's Mr Steen. The defence's tame gynaecologist was a M.A., M.B., B.CH. (Cantab.), F.R.C.S., F.R.C.O.G. examiner for the University of Cambridge and lecturer in obstetrics at the Chelsea Hospital for Women. This careful list of Steen's credentials was a masterstroke on the defence's part – particularly as the prosecution counsel, perhaps weary of hearing it all, had not bothered with the usual curriculum vitae for the famous Alfred Kemble. Dora saw the man open his mouth and close it again as he realised too late that he had missed this all-important preliminary.

'Mr Steen, did you examine the body of the infant found at 72 Blenheim Buildings?'

'I did.'

'And was the infant, in your opinion, stillborn or born alive?'

'There was no indication of any injury, or any attempt at suffocation. The infant showed no abnormalities. It was perfect in every way . . .'

The merest suggestion of a pause but time enough for a woman in the jury to begin dabbing at her eyelashes beneath the veil of her bought-for-court hat.

'Unfortunately a lack of professional care during delivery had, *in my opinion*' (the irony in this echo of Kemble's courtroom catchphrase was unmistakable), 'resulted in its death before or during its birth. The condition of the body was entirely consistent with natural perinatal death.'

'Are you familiar with the hydrostatic test whereby the point of death of an infant is established by placing a portion of the lung in a beaker of water?'

Of course he jolly well was. He was a consultant obstetrician for heaven's sake.

'Did you apply this test?'

'I did not. The so-called "flotation test" is a crude, old-fashioned device and does not, in my opinion, prove or disprove live birth. If the body has actually begun to decay, the formation of gas will in itself cause the portion of lung to float. Conversely, if the child survives only a few minutes the lungs will not be well aerated and will sink just as those of a stillborn child would.'

Time to recall Dr Kemble from his corridor. Was Dr Kemble aware that current thinking was of the view that the, ahem, flotation test (the procedure had acquired lawyerly inverted commas now that Mr Steen had discredited it) was a somewhat crude indicator? Was he aware that a portion of lung might very well sink if the infant survived only a few moments?

'I have heard of such cases but I have very little experience of infants whose lungs do not float in water after surviving the first few minutes of life.'

' "Very little experience"?' The young lawyer knew that he was punching above his weight and had to take care not to seem puppyish or arrogant. He looked again at the scrap of paper on the table in front of him. 'Might the court ask how long it has been since you last attended a woman in childbirth, Dr Kemble?'

Dora thought of Constance running off to mother's in Guildford and of the first Mrs Kemble, making her final fuss by the hall telephone. Alfred Kemble frowned slightly, reliving his student days, trying to find clean linen and hot water in the filthy rookeries of Paddington

'Sixteen years.' His voice was slightly furry. Perhaps his trusty silver flask had been keeping him company on the witness bench. 'But I doubt the process has altered much during that length of time.'

The court was ready and willing to oblige with a ripple of laughter but the defence beat them to it.

'Not *altered*, you say? Not altered since *1913*?' Bonnets, Hansom cabs, horse-drawn omnibuses seemed to crowd into the courtroom. 'You are of course entitled to your opinion, Dr Kemble, but I think we might perhaps leave that to those more experienced in the field to determine.'

The very air in the court felt different. A change in the atmosphere as palpable as the drop in pressure before a thunderstorm. The tide of sympathy had turned and the defence sensed it.

'Might one ask when you last examined a live patient of *any* sort, Dr Kemble?'

The pathologist shot a furious glance at the prosecution, who remained rooted to his seat.

'It is an unchallenged fact that the number of criminal abortions is stupendous in all civilised countries.'

His Lordship seemed rather taken aback by this violent change of subject.

'That may or may not be the case, Dr Kemble, but could you please answer the question put to you by the defence.'

The long, handsome face had drained of colour and Dora could see the masseter muscle twitching on the side of his cheek as he clenched his jaw, like a worm burrowing under the skin. His mouth opened but he didn't speak and the barrister had to repeat his question.

'I can't remember.'

Dora closed her notebook and crammed it into her coat pocket.

Once the witness was safely back outside, the defence launched into his closing speech.

'For some reason or other Dr Alfred Kemble has arrived at a position where his utterances in the witness box receive unquestioning acceptance from judge, counsel and jury. This reputation for infallibility that has been thrust upon Dr Kemble (I am sure he would never have claimed it for himself) is quite out of place in medical and surgical matters.'

Every word he uttered systematically robbed the jury of all its comforting certainties. It had been their instinct to believe the famous Alfred Kemble but the local doctor seemed a decent sort and the rival expert – so compassionate, so emphatic, so well informed – unsettled them completely. Besides which babies *did* die. You couldn't always account for it.

Dora tiptoed out of the gallery and left the court without bothering to see if Kemble had stayed to learn the outcome. In the time it took her to walk the long walk home to Warwick Square the jury had returned their verdict ('lack of professional care during delivery,' just as Steen had maintained) and the death of Matilda Waite's perfect baby boy had inched along the scale from crime to tragedy.

Chapter 25

Dora was lying on the slab yet again and Kemble was hovering over her. The fingers of his right hand were holding the skin of her throat on the stretch while the left wielded a quarter-inch wood chisel with a blond wood handle. The breasts, he explained, should only ever be examined from within.

She woke with a start as Mrs Frith did her usual knocking-and-entering trick with the news that there had been yet another abuse of her precious blasted instrument and that Theodora was to meet Dr Kemble and various others of a similar persuasion at a block of service flats in Maida Vale.

'You are to take a taximeter cab,' continued the landlady, mysteriously mollified by this departmental largesse. 'I have sent Ivy to call one from the rank.'

'Daisy.'

'Daisy?'

'The girl. Daisy, not Ivy.'

Madeleine Frith raised her eyebrows, closed her eyelids and shook her head in one of her favourite don't-weary-me-with-details mimes.

'*Why* a secretary's services should be required at this early stage in the proceedings I cannot begin to imagine. It isn't as if you had shorthand. You ought to put your foot down.' She straightened a framed print of Rouen cathedral (companion to a long-lost study of Notre Dame). 'I expect the newspaper people will be there; better keep your veil down.'

Kemble and the police still seemed to be a few steps ahead of Fleet Street because there were no reporters to be seen when Dora's taxi pulled up under the sweeping porch of the eight-storey block of luxury flats. Her veil was still down and the unfamiliar gauzy view of the world made the whole morning seem stagy and unreal.

One of the two police constables on duty held open the plate glass door to the entrance hall which smelled cleanly but oppressively of the floor polish used to buff the marbled linoleum that stretched across the lobby. Dora thought of the late Oswald Jelly and his abnormally shiny shoes.

Dr Kemble was sharing cigarettes and laughter with a few plain-clothes men and a police photographer. Hubbard (back on duty after Wednesday's mysterious truancy) was standing at the edge of the smiling circle holding the precious bag. He turned as Dora approached and flashed her an almost friendly frown.

'They've found a tin trunk on the fifth floor. Flat rented by a Mrs Clarissa Pope.'

Hubbard poured a cup of tea from a thermos flask and passed it to Dora together with a buttered currant bun.

'Better get this down you. You won't be able to later by the sound of it.'

'Why was I called if you're already here? He only needs one of us to take notes, surely.'

Hubbard didn't answer. The automatic lift claimed to hold eight and once Mrs Strange had been introduced they all crowded into it, avoiding each other's eyes and instinctively turning round to face the metal gate and watch the neatly stencilled floor numbers glide by on the lift shaft wall. The policemen and Kemble took off their hats as Mrs Strange stepped in but Hubbard's new-found chumminess didn't seem to stretch as far as basic good manners.

Number 178 Blythe Court was a very modern flat: steam heat in every room, hot and cold, a chute that sent tea leaves, potato peelings and items of an intimate feminine nature hurtling down to the sub-basement – but that seemed to be where the luxury ended in this particular instance. Only the bedroom, which could be glimpsed at the end of the uncarpeted corridor, showed any normal signs of occupation. It had been decorated in the Van Rooden manner, the walls covered in pink watered silk and the gilded dressing table wearing a fancy skirt of matching frills. The unmade bed was draped with a luxurious eiderdown of white gold satin but the sheets were none too clean.

The windows of the stiflingly hot sitting room had been smeared with whitewash in lieu of curtains, the light bulbs were bare and the only things to sit on were an empty tea chest and a large tin trunk. There was nothing luxurious about the smell coming from the trunk.

The police constable had already been sick and everyone else was trying to mouth-breathe through their handkerchiefs. Dr Kemble opened one of the whitened windows. He alone remained unperturbed by the stench.

'As Mr Box so helpfully puts it in his standard manual of post-mortem practice: *the presence of decomposition is a positive sign of death.*' (Medical students usually laughed at this point but the police had more taste.) 'Perhaps we could get the preliminary photographs over with and then I can get to work, eh Barker?'

A rope had been knotted around the upended trunk and there was a damp brown stain on the floorboards beneath it. The police inspector told the constable to undo the knots.

'Wilkins here was in the navy two years weren't you, Wilkins?'

But Wilkins had forgotten any knots he ever knew and after tugging helplessly at the rope with trembling fingers, cut through the hemp with his pocket knife and loosened the brass fixings.

It was very much like the cover of a book. A cheap, thin, common little book of the kind sold at railway stations. The unclothed body slithered free of the trunk's interior like meat slipping from an opened tin. A length of cord had been doubled round the knees and tied round the neck. Mrs Pope slumped out face first, her yellow arm flopping on to the carpet followed by a puddle of blackish ooze. A charm bracelet glinted brassily on the wrist in the filtered morning sunlight, there was a dirty sticking plaster on her finger. 'c/o Kemble' had been carved on her naked back in the murderer's neat, left-handed script.

The newspaper in which the body had been loosely wrapped unfurled on to the floor beneath the arm: 'Charm bracelet verdict: porter to hang.'

The smell, which had been bad enough before, hit them all like blast. Dora could feel the sick rising in her throat so fast she barely had time to turn her head. The constable hastily grabbed an old newspaper from the tea chest just in time for her to spew into the improvised cone. He stood awkwardly holding it, like fish and chips. 'Alley murder: uncle held.'

The inspector automatically reached for his cigarette case but Kemble checked him with a wave of the hand.

'You mustn't smoke. I can't smell the smells I need to smell.'

The other detective, who had been coping quite well until this point, ran from the room and down the passageway.

The police photographer (who always came prepared) tied a large, red spotted snuff handkerchief over his mouth and nose and began recording the scene, methodically tracking from angle to angle before moving in for close-ups of the bracelet, of the cords around the neck and of the deep scratches in the smooth skin of the back.

The inspector was the first to recover. The scale of the problem flashed upon him as if lit up by sheet lightning and he acted quickly. He rested his hand on Kemble's sleeve and explained quietly but decisively that he hoped Dr Kemble wouldn't mind but it would probably be best to telephone to Sir Godfrey Mason at St Mary's and get him to do the preliminaries. The pathologist looked at the hand on his arm as though wondering how it had got there.

'I wouldn't trouble if it were up to me, sir. No real need, obviously, but it might be better to get in a third party – just for form's sake. Perhaps you could seal the room, constable.'

His touch changed to a light but firm grip as he steered Kemble away from the trunk.

'Is your driver waiting? We'll get Wilkins to send him across to the other entrance if you don't mind, sir. I expect the newspapers will be downstairs by now.'

The inspector then ushered Kemble, Hubbard and Dora out of the flat and down a narrow steam-heated corridor that ran like an escape trench between the north and south wings of the vast block then down the lift on the other side.

The outside air had a bracing smell of petrol and the japonica that grew by the main door. Hubbard stepped away from the group and was explosively sick into the bush but parted the blossoms so tidily that none of it landed on the petals but formed a strange, curranty mulch around the base of the stems.

They could just glimpse the north entrance through a screen of ornamental cherry. A motor car had pulled up and two men in grubby Burberrys were leaning against it, one of them wearing a camera and flash apparatus.

'We'll get Sir Godfrey brought to this entrance and see if we can't get the body taken out the back way,' whispered the inspector. 'Try and keep them off the scent as long as we decently can. It'll just be "Body found in Maida Vale flat" for the moment.'

Dora kept her veil down as they drove in silence back to Willcox Wing, where Hubbard used the burner in the lab to make tea for Kemble. The pathologist, still wearing his coat, sat down at Dora's desk taking slow, careful sips at his cup and staring dumbly at the great black telephone, as if the slightest movement might cause it to explode.

Chapter 26

The 'phone was already ringing as Dora turned the key in the lock the following morning and it rang and rang and rang until she finally answered it. One always did answer the telephone. Rude not to. No, Dr Kemble's department was not involved in the Maida Vale murder investigation. No, the department had no comment to make at this juncture. The bell on the wall started up again the moment she replaced the receiver.

Hubbard watched her fielding the calls as he filleted his way through the latest batch of newspapers.

'I really couldn't say. That would be a matter for Sir Godfrey's people at St Mary's,' cooed Dora for the umpteenth time.

There was a sudden twanging thump and she looked up to see Hubbard's scalpel sticking out from the scratched wood of his desk. There were rustling sounds from the supplies cupboard and Hubbard emerged moments later with a small bale of tow, a piece of sacking, a length of twine and the stepladder. He proceeded to pack the fluff around the still ringing bell, reducing its urgent cry to a muffled death rattle which they both did their utmost to ignore.

It was eleven thirty before Kemble arrived. There had been two post-mortems that morning (ruptured appendix at Finchley, cerebral haemorrhage at Marylebone) but Alfred Kemble FRCS etc. had not conducted either of them. He had visited a barber's shop in Cleveland Street on his way to the office but it would have taken more than soft soap and a lick of pomade to disguise the evidence of a sleepless night spent crawling inside a bottle of brandy. He greeted Dora with an approximation of his usual sardonic smile but he looked older suddenly. Thinner. His skin a shade yellower. Hair was growing out of his nose and ears, she noticed, and he had a shiny curl of wire tucked around one of his back teeth. He checked his fob watch then rattled back down the stairs.

Public house opening time slowed the 'phone calls to the merest trickle but Dora still couldn't settle down to the last few dozen index cards – the nearer she got to the end of her Sisyphean task, the more fiddly and fantastical her cross-referencing became, as if she were trying to put off the day when every last card had found its place. Nor was she in any hurry to type up her letter to the bursar's office. What did the agency do when one of their clerks resigned from a post? Would they find her another? And how would papa react when he learned that Theodora's precious experiment had lasted all of four weeks?

The parting gift from the filing instructress at the secretarial academy had been what she called the Golden Rule of office life: Look Busy. Dora began feeding sheet after sheet into the typewriter and hammering her way through a string of imaginary exercises: 'A partial pathologist has a quaint packet of lemon yellow paper; I saw you at my trial in a red carnation.'

The newspaper men, suitably refreshed, resumed their enquiries a few minutes after their various watering-holes had closed for the afternoon – an event that coincided with the pathologist's unsteady return to the office.

'Hello. Hello, Hubbard, old fellow. Hello, young Strange.'

He squinted at the mummified telephone bell as the rattle started up yet again.

'Can somebody not answer that infernal machine?'

Dora affected the melodiously elocuted tones of the telephone room: 'Yais? Yais? No. No. Dr Kemble's department has no information at this time. No, Mr Kirkby, I'm afraid not.'

'Kirkby? Lemme speak to him.'

He leaned across Dora's desk and gave a swift snarl of apology as he grabbed the receiver. There was a smell like Christmas on his breath.

'Kirkby? Hello, hello, Kirkby, Kirkby, Kirkby. What can we do for you, old chap? Has it?' He rolled his eyes in mock surprise. 'All morning? Tut tut tut. I'm afraid my people can be a trifle over-zealous.'

He leaned back against the bank of filing cabinets.

'Miscarriage of justice, you say? Harsh words, Kirkby-old-chap. Far too early to pass judgement. Might easily be what our American friends call a "copy-cat" crime . . .'

Dora stopped even pretending to type. It was hard to tell from the one-sided conversation whether the pathologist retained any credibility with his once tame newsman. There were, admitted Kemble, *extraordinary* similarities between the two cases. *Highly* unusual for such criminals to work in pairs hence the police's understandable *failure* to look for an accomplice . . .

Dora very nearly gasped out loud at the sheer brass neck of the man. The police's failure? When it was Kemble who had asserted on oath that (in his opinion) the murderer had worked left-handed with a quarter-inch wood chisel, Kemble who supplied the prosecution's little yellow cribsheet chronicling the feckless fecundity of Mrs MacDonald's very special schoolboys, Kemble whose matchless reputation had been enough to spin all that circumstantial straw into gold.

Mr Kirkby, evidently undaunted, seemed to be ploughing on with his list of awkward questions and had clearly just asked quite why Dr Kemble been taken off regular post-mortem duties?

'Nothing sinister, old fruit. We thought it best if Sir Godfrey took this one and then he and I can compare notes as and when the Yard sees fit. Obviously we can't rule out an exhumation of the Delgado female at this stage.' The confiding tone grew oilier still as he lowered his voice to an off-the-record murmur: 'Look, Kirkby old bean, you were in court, you saw the little tick. You heard them giving the low-down on his record. Would you want that kind of moral defective polishing floors anywhere near Marjorie or young Jane? Would you want him squirreling away their stockings and powder puffs?'

Kirkby dashed off to write up his story and when the messenger boy came round with the final edition it was clear that Kemble's blustering bonhomie had failed to impress the seasoned reporter: 'Second charm bracelet victim puts Jelly verdict in doubt'. True, there were two paragraphs on the pathologist's war record, on the death of his brothers, the loss of his wife, the recent passing of his younger son and 'Our Crime reporter' paid tribute to the fact that Dr Kemble had performed a thousand necropsies in the last year alone. But, while everyone could appreciate that such a workload would place that most expert of expert witnesses under a considerable mental strain, it did not alter the shocking fact that the wrong man had eaten a hearty breakfast.

Chapter 27

Dora very nearly didn't recognise Vazard at Victoria Station the next morning. He was waiting, somewhat anxiously, beneath the announcements board while the destinations clicked from Arundel to Worthing and back, like the rattle of a never-ending mah-jong tournament. His hat and clothes were different from his usual donnish tweeds and his blue tie exactly matched his (unholey) socks. He was standing quite close to a fur-trimmed female and Dora saw her looking at him from under her stupid little hat, slyly admiring his tow-headed, captain-of-cricket looks. Handsomer still when he caught sight of Dora.

'You came! I was afraid you mightn't after last week's horrors.'

He was clutching a brown paper carrier bag containing a vacuum flask and the greaseproof paper picnic his landlady had made (no meat). He had bought a copy of the *Morning Post* and the latest issue of *Tatler* ('I wasn't sure – you could always draw moustaches on them all').

Vazard didn't care either way about Crystal Palace but he was rather looking forward to the train journey. Where else would he be able to hold her hand? Maybe steal the odd kiss or two? Spooning in picture palaces wasn't really on, she was hardly park bench material and he couldn't really afford taxi cabs.

'Hurry along.' All bossy and I'm-in-charge suddenly. 'We shall lose our train.'

He strode down the platform, past the crowded excursion carriages to the first-class compartments. No corridors (no surprise).

The overheated interior of the train had the unmistakable smell of lightly toasted house dust. It was so hot that Dora had to take off her coat and as he reached to help tug the sleeve she was back in the Upper Fifth, having her arm stroked in the darkness by a strange young man who whispered in a foreign accent. Her coat brushed Vazard's newspaper on to the carriage floor and she felt almost queasy with desire and disgust.

'I dreamed about you last night, Dr Vazard.'

His cheeks grew rosier still.

'Golly. Was I at your feast in a pink dress?'

'No. Dr Kemble was trying to find the missing biscuit tin leg and that shifty porter person who telephones kept ringing to say that there was "another one" in Alexandra Ward. You kept being sent across to bandage it and fetch it on Mrs A's trolley only to have Hubbard throw it out of the supplies cupboard window and send you off for another until there was a huge pile of them down in the ambulance yard. Vile.'

Vazard scratched his head.

'Mmm. I see the chief's told you the Hubbard human centipede story. Enough to give anyone nightmares. You really mustn't let the work follow you home, you know. In any case, I'm not sure I believe that particular atrocity: up there with babies on bayonets, I reckon. Germans aren't animals. And the sheer practicalities of it. Think of the *flies* . . .'

'But why lie?'

'Not *lying*, exactly.' Vazard looked uncomfortable, like a schoolboy being made to tell tales. 'War stories are like that: shared out, twisted round, dressed up. They don't abide by the usual rules of evidence. It isn't as though anyone's going to call Hubbard to the stand to corroborate.'

This wasn't at all the kind of conversation he had in mind. She had appeared faintly out of sorts when they first sat down on opposite sides of the carriage, as if afraid that he would pounce, and it was hard to know how to make the first move. 'May I kiss you?' would have been absurdly Edwardian and the slow, steady motion of the Saturday service offered little prospect of lurching lustfully into her lap. Perhaps he should pretend that he felt groggy if he didn't face the engine? There was an unreadable, almost angry light in her eyes as she scanned the newspaper lying on the dusty carriage floor. Her mouth was moving but he couldn't hear her for the chug of the train over the points.

'Sorry. What did you say?'

'Kiss me.'

Dora thought for a moment that he wouldn't. He looked so taken aback. Then with one leap he was beside her, like the hero from Matthew Arnold's *Culture and Anarchy*, 'enfolding the slim, wool-clad form in his manly arms, raining kiss after burning kiss upon her sweet mouth, raising her to the seventh heaven of bliss'.

The minutes between the last two stations passed in one long embrace. Vazard smelled of Pears soap and tasted of peppermint. One arm was round her waist while the other stroked her hair, her neck. Dora leaned back as he kissed her throat, watching the clouds whiz by, imagining a host of four-eyed faces at the window, tracking the progress of Vazard's hand.

The day was bright and almost boaterishly warm by the time they arrived at Sydenham and the pleasure grounds were filling fast with earnest, stamp-collecting, caterpillar-boxing, infection-prone little children who had been lured to the Palace by the promise of life-size dinosaurs only to be forcibly improved for an entire afternoon, being dragged from Alberta to Zanzibar on the ends of grown-up arms.

'You'll find it jolly interesting, Horace,' insisted a voice. Horace found it nothing of the sort and said as much. No ice cream for boys who did not behave, apparently.

Did Dora want to see inside?

'No. Please don't let's. I'm sure it is all *jolly interesting* but I do so want to be outdoors.'

'No ice cream for girls who do not behave,' teased Vazard happily. How pretty she looked.

They ate their sandwiches on a bench in the gardens watched over by an implausibly green ten-foot megalosaurus that peeked mildly out at them from behind the shrubbery while Vazard pondered the fate of the theropods. You half expected him to produce one from a matchbox.

'Evolutionary failures,' twittered Dora (he had paused for breath and one had to say something).

'Hardly. A lesson to us all, the dinosaurs. Brains the size of pickled walnuts but they jolly well bestrode the earth perfectly happily for umpteen millennia. A triumph of feeble-mindedness and one in the eye for the human betterment buffoons.'

Oh Caractacus, thought Dora. *Please* not another germ plasm row.

'We shall be lucky to last as long,' he observed.

He really did look very handsome sitting there on the bench working his way through two rounds of shrimp paste, but he was a dull old stick just the same.

'Snobs and racist cranks,' munched Dora.

'Come again?'

'Papa has a very low opinion of the human betterment people.'

'Sound egg, your pa,' agreed Vazard. 'That paper of his on Mendelian analysis really blew them out of the water.'

Dora could see that Vazard was wound up and ready to go and that unless evasive action were taken pretty sharpish she'd be up to her neck in the gene pool before you could say *rassenhygiene*.

Talking of medicine, had Vazard ever come to a decision about pathology?

He shook his head.

'My heart's not in it. Ealing mortuary telephoned yesterday. Was I free for a quick once-over on a pulmonary embolism? I made my excuses. I haven't told the chief the news yet. I was going to last week and then there was this business with the boy and now the Maida Vale fiasco. I'll try and broach the subject on Monday.'

'He'll be disappointed.' It sounded nonsense even as Dora said it.

'No, he won't. He was glad enough to have a willing and capable assistant but I don't think he's an evangelist for the calling. The fewer pathologists the better – all the more for him. All the more bodies to open and shut. Not for me, I'm afraid. I'm a doctor not a policeman. I want to find out what's wrong and make it better. Kemble just wants to find out what's wrong for his own satisfaction so that you and Hubbard can put the whole show in alphabetical order, fully cross-referenced. Ten thousand autopsies and he hasn't even got a textbook to show for it.'

'What made you decide to go in for medicine in the first place?' Kemble was right: a dreary but very serviceable gambit. It wouldn't do for all professions – 'Tell me, Mrs Frith, what made you decide to share your house with a series of impecunious strangers?' – but it certainly seemed to touch a nerve with Vazard.

'Funnily enough, I can probably tell you the exact moment.'

This was obviously going to take time. Dora surreptitiously turned up the collar of her coat against the breeze.

Vazard was leaning forward with his elbows on his knees and staring at the path under his feet.

'Mother was an extremely keen hospital visitor. I can only have been nine or ten but she used to drag me round with her, supposedly cheering the blind and limbless. She was a seasoned brow-mopper. If she were distracted for any reason at the end of a row of beds she was perfectly capable of working her way back up the same line of men, cooing the same drivel about their bravery and sacrifice, mopping away seraphically. I remember some of the perkier ones winking at me, too polite to point out that they'd already had theirs.

'Once we were visiting a ward full of Blighty wounds and the matron ordered the mater to leave me outside (I honestly don't think she would have done otherwise). I was sitting on a long, French-polished bench – I remember sliding the seat of my short trousers from side to side across the surface. The big double doors to the ward were partly open and I could still see some of the beds, the mouths of the pillow cases had all been turned so that the stripey smiles of pillow ticking faced away from the matron's office and towards the door. There were three old poison bottles on the window sill, each with a poppy stuck in its neck.

'It was near the end of the half hour allowed for visiting and the nurses were getting ready to change the men's dressings in their station near where I had been planted. They had a steel trolley all laid out with trays of stuff (I didn't know the words then): demijohns of Condy's and Dakin's fluids and little pots marked with red and blue poison labels, neat little coils of bandaging, snowy pre-cut squares of gauze and cotton wool and lint. There was a great sweet-shop jar full of sterilised probes and tubes and a long line of needles and sounds and forceps all laid out in readiness on a white linen cloth.

'One of the nurses opened the doors and another began pushing the trolley into the ward and all the instruments and bottles began to rattle against the metal rail around the top. And the noise – it was very like the row Mrs A's tea trolley makes, it always makes me think of it – set off the most awful groans from the men in the ward. The one nearest the door had his leg in a great Liston splint. He was still having his face sponged by my mother and at the sound of the nurses' cart – the Agony Wagon, the men called it – he began to scream. Like something caught in a trap. I remember seeing my mother through the half-open door. The disgusted look on her face . . .' Vazard took a gulp of cold tea. 'And I remember a door opening at the very far end of the ward and a man – quite a young man – in a bright white coat striding briskly across to the bed holding a hypodermic ready-primed in his hand and the screaming stopped and the man in the bed lowered his head back to the pillow. And I remember thinking how kind and how clever he was to be able to do that: to make the screaming stop.

'And then everything just carried on. The smiling nurses told him to be brave while they committed their antiseptic atrocities, draining the holes in his body, shearing away a few more inches of lifeless flesh. And of course mater carried on mop-mop-mopping. The look on her face – two looks really . . . Contempt at the man for screaming but thrilled, really honestly *thrilled* to be part of it all.'

There was something disturbing about the way Vazard stifled his cigarette under the heel of his shoe, grinding it into the path long after it had been extinguished.

'Florrie, my sister, really, really enjoyed nursing. Not endured. Not survived. *Enjoyed*. Had the time of her life in France. She trained at the military hospital at Wimereux and I remember her coming home and talking wounds for hours at a time with mother. She'd describe how whole trainloads of men with hideously infected wounds would be unloaded into the wards. How excited they'd all get preparing for a rush, how they'd *look forward* to the second wave with the really *interesting* cases. Jealous – actually *jealous* – when a neighbouring station had more customers. Then, when the novelty wore off, she volunteered for some special . . .' Vazard hesitated very slightly, took a long puff of a fresh gasper and soldiered bitterly on '. . . some *special* GU place over on Salisbury plain. The coy chats with mater came to an end then, of course. Mother dear, for all her voracious visiting, never did learn what the letters stood for. It was only when I began studying medicine that I realised that my sister had spent half the war behind barbed wire blithely torturing syphilitic Anzacs. And *loving* it. "Time for your mercury inunctions, Corporal." What the good doctor Stänker of Berlin would probably call "sadistic". She'd have loved that post-mortem the other day. I don't expect she ever saw a naked man who wasn't wounded or diseased. Sometimes I tell people how much Florrie enjoyed it all,' he looked sharply up at Dora, 'to see how they react.'

Dora felt herself adjusting her face, hoping somehow to register the correct blend of sympathy and distaste.

'The chief came up trumps. When I told him what fun she'd had he said, "What an utterly appalling woman. Do you ever speak to her?" Good old Kemble.'

Vazard gave a little choking chuckle at the memory.

'And funnily enough I don't, not since ma died. Used to see her once in a while when she had a fiancé – or half of one – but he died of his wounds a few years after the war. She now lives in a rather damp little cottage up in Lincolnshire with a fellow VAD and four Irish setters. We manage to swap Christmas and birthday cards. Ghastly woman. Did the war make her like that, do you think, or did it just give her an outlet? In ordinary life we punish murder, sadism, wholesale destruction of property: war gives prizes for it all. What kind of a woman wants anything to do with medicine?'

Dora was taken aback by the ferocity, the unreasonableness of the question. From *Vazard*. Such a sensible sort. It was the kind of question papa used to ask.

'I found it interesting.'

'Exhilarating?' Still strangely fierce.

'No. Just interesting. But as things turned out I wasn't able to … My father … had very fixed ideas about women doctoring.'

Less mortifying than a full confession. Vazard didn't need to know that in actual fact Miss Strang, although 'a conscientious candidate who had obviously worked steadfastly', was not the sharpest scalpel on the tray.

All in all, the train had been a jolly good idea, Vazard felt. A clear eight minutes between Herne Hill and Victoria (he'd checked beforehand in Hubbard's *ABC*). It was like Tuesday afternoon in the stationery cupboard only much, much more so. They were nearly joined at one point by a vinegary old woman who drew up alongside the window as the train pulled into Streatham Hill. She was dressed with the unlikely care of a vital witness in a hat shaped like a biscuit barrel and a pre-war coat of rusty black. Vazard stroked a speck of soot from Dora's cheek and the old lady trotted on to the next compartment, quivering with disgust.

As the train wheezed back into life, Vazard realised, with a vague sense of panic, that he had only a few more minutes and he found himself burbling away about probably being taken on as registrar with old Steen by the end of next year and the screw for that being just about enough for a little flat in Pimlico or Camden Town or Marylebone or somewhere . . .

Dora shut her eyes. And then what? Rooms over the shop in horrid old Harley Street? A life in "the valley of the shadow"? A Frith to man the telephones? A wife to warm the bed? Little Vazards to fill the silver frames? She could see Vazard's castle in the air as clearly as if he'd sketched it in pastels but she wasn't entirely sure that she wanted to share it.

For a moment she allowed herself to dream of a wifeless, childless Alfred Kemble lying on a nice plain bed in a nice plain bedroom, the incarnation of all her bedtime reading. A husband who came complete with everything the Sixth-form common room had held most dear: dry wit, decent tailor, smart address, a good war . . . 'sharp, clean-cut almost classical features: a long, thin nose, a firm cleft chin, eyes dark, flashing and deep set and the most fascinating head of hair.' And then the memory of those nasty, brutish minutes in the supplies cupboard swept over her in a beastly great wave of misery and shame.

Vazard mistook the blush for maiden shyness, which he felt was probably rather a good sign. The look on her face when he first launched into his not-quite-proposal had warned him not to offer his hand outright. She might license the odd kiss but there was still that bluestocking streak to contend with, which was bound to make her say 'no' at first. He needed to take it more slowly – no need to make an ass of himself. He began gently back-pedalling, smoothing the way for subsequent attempts (if any) while making it appear that his talk of marriage had been general, not personal.

'As far as I know there's only ever been one honest-to-goodness married person in the department (apart from the great man himself) and that was Mrs Culvey. Poor Mrs Culvey. The chief is a bit of a surprise packet. I don't think I'm revealing any state secrets if I say that he may very possibly have *been man to her woman* . . .'

He fell silent as the train trundled across the Thames, frowning at the thought of the department's late (and unlamented) secretary. Mrs Culvey had been rather *fast* (as his mother used to say). Still, it was a comfort to know that the hospital had no cast-iron objections to working wives. He couldn't really believe that Kemble was a menace to female staff in general and the money would be jolly useful at first. The happy dream played on in his head: a snug Marylebone flat, cosy little suppers, jolly breakfasts and the thrilling hours between . . .

Chapter 28

Mrs Frith set an early alarm and trotted down to the station to get her own copy of the *News of the World* (taking care to pencil next door's address on the corner of the front page with a newsagent's careless scrawl). The *News of the World* was unquestionably a 'despondent voice' but she felt it was her duty to learn all she could about young Theodora's employer.

The newspapers were like a dog with a bone about the charm bracelet case. They'd run interviews with the directrice of the late Mr Jelly's special school (eager to set things straight after her mauling in court) and with a long-lost sister (married to a high street optician and not the least bit simple-minded apparently). Miss Jelly (as was) who had lain low throughout the shame of the trial now pitched up to say that he'd been a sweet-natured boy but that mother (a Ladysmith widow) hadn't been able to manage and that, while they'd none of them liked the idea of it, an institution had been the best place for him and that he had been taught to carve wood and make lovely wicker baskets. Why was it always wickerwork? wondered Mrs Frith. She could hardly look at a basket without thinking of some drooling idiot puzzling away at its making.

The head porter, loyal to the last, had been perfectly willing to repeat his testimonial for the newspapers. Oswald Jelly may not have been the full shilling but he was never any trouble and he kept the floors spotless.

In short, a man less likely to rape, mutilate and crate up that nice blonde lady on the sixth floor who had given him a half-crown Christmas box had never drawn breath. And no, he wasn't left-handed. And no, he hadn't been taught to read or write and yes, looked at again, Jelly's alibi – a mild and bitter in the public bar of a Camden Town pub happily watching other men playing some wonderful, unfathomable game with dotty bits of wood – was perfectly sound. Witnesses who'd never said (because nobody never asked) now remembered seeing him: small bloke, bit backward. But harmless enough. Harmless.

The press were already calling for the Home Secretary to sign the order to have the innocent Jelly's remains moved from Pentonville to somewhere near Colchester at his sister's request. There was a good half page on Theodora's pathologist: picture of son, picture of pregnant wife and a news feature on the famous Dr Kemble himself. Dr Kemble, who had been so unshakably convinced that the backward porter person was the culprit. But he couldn't have been, could he? Not from Pentonville?

Mrs Clarissa Pope's body had been discovered on a Thursday, giving plenty of time for a lovely big splash in the Sunday papers. When Mrs Frith had first glanced at the charm bracelet headline at the news-stand she was surprised and rather disgusted to see that they were still eking out the same old blonde-found-slain material, but as she read on, she realised it was another blonde entirely. The picture was quite, quite different – not that the body found in the trunk had borne much resemblance to that carefree snapshot by the sound of it: 'Mrs Pope's facial injuries were of such severity that she was identifiable only by her various scars and moles.'

There was no longer anyone living who could have recognised Mrs Frith by the moles on her shoulder, by the striae on her chest and abdomen. Would the dentist even remember her? Was he even alive still? She bared her teeth at herself in the polished lid of the silver cigarette box on the chimney piece. Only eight stoppings but the enamel had never recovered its colour.

The dead woman had been thirty-nine, the same age that Mrs Frith admitted to, but the photograph (a recent one, to judge from the hat) looked far younger. She too was a war widow. 'Regret to inform you that a report has been received from the War Office to the effect that . . .'

War kept the post office very busy. A telegram first, the standard regrets, then either 'wounded', 'dead' or (as in Lieutenant Frith's case) 'missing presumed dead'. The handwritten follow-up letter from the commanding officer would paint a fuller picture (if not an exact likeness). German snipers were seldom given a moment's peace in those kindly communiqués which broke the news of heroic, well-liked men with bullets through their heads. Madeleine Frith thought bitterly of how her pulse had raced when her own envelope arrived, how she had prayed silently to herself as she unfolded the telegram, reading it through again and again to be quite, quite sure.

Mrs Frith's usual doctor had been sent to France in 1916, about two years after her marriage, and the medic called out of retirement to replace him had been treating her with an iron tonic. She was run down, he said, and these rashes were very common in her condition. Was she eating properly? Idle old fool.

Some instinct had told her not to give her own name to the physician she found down in Vauxhall who sent her for a course of kill-or-cure treatments at the 'skin' hospital in Leicester Square. It had vaguely occurred to her when she first moved up to London that there must be an awful lot of skin disease about – scurvy, impetigo, scrofula. Scabby, working-class ailments – to warrant so many hospitals for it. It was only now that she realised what really went on inside them.

She became very familiar with the various routes from the two-room flat in Marylebone to Leicester Square, walking across town in a shabby old coat and a cheap veiled hat with cherries on it. She went a different way each Wednesday once a week every week for an endless succession of injections and inunctions. Twenty-four months rubbing ulcerous elbows with the very dregs of the metropolis, absorbing enough mercury and arsenic and bismuth and calomel to poison an entire genteel boarding house. Home was no refuge. The bathroom cupboard was overflowing with yards of rubber tubing and gallons of picric acid and purple disinfectant to be self-administered by the patient herself at excruciating bi-weekly intervals.

She used sometimes to imagine what she would say to Archibald when he next got leave and she found the stage management of the scene oddly comforting. Madeleine Frith would be discovered by the fireside, knitting away disconsolately at a little white garment that would never now be worn. Her errant husband would turn away from her ashen face and hide his head in shame while she made a rather fine, Duse-like speech on his vices and the recompense he should make.

It was quite a long speech. Every ounce of disgust and disappointment distilled into it by the agonised hours spent in the tiled torture chambers of the skin hospital where stern, starchy women performed unnatural acts with clips and tubes.

But the speech was never made because he never did get leave again and Mrs Frith eventually lost her taste for melodrama, opting instead for a short but decisive visit to Warwick Square. Her mother-in-law was not at first cooperative. Archibald wasn't to blame, bleated the old lady. The war was making beasts of everyone – especially young soldiers: leaflets egging them all on, licensed places full of filthy Frenchwomen. War did terrible things. Then a nasty thought seemed to strike her and Mrs Frith Senior embarked upon an irrelevant and highly insulting anecdote about a recent visit to the cinema during which the manager had announced that a soldier was waiting outside to surprise his wife with her fancy man and that a dozen couples had promptly stormed the fire exit ...

Mrs Frith didn't know her daughter-in-law particularly well and was entirely unprepared for the fury unleashed when the bride wheeled round to demand exactly what she was insinuating. The old lady apologised. Then she wrote a long, grovelling letter apologising more thoroughly. Then she sent poor, dear Madeleine a cheque for two hundred pounds.

It was about six months after all that that the war office's telegram came. Followed by the commanding officer's bread-and-butter letter thanking her for her sacrifice. 'He didn't suffer,' wrote the colonel, his pen practically forming the words on its own, forgetting that Lieutenant Frith's sufferings were an entirely unknown quantity given that his body had not been found after the bombardment. And the new widow had wrung the letter to shreds between her numb and peeling fingers. Her own sufferings had more than a year left to run before the ratty man in the lab coat would give her the second negative test result.

And then, nearly a year later, another letter came. Three letters really, one inside the other like a game of pass-the-parcel. The outermost part of the package was a manila envelope bearing her Marylebone address on a typewritten label, containing a printed slip about forces mail going astray. A second envelope, opened and resealed with an official wafer, was addressed to a soldier in France in Archibald Frith's unformed, boyish hand. The franking mark was from a hospital in Salisbury dated nine months before the army's 'missing' telegram arrived. Nestling inside that was a letter for Mrs Frith (undated) which her husband had wrapped in a note scribbled on a half sheet of cheap paper. 'Dear George. Be a sport and bung this in the regimental post for me like a good chap. Should get the all-clear in a month or two. Mum's the word. Archie.'

The letter to Dearest Maddie was exactly like all the others he had sent (she had often wondered if he had written them in one sitting). He was in the pink and very grateful indeed for the chocs and socks. All leave cancelled again. Hope this found her as it left him (which it did, of course. Very precisely so).

The letters proved to be rather valuable documents. Proof of her own innocence. Proof of her husband's crimes to old Mrs Frith, who now learned that her beloved only child had spent six months of the war behind barbed wire in a military lock hospital. She wept a great deal and said 'my poor, poor Archie' a lot but when she herself died nearly ten years later the Warwick Square house was left to her daughter-in-law in lieu of husband, baby, health, happiness.

Mrs Frith had burnt all the letters (maids were so nosy). All that was left was a cheap little postcard portrait of Archibald Frith as a young lieutenant. It lived at the back of a sideboard drawer and she seldom looked at it but something made her fish it out that Sunday morning. It was a good likeness. His freckled face wore only the slightest of smiles so one couldn't see the gold tooth that had seemed so roguish and captivating at the dance where they had met.

She remained motionless, holding the snapshot in her hand when out of the corner of her eye she saw a movement from under the chiffonier – exactly the spot she had peppered so thoroughly a mere fortnight ago. How could something so astonishingly small move so quickly? And *white*? Surely that was only the pet shop sort?

She surprised herself by the speed with which she climbed on to the seat of her Louis Quinze *fauteuil*. The mouse retreated under the Davenport at the sound but emerged again moments later, believing the coast to be clear and scooted to the far corner of the room, where it began breakfasting on the cracked saucer of plaster of Paris and icing sugar intended for the black beetle population. Would the same method work with mice? And if so would it mean skirting boards full of decomposing albino rodents? The landlady tore a strip from the card in her hand and crushed it into a pellet. The animal twitched its head clear of the saucer as the missile whizzed past it but showed no sign of retreating. It seemed almost tame ... Mrs Frith's heels were beginning to dig into the *petit point* upholstery but that insanitary little bundle of whiskers and claws made descent impossible and she could hardly call out for one of the PGs. Mr Stone would never let her hear the last of it.

The room looked different from her perch on the chair – much more crowded than she had realised – and from this height she could see almost all of herself in the great tarnished overmantel. The morning sun streaming across the square had no mercy on her reflection: old, tired, mean. She looked down at the youthful, smiling postcard and saw with a sudden pang that she had torn off the top of its head: 'for ever wilt thou love, and he be fair ...' The unsuspecting mouse carried on enjoying its hearty breakfast while Mrs Frith ripped the remains of the precious photograph to shreds, tears streaming down her ugly grey face.

Chapter 29

The mountain of green ink had dwindled to a fat handful of index cards but Dora's increasingly obsessive cross-referencing now meant that each case was running to nearly a dozen entries.

She stepped into the supplies cupboard on Monday morning for what would probably be her last packet of cards and was immediately joined by Kemble, who softly closed the door behind her and began scanning the shelves of stationery.

'There still don't seem to be any PM forms.' Dora shrivelled with dread at the familiar whispering tones. 'I'm down to my last one. I assumed you would requisition some more from supplies.'

He caught her by the wrists and began pushing his face roughly against her neck like a man who had read caresses described but never actually got as far as the practical.

'Dora,' a clueless pause, 'Dora, *darling*.'

'No.'

'Like Tuesday.'

'I said no.'

The hand round her arm tightened its bruising grip while the other pinched at the fabric of her skirt, hitching it up and feeling for the pearl buttons between her legs.

'You want to.'

'No I don't. Let go of me. You're hurting my wrist.'

He should have swept her into his arms like that imaginary morning in Holborn mortuary and carried her into the septic theatre, where he could have laid her on the slab, ambidextrously palpating and weighing her body while his straining shaft plumbed the silken depths of her being and an adoring audience of eager young housemen took careful and copious notes.

'Let go.' She struck out wildly with her knee and he suddenly seemed to loose his footing and crumpled awkwardly, releasing his hold as he reached for the edge of a shelf to prevent himself from falling. His other hand began rubbing his leg.

'I said no.'

He tried sliding his right hand around her waist but she turned clockwise out of his caress.

'I'm sorry.'

He raised his hands in surrender as though waiting for Vazard to glove them.

'How about a morsel of dinner? A chance to escape Monday's menu? What delights are in store on Monday? Mutton pie? Mashed swede? Marzipan?'

'I can't.'

'Tomorrow then?'

'I can't.'

She was in fact going to the cinema with Vazard. She could pretty well picture the scene. She'd watched couples before. An arm would be laid across the back of the seat, then creep sheepishly around her shoulder, fingertips squeezing hers as they fumbled among the chocolates.

Had her breathing changed? Was there a silly look on her face? Because the pathologist was suddenly angry. As if he too could picture Dora and Vazard in the dress circle of the Biograph.

'Can't? Or won't?'

'It makes no odds. I'm just not coming, that's all.'

Chapter 30

'Well, our esteemed hostess has certainly excelled her little self this morning.'

Mr Stone hoisted a rather small, very dry, unnaturally yellow little fish from his plate with the tine of a fork and tapped it thoughtfully against the willow-patterned rim.

'What is it, do you suppose? Cadet branch of the sprat family? Do you think she spears them herself in the Thames down at Millbank? Or do they die of natural causes?'

Mr Stone was on repulsively good form despite his inedible breakfast because Mr Stone had just paid a month's deposit on an altogether delightful room-with-bath in Cadogan Gardens ('hot and cold, no vexatious extras') and was already counting the days to his final Frithy feast.

'And how is our Miss Strang?' He all but hissed the *Miss*. 'What a thoroughly enchanting cardigan. Did you make it yourself?' Haddon had begun blowing bubbles into his teacup. 'I see it's to be toad and tapioca for you this evening after all.'

Mrs Frith had, as always, left the morning's letters on the hall table and there had been two postcards for Dora. One was from Aunt Jacaranda complaining about the service at her Worthing hydro and the other was from Alec Vazard informing her that he wouldn't be holding her hand in the cinema that evening as arranged. Mr Stone and Mr Haddon had clearly both read it

– as had the landlady herself. Was it even *done* to send regrets by postcard? Dora rather thought not. Particularly not on such a glum, thrifty, scrap of pasteboard and with so little attempt at civility: 'Obliged dine Steen Tuesday. Apologies. Vazard.' Her father would have been proud.

'Good morning, Theodora. Did you sleep well?'

Mrs Frith's yellow head was on one side, making her look exactly like a Marcel-waved canary.

'Will you *Haz-ard* joining us for supper this evening?'

Another snigger from Haddon at this leaden piece of wordplay.

Dora choked down a charred slice of stale bread then headed for the Belgrave Road. She managed to hail the early omnibus she had caught on her first day at the department and the same trio of office cleaning ladies climbed in when the bus reached Whitehall. An arrest had been made in the charm bracelet affair: the brilliantined salesman from the Oxford Street jeweller where both victims had purchased their nine-carat novelties (and where one of the charladies had once bought a cameo brooch). The arrest earned a column of speculation but the papers were far more interested in chewing over the famous Dr Kemble's sudden fall from grace. The cleaning women were in two (if not three) minds about the whole business. He wasn't as black as he was painted but there was no smoke without fire and still waters ran deep (no good saying they didn't).

The department door was still locked when Dora arrived at half past eight. The outer office was in darkness but there was a telltale glow visible through the fanlight as though someone were at work in the laboratory. A gloved, gowned someone with a beaky profile and penetrating green eyes.

As she hung up her hat and coat she saw an envelope propped against the typewriter addressed to Hubbard in Kemble's scratchy green hand. She walked across to the corner of the room and rapped faintly on the laboratory door. No reply.

The lab bench was littered with the ripped cardboard covers of eviscerated diaries and notebooks. The metal waste-paper bin was filled with their charred pages and the twin bin from Hubbard's desk had been placed alongside so that each batch of ashes could be decanted into it. Two singed fragments of lemon yellow paper had fluttered clear of the blaze – 'Jelly', 'moral imbecile' – blown free by the icy draft coming from the septic theatre whose door had been left half-open. You could just see the great porcelain post-mortem table through the opening, just see the two socked feet of the body that lay on the slab.

The precious case of specialist blades was laid out on one of Vazard's enamel-topped tables. A large (empty) syringe had been placed neatly alongside the final sheet of the final pad of post-mortem forms. The document was already partially completed in viridian ink, giving name, age and a brief description: 'well-nourished male, heavy scarring to the left thigh. A range of burns and abrasions on the skin of the legs, chest and urinary meatus, some healed, some of recent origin.' There was a practised sketch of the herringbone pattern.

Dora sleepwalked into the supplies cupboard for a sheet to cover the body and a fresh pair of surgical gloves. She then pulled a couple of large brown envelopes from Kemble's desk drawer and slotted the torn covers into one of them before carefully tipping the ashes into the other together with the gloves (now hopelessly soiled). She took the blackened steel dustbin and swapped it for the one tucked away under her own desk and sat down, staring blankly at the manila packages. She briefly toyed with the idea of sending them to herself *poste restante* at Trafalgar Square but decided instead to cram them into the deep pockets of her coat. They could join the remains of her torn blouse on the area steps of the derelict house in Pimlico. More potential exhibits in her nameless little murderous mystery.

Hubbard (who was never late) was late. Very late. It was ten past nine before he finally materialised (not a good start). He looked seedier than usual and there were blackish circles under his eyes and a black band on his coat sleeve. Dora frowned at it with what she hoped was concerned inquiry but he didn't elaborate.

'Guvnor not in yet?'

'There was no one in the office when I arrived,' hedged Dora. What did one say? 'I think you'd better read this.'

Hubbard's gaze flicked to and from her face as he reached for the envelope. Something in her manner, something in the atmosphere in the room seemed to put him on his guard, and he held the letter by its edges as if handling vital evidence and unwilling to disturb fingerprints, spores, traces of mammalian blood. He opened it with the rusty old scalpel in his usual disembowelling way then sat heavily down at his desk, still wearing his overcoat.

'Mrs Strange is to telephone to Sir Godfrey. The number's in the box.'

He struck a match against his bitten thumbnail and dropped the blazing sheet into the ashtray on his desk before disappearing into the supplies cupboard.

Sir Godfrey Mason's housekeeper said that the great man was just that instant leaving the house and was on his way to the mortuary at St Pancreas (Sir Godfrey enjoyed the mistake so much he had never bothered to correct it). She was eventually persuaded to shout after him and bring him back to the telephone so that Dora could tell him that his erstwhile colleague, Alfred Kemble, awaited him in the septic theatre at Willcox Wing.

Had Mrs Strange called the police? Had Mrs Kemble been informed? If she would be so good . . . The widow would probably want to view the body. Sir Godfrey had a post-mortem to attend to but it was a straightforward case – motoring accident – he ought to be with them by eleven thirty. Open and shut.

The Lexham Gardens telephone was answered by the cook, who then grumbled off to find Nanny.

'Miss Lynch? This is Mrs Strange at Dr Kemble's office. I'm afraid I have some rather bad news. I think you should prepare yourself and young Master Kemble for a shock.'

But Nanny didn't really seem to need any particular preparation for shocks. Her sort never did. They gasped and tutted when bad news was told to them, like the old vultures on the omnibus, but they prided themselves on never actually being surprised by it. On having *known*, Cassandra-like, that such a thing – whatever 'thing' it might be: cancer, bankruptcy, twins – was bound to occur sooner or later but not liking to cause offence by mentioning it.

'I suppose it was only to be expected,' she sighed, almost contentedly, 'after poor Bertram's passing. I must go to Alfred. Mrs Kemble is away visiting her mother in Guildford – Guildford 217.' The note of instruction in her voice was unmistakable – didn't even say 'please'.

Constance Kemble's breathy purr had a sleepy, pink-satin-and-cold-cream quality to it at that time of the morning. She recognised Dora's voice straight away (six months on the switchboard at the Strand Palace Hotel gave one a knack for it). Dora fully expected hysterics but she took it very calmly. Very calmly indeed. Dora thought again of the brown bottle on the pink dressing table. Had *Missistrange* phoned Nanny? Jolly good. Nanny was a jolly good sort. Nanny could tell poor little Bertram. Bertram? *Alfred*. Poor little *Alfred*. You could practically hear her brain grinding into gear, wondering whether Dottie and Tonto could be persuaded to stage another funeral . . .

Would Constance even want to look at the body? And how in blazes did one go about asking? What would Miss Parker advise? Mrs Strange requests the pleasure of Mrs Kemble's company at a private view? Dora eventually managed to stammer out some form of words.

'Sir Godfrey's people won't be coming to deal with things until later on today if you wanted to ... er ...'

To Dora's surprise Constance rather thought she did want to ... er. It wouldn't take her very long to get up to town. *Marvellous* service. The barbitoned voice sounded even vaguer as her mind's eye wandered off to the burr walnut wardrobe in the corner of her mother's spare room. She could hardly wear the same two-piece she'd worn to the boy's funeral. A husband demanded the mattest, blackest, widow-of-Windsor show of grief one could find. Mummy had a hat that might do ...

Dora pressed the exchange button for a fresh line and dialled Whitehall 1212 (he'd hardly have wanted the local lot to come blundering in). They arrived in force twenty minutes later. Dora made a statement and then an almost catatonic Hubbard made a statement confirming Dora's statement (jolly insulting considering he hadn't even been there). Sir Godfrey arrived on the stroke of eleven thirty having cantered through his motor accident with unseemly dispatch. After a cursory glance at Kemble's naked corpse he decided that, while the dissecting table in the septic theatre had been impeccably laid, he would prefer to work at St Mary's with his own instruments and would send for the body as soon as Mrs Kemble had ... er.

Sir Godfrey jotted down some preliminary remarks, took the body's temperature then hastened away to give evidence in a case of suspected chloroform poisoning. Would she mind typing up his motor accident notes? Mrs Strange, wasn't it?

'Miss.'

'Miss?'

'Miss. Not Mrs. Miss Strange.'

Not even Strange.

Sundry sergeants and inspectors dithered around the department for another hour or so, making nuisances of themselves and taking down blasted particulars before heading back to the station, where the usual lurking hack got wind of the whole juicy business. By the time the grieving widow arrived (very convincingly turned out in borrowed weeds hastily remodelled with slit seams and elastic to make room for the growing Cuthbert) there was a photographer on hand to record the moment for posterity (if you could call the cuttings library of the *Evening News* posterity).

She had come straight from her mother's house but had already arranged for all her things to be moved back to Lexham Gardens. No need to bolt now and anything was better than life back at mother's where the absence of fortified wines was proving a very great trial.

'May I see him?'

The constable left on duty (one of a split pair: the other was lurking at the street door) looked doubtful but could hardly deny the grieving widow and he remained outside as the two women filed into the lab and through to the septic theatre.

Constance had been dabbing her handkerchief in the general direction of her face when she first arrived but she swept back the veil and filed the lawn square in her bag the moment Hubbard and the constable were out of range. She pulled the sheet back – all the way back to the gartered black socks – and the two women looked at the corpse in silence.

There was a hideously twisted purple scar running down the left thigh where shrapnel had ripped a great shred from the quadriceps muscle. More than enough for a limp, a stick even. Lucky not to lose it. The schoolbook engraving of the heroic Hubbard carrying his precious burden back to the aid post popped into Dora's head once more. She tried to picture the months of visits from the agony wagon, nurses shaving away mortified flesh, sluicing the wound with Lysol while Mrs Vazard (or one of her ilk) mopped away at his furrowed forehead.

Constance ran her gloved fingertip along the scar's bumpy length, like Mrs Frith checking for house dust.

'No wonder he never swam. Spent our entire Riviera honeymoon sitting on the terrace in white flannels.'

They continued to stare, rather awkwardly, at the naked body between them.

Was it possible that Constance hadn't noticed the herringbone patterns ornamenting her husband's chest (in places so densely imprinted he seemed to be clad in a pinky Harris tweed)? Dora felt herself blushing with horror and something unpleasantly like arousal at the guilty memory of Alfred Kemble lying on the bedroom carpet of his wife's boudoir, wincing at each swish of the leather crop, but not all of the lashes were of her making. The results of her own little experiment had been joined by other marks of more recent date and by a row of neat, round burns dotted all along one collarbone and down the inside of the left arm. Constance lit a cigarette and gazed abstractedly at its glowing tip.

'Will anyone cry, do you think? Imagine *no one at all* being sorry. I suppose one should live one's life with that in mind, shouldn't one?'

The starched calico sheet snapped smartly as she whisked it back over the body, like a housemaid making up a bed.

'Where shall you have your baby?' wondered Dora, desperate to change the subject.

'Lexham Gardens, I should imagine. As a matter of fact I think Nanny's done babies and all that: six months at Queen Charlotte's or similar. And I've found a marvellous man (as I think I told you in Bournemouth). Telephoned him this morning. He says I mustn't allow myself to get upset. Babies inherit the mental peculiarities of the mother during the earliest stages, he says. Recommends the finest brands of milk chocolate to avert miscarriage. *Mar*-vellous man.' She puffed crossly at her cigarette. 'And I'm damned if I'm calling it Cuthbert. Poor little chap – or chap-ess.' She smiled at the thought. Then the familiar green scrawl of the post-mortem form caught her eye: 'feet well-kept; five grains of morphine sulphate, self-administered intravenously'.

For the first time since her arrival Mrs Kemble looked genuinely troubled.

'Does one inherit in the usual way after a suicide? Or does it all go to the Crown like buried treasure? That would be jolly unfair. But we can hardly make a case for accidental death. Not with all this.' She looked again at the half-completed form.

'I think it's only insurance that's the difficulty,' murmured Dora.

'It's a wonder he didn't make a start on himself. He was always so frightfully par*ti*cular.' The voice her husband had imitated so cleverly.

Constance flicked the ash from her cigarette into the corpse's cupped right hand.

'Do you know,' she retched up the confession like a cat being sick. 'Do you *know* what he did? Didn't always wash his hands once he'd peeled off the gloves. Six weeks with catheters and rubber tubes. Picric acid and God knows what-all. Cuthbert here was a major surprise after all that.'

She retrieved the tear-less handkerchief from her bag like an actress making sure of her props and tweaked the veil back down on her smart felt hat. She looked at Dora and smiled – quite kindly.

'Poor Hubbard. Is Hubbard all right?'

'I'm not sure. I have a feeling his mother may have died. There's a black band on his coat and today's sandwiches appeared to have corned beef in them – it was oxtail and carrots this time last week.'

'Sounds pretty conclusive to me. Poor Hubbard. He and Freddie tried to drown me in a bath once, you know . . . I was to sit there in my bathers and fight back as hard as I could while the pair of them worked out whether it could be done – trickier than you might think. They spent twenty minutes desperately trying to push my head under to no avail because I grabbed on to the sides, until finally Freddie had a brainwave and hoicked me up by the knees. Hubbard brought me round. Breathed right into my mouth. Rather enterprising. Freddie didn't know how of course. He'd have known if you did it to dead people, probably. Poor Hubbard. He got my lipstick all over his mouth. He looked completely different with lips.'

She glanced sharply at Dora.

'Did Freddie ever use you in his experiments?'

The beady brown eyes were scanning Dora's powderless face.

'Unusually fine pores.' She smiled 'You all right? You mustn't fret about any of this, you know. You're still very young and he was a really ghastly man underneath all that charm. Really, truly ghastly.' She said it as if remembering something else he had done. 'But so dashing. And so funny. And so handsome.' The praise was reeled off in a strange, almost questioning tone as though doubting his power to attract. 'But ghastly.'

She took a farewell look at the slab as this last, unlikely adjective hung in the air.

'Anyway. I'm *sure* you'll meet someone *nice*.' Only she wasn't really sure of any such thing because she was frankly incredulous when Dora told her, as they walked back to the laboratory door, that she was in fact engaged.

'To be married?'

As opposed to engaged to be what? Cook housekeeper? What a goose, honestly. Constance looked rather put out by Dora's unlikely news and rather surprised, which was downright rude.

But of course it was unlikely and of course she wasn't (strictly speaking) engaged at all. She made a quick visit to the ladies' lavatory when she had seen Constance out and took a look at her face in the mirror. The headache had pinched a little pleat between her eyebrows and her skin looked sallow and unappetising in the dim glow of the electric light. She thought again of Vazard's hastily scribbled postcard.

The office telephone had been ringing unheeded for the last half hour. The next time it paused, Dora quickly asked the exasperated switchboard girl to connect her to Mr Steen's department. Dr Vazard was not available, huffed the secretary. Was the woman telling the truth? Or was Vazard on the other side of the room shaking his head and pulling faces?

Meet someone nice. It was dawning on Dora, slightly too late, that she had already met someone nice and that she had very definitely spurned his nice half-proposal and that this morning's not frightfully nice postcard was the result. *Dr and Mrs Vazard.* She tried to imagine herself preparing dainty dishes for slender incomes in a two-roomed flat in Marylebone, struggled to picture Sir Alec and Lady Vazard (FRCS ad nauseam) installed in disinfected splendour in a swanky new house at the smart end of Harley Street. And wouldn't papa be pleased – or not be *dis*pleased, at any rate. A young man of his own kidney.

She made one last call to the baby department. Dr Vazard had just left. Yes, he had been told of Mrs Strange's call.

The bell began ringing again almost instantly. At first she passed the calls to Hubbard, who met Fleet Street's questions with a dead bat which only succeeded in irritating them, but then Dora had a brainwave and let the phone ring five times before picking up the receiver, once again assuming her telephonist persona: 'Hi'm afraid there is no reply on that extension, caller. Please call again later.'

Hubbard seemed pleased. So much so that he gave Mrs A the threepence for Dora's cup of tea (strong, with, without). He had dashed down to the basement and through the tunnel to buy the early evening papers from the boy stationed outside the main hospital – hadn't even put on his coat – and devoured all three in silence together with the second half of his corned beef sandwich. He passed each newspaper to Dora as he finished it but seemed abashed by his own largesse.

'Kindly keep the pages together. I still have the cuttings to do.'

The news desks had very little to go on in the early editions, which confined the story to the Stop Press: 'Eminent pathologist Alfred Kemble has been found dead in his laboratory by his assistant. Cause of death not yet established. Dr Kemble was 44.' By two o'clock they had the photographs of the grieving Constance with her Honiton hanky and her 'delicate condition' but by the time Hubbard came back with the 5 o'clock they had worked it up to something far meatier.

Nanny Lynch had made the mistake of answering the Lexham Gardens telephone and her idea that it was only to be expected after the death of poor little Bertram was more than enough for the reporters to be going on with. They had obviously laid siege to the house and eventually Kirkby of the *Standard* had persuaded the parlour maid to hand over the portrait of Alfred Kemble MO and the gallant Berties. Meanwhile a dame school in Kensington had supplied what the headmistress believed to be a fuzzy photograph of Kemble Minor in a cap and striped blazer culled from the previous year's school photograph. It was in fact a picture of his best friend whose father's indignant letter to the editor resulted (a whole week later) in an apology at the bottom of an inside column on page eight, in which his name was (quite deliberately) misspelled and the family's Onslow Square address described as Earl's Court.

Sir Godfrey had been mobilised by the hospital governors to feed the press a suitably sympathetic line: death of both brothers, sudden death of beloved first wife, recent death of son, war wound and chronic insomnia (as a pathologist of thirty years' experience he had no hesitation in saying that 75 per cent of suicide cases were due to lack of sleep). The press dutifully reproduced the various mitigating circumstances but nonetheless ran the story in parallel with the Home Secretary's consent to the transfer of the earthly remains of a man who should still (by rights) be buffing North London linoleum.

It was raining hard when the men arrived via the hospital tunnel to crate up the body, manhandle it into the goods lift and down to the loading bay, where an ambulance was waiting to take it to Sir Godfrey's laboratory. Hubbard took this very badly, seeming to feel that the chief's autopsy ought to be conducted on his own territory – like giving birth at home or dying in your own bed. He insisted on accompanying the chief's remains to Paddington, like the faithful hound he was, leaving Dora alone with the still screaming telephone and a supplies cupboard full of ghosts busying themselves with blotting paper and pinky-panky.

'Hi'm afraid there is no reply on that extension, caller. Please call again later.'

'Dora, is that you? I've been telephoning all afternoon on and off. You poor old darling, it must be hell. How's Hubbard taking it?'

Poor old darling. But not his poor old darling, just any old darling. She might just as easily have been Curtis.

'I'd have come right away but I was in theatre – intestino-uterine fistula – Mr Steen asked me to assist.' She half-smiled at the stupid note of pride in his voice. 'We've only just finished. My dinner with Steen isn't till eight. I'll pop along, shall I, and see how you both are?'

Both. Dora and Hubbard.

'I'll wait here.'

She sat up straight in her chair and slid the typewriter towards her. Her blouse inched up her arms as she stretched, revealing the ripening bruises on her wrists. She covered them with her cuffs and began mechanically typing Sir Godfrey's very dry, very matter-of-fact notes, hitting the keys so hard she split her index fingernail. It seemed like hours before Vazard came.

He had rushed from the main building during a sudden heavy shower and the rain had darkened his blond hair, which he had swept back from his forehead with an impatient hand.

'What you need is a little healing elixir. Gin and French?'

She pulled on her coat and followed Vazard down the stairs, through the tunnel and out of the hospital's front gate. It was still raining hard as they dashed along the crowded evening pavement toward the foggy glow of the public house in the distance.

Whenever she blinked the image of Kemble's corpse seemed to slide down into view again like a magic lantern show when the blinds are drawn: the feathery strokes of the riding crop against the dead white skin, the cigarette burns like little red rivets holding the body parts together. She almost swooned with nausea at the memory and lurched forward from the pavement just as a huge motor van squealed around the corner into Charlotte Street. She felt her shoe fill with freezing puddle water as she stepped off the kerb and felt Vazard take hard hold of her arm as he wrenched her clear of the road: furious, like a panicked parent.

'For God's sake be careful, Dora!' He almost shook her, like someone waking a heavy sleeper. 'Dora, darling.'

Darling. She looked dumbly down at her wrist. Yesterday's bruise looked nearly black by the sickly yellow light of the street lamp and it was now joined by the fresh, pastry-cutter pattern of Vazard's hard, clean fingernails. A familiar thrill trickled through her as he enfolded her in the pavementy smell of his wet overcoat. She turned her tearless face to his and slowly lowered her eyelids once more.

'Kiss me.'

A NOTE ON THE TYPE

The text of this book is set in Adobe Caslon, named after the English punch-cutter and type founder William Caslon I (1692–1766). Caslon's rather old-fashioned types were modelled on seventeenth-century Dutch designs, but found wide acceptance throughout the English-speaking world for much of the eighteenth century until being replaced by newer types toward the end of the century. Used in 1776 to print the Declaration of Independence, they were revived in the nineteenth century, and have been popular ever since. There are several digital versions, of which Carol Twombly's Adobe Caslon is one.